"Sure to satisfy both dedicated foodies and ardent mystery
lovers alike."
             —Jessie Crockett, author of _Drizzled with Death_

Also
by Ellie Alexander

Meet Your Baker

A Batter of Life and Death

On Thin Icing

Caught Bread Handed

Fudge and Jury

A Crime of Passion Fruit

Another One Bites the Crust

Till Death Do Us Tart

Live and Let Pie

A Cup of Holiday Fear

Nothing Bundt Trouble

Ellie Alexander

St. Martin's Paperbacks

This is a work of fiction. All of the characters, organizations, and events portrayed in this novel are either products of the author's imagination or are used fictitiously.

First published in the United States by St. Martin's Paperbacks, an imprint of St. Martin's Publishing Group.

NOTHING BUNDT TROUBLE

Copyright © 2020 by Katherine Dyer-Seeley.
Excerpt from *Chilled to the Cone* copyright © 2020 by Katherine Dyer-Seeley.

For information, address St. Martin's Publishing Group, 120 Broadway, New York, NY 10271.

www.stmartins.com

ISBN: 978-1-250-21436-2

Our books may be purchased in bulk for promotional, educational, or business use. Please contact your local bookseller or the Macmillan Corporate and Premium Sales Department at 1-800-221-7945, ext. 5442, or by email at MacmillanSpecialMarkets@macmillan.com.

Printed in the United States of America

St. Martin's Paperbacks edition / July 2020

10 9 8 7 6 5 4 3 2 1

Acknowledgments

Writing this installment of the Bakeshop Mysteries gave me a deeper understanding of Ashland's past. I felt a bit like a time-traveler as I researched life in the Rogue Valley in the 1980s. In the process, I learned that while some things have changed—housing prices have skyrocketed and pay phones no longer exist—Ashland's sense of community still runs strong, in part due to many of the business owners and families who put down roots in the decade of neon.

I'd like to share a special thanks with Valerie Rachelle for providing me with background, insight, and a behind-the-scenes tour of the Oregon Cabaret Theater. If you ever find yourself in Jules's hometown, be sure to catch a show at the Cabaret.

Also, thanks to many longtime locals for lending their perspective and memories, including Steve Sacks, Jamie Palomino, Wendy Ray, Pam Denke, and Stefanie Nagata.

Last, but certainly not least, my deepest thanks to all of you for coming along on this journey with Jules and her team at Torte. I hope you enjoy this glimpse into her past.

Chapter One

They say that the future is mutable. That our choices and actions influence every outcome. That could be true, but the only way I was going to be able to embrace my future was to understand my past. Moving into my childhood home had quickly reacquainted me with years of long-forgotten memories. Like the hallway floorboards that squeaked with the lightest step. It was a good thing I had never tried to sneak out when I was a kid. There was no chance I would have been successful. Maybe that's why my dad had never bothered to fix the creaky floor. After he died, I guessed that loose pieces of hardwood were low on Mom's priority list. So here I was almost twenty years later, tiptoeing down the hallway in my slippers, trying to avoid the squeaky sections of the floor.

My parents' house—now my house—was tucked in amongst towering ponderosa pines, sequoias, aspens, and blue spruce trees on the aptly named Mountain Avenue in Ashland, Oregon. The view from the back deck offered a panorama of Grizzly Peak and the sepia toned hillsides across the valley. As a kid, I had always felt like I lived in a tree house. I would fall asleep watching the spindly

branches of the pine trees waving in the window and staring up at the star-drenched sky.

When Mom and her new husband, the Professor, had
offered to pass the house on to me, I resisted. It wasn't
because I didn't love the house. Quite the opposite. It was
that I didn't want to take advantage of their generosity. They had done so much for me since I had returned
home to Ashland. However, they had made it clear that
keeping the house in the family was important to them.
After their wedding last summer, they had opted to leave
both of their old worlds behind and start a new life together on the wind-swept banks of Emigrant Lake. I hadn't
seen Mom this happy in years. Her enthusiasm was contagious. For the past week she had been over every day
helping me unpack boxes and rearrange some of the furniture she had left behind.

The holidays were also behind us, which meant that I
actually had time to focus on organizing my new space.
Ashland is a tourist destination and mecca for theater
lovers. When the Oregon Shakespeare Festival is in
season there's never a dull moment at Torte, our family
bakeshop. Most small business owners in town (myself included) know that there is a small window of time each
year to plan a tropical getaway or tackle the list of tasks
that fell by the wayside during the rush of the tourist season. Rather than jetting off to a sunny island or trekking
through the snowy Siskiyou Mountains, I had decided to
use the downtime to officially move in.

Since I had spent nearly a decade sailing from port to
port in my position as head pastry chef for the *Amour of
the Seas* cruise ship, I hadn't had a need to accumulate
things, which made unpacking a breeze. My move had

consisted of packing my clothes, my collection of cook-books, and my kitchen tools. The apartment I had been renting above Elevation, an outdoor store on the plaza just a few doors down from the bakeshop, had come fully furnished. My challenge now was finding enough furniture to fill the four-bedroom house.

Mom had left a few pieces of mission-style furniture, including a large dining room table and chairs, a couch, side tables, a coffee table, and a desk. I'd been sleeping on my old twin bed in what was my childhood bedroom. Mom had converted it into her sewing room when I left for culinary school. I figured it was probably time to graduate to an adult bed, so I had ordered a custom queen-size four-poster bed and mattress. It was due to arrive this afternoon, and I couldn't wait.

As if on cue the doorbell rang. I went down the oak staircase to answer the door.

"Hello, darling." My friend Lance stood on the porch, holding a bouquet of pale white roses dotted with greenery in one hand and an expensive-looking tool kit in the other.

"You're early." I greeted him with a kiss on the cheek and showed him inside. Lance had offered to come help me set up the bed and dressers.

"Better early than late." He handed me the flowers as I shut the door behind him. "I figured I should be here to oversee the delivery. We wouldn't want the delivery crew to ding up your walls, would we?"

"No." I chuckled. "Imagine the horror."

Lance set his tool kit in the entryway and tugged off his charcoal gray wool coat. Beneath the coat he wore a pair of perfectly cut khaki slacks, a cornflower blue shirt, and expensive leather shoes. He hung the coat on a rack by the door. "You jest, Juliet, but you'll thank me later."

"I'm sure I will." I pointed down the hallway to the kitchen. "Come on in. I'll put these in some water." I was in my usual weekend attire—a pair of fleece yoga pants, thick cozy cabin socks, and my favorite well-worn fleece hoodie. I had acquired the two-tone yellow and gray hoodie with front pockets and cowl neck from a vintage shop in the plaza not long after I returned home to Ashland. There hadn't been much need for fleece clothing or wool socks on the cruise ship.

We walked to the kitchen where sunlight flooded the room. The original pressed-glass windows reflected a greenish glow from the trees outside. I had planted a row of herbs above the sink that were just beginning to sprout.

"I see you've wasted no time getting the kitchen organized," Lance noted, pointing to the display of cookbooks near the six-burner gas stove and my copper pots hanging on a wire rack above the butcher-block island.

"It's my happy place. I had to start here." I filled a vase with water and arranged the roses.

"Trust me, we are all the better that the kitchen is your happy place." Lance lifted the lid on my canary yellow Dutch oven. "My lord, what smells so divine?"

"That's meatball soup for later. I couldn't beg for your assistance without feeding you. I made a batch of butter rolls, a simple Italian salad, and a bitter chocolate cake. If your handyman skills are really as good as you claim, then I just might feed you when we're done." I tried to wink.

"For a spread like that, you can work these muscles to the bone." Lance flexed. He was naturally lanky with a thin frame and angular features.

I rested the vase of roses on the island. "How are things at the theater? Are you ready for the new season?"

Lance undid the top button of his pale blue shirt and rolled the sleeves up part way. "It's fine. Have you heard the news about the Cabaret? That's where the *drama* is these days."

"No." I poured us cups of French press that had been steeping. "What's going on?" Despite Ashland's small population at around twenty thousand residents, the entire Rogue Valley was ripe with talent. There were dozens of theaters (large and small), music venues, and countless pubs and restaurants that offered a range of entertainment from open mic night to stand-up comedy and poetry readings. Our little hamlet was truly an oasis of entertainment. On any given night you could take in a fun and raucous musical at the Cabaret or catch a serious production of Shakespeare under the stars on the Elizabethan stage.

"The new owners have taken over. Truly wonderful people. Such great vision. They're a young couple from LA. They've been on the scene for years and I can't wait to see how they transform the Cabaret over the next few years."

"Cream?" I asked, pointing to a pitcher resting on the island.

"Always." Lance looked miffed that I had even asked.

"What's the issue, then?" I poured a generous splash of heavy cream into Lance's coffee and swirled it into the dark brew.

"Where to start? The stage has been rife with emotion. I never should have agreed to provide my expertise. I blame it on my benevolent nature."

"You're so kind, *and* so humble." I poured myself a cup of the French press.

"I am. I truly am. Sometimes I astound myself at my generosity." Lance raised his coffee mug in a toast to himself. "I mean after all it is my duty to give them the lay of the land here in Ashlandia, so to speak. But I hadn't counted on the fact that I would be spending so much time hand-holding and refereeing petty arguments. I've been burning the midnight oil running back and forth between campus and the Cabaret."

"You should have told me that you've been busy. I wouldn't have asked you to come help me put furniture together."

Lance dismissed me with a flick of the wrist. "Nonsense, darling. I would never pass up an opportunity to spend a day with you. Plus I need a reprieve from *Mamma Mia* for a few. If I hear that song again, my ears are going to bleed."

"Gross." I shuddered at the thought. The Cabaret had been running its latest production, *Mamma Mia*, to sold-out audiences for a month. I had read in the paper that they had extended the show due to demand. "Don't ruin it for me. I bought tickets for Mom and me for next week."

"You'll love it. It's a fabulous production and Amanda—the new artistic director—her use of space and set design is nothing short of brilliant. If you've seen it fifteen times though, those catchy musical numbers begin to stick in your head." Lance shoved a finger in his ear and pretended to try to rub away the lyrics.

"I can't wait. I scored front-table seats and I'm surprising Mom with dinner too." The Cabaret served a full dinner menu and drool-worthy desserts and cocktails as part of the show. It added to the ambiance of its intimate setting in an old refurbished church. Seeing shows at the

Cabaret had been a family tradition. My parents were friends with the original owner and had helped launch the new theater when I was young.

"As long as the cast and crew don't implode in the next week, you'll be fine."

That sounded ominous, but the doorbell sounded again, interrupting our conversation.

"That must be my furniture." We left our coffees and went to show the delivery crew where everything went.

Lance removed a tape measure from his tool kit and proceeded to direct the poor delivery guys as if they were actors in his company. Fortunately, they had a good sense of humor and played along when he stopped to measure each doorframe before allowing them to bring my bed upstairs. It didn't take long for the crew to unload the boxes. When they were done, I offered them home-made Amish sugar cookies, and then Lance I got to work on the hard part—assembly.

"These floors are magnificent," Lance commented as he placed pieces of painter's tape to mark the spot where each of the four-posters would be placed. "They don't make hardwood like this anymore. It's all manufactured and processed laminate now. Is this oak?" He massaged the smooth surface of the shiny floor.

"Yeah. It was already here when my parents bought the house, but they had the floors sanded and stained. The house was not in great condition when they bought it, but guess what they paid for it back in the eighties?"

Lance made an X with the tape and moved near the window. "Do I even want to ask?"

"Probably not. Mom showed me the original deed and I thought she was pranking me. They bought this house, which is over two thousand square feet on a ten-thousand square foot lot, for fifteen thousand dollars. Can you believe that?"

"No. I can't. Don't even ask me what I paid for my place." He made a choking motion.

Lance's house was on Scenic Drive, one of the nicest streets in Ashland. Given its size, ornately manicured grounds, and views, I would guess that he paid close to a million dollars. Housing prices in Ashland had skyrocketed in the last decade. Even cute cottages in the railroad district were selling for half a million dollars or more. Many of Ashland's restaurant and hotel workers had been priced out of the city. They couldn't afford the rising cost of rent or the down payment for a tiny two-bedroom fixer-upper for prices that would normally be found in a city like San Francisco or Seattle. It was an ongoing source of stress for Mom and me. We paid our team at Torte a fair wage, but even with that, many of our staff had been priced out of Ashland's rental market.

"I think we're ready to start arranging the slats for the base," Lance announced, balancing a stack of narrow slats of wood.

Surprisingly, the bed went together more easily than I had expected. In less than an hour we managed to assemble it, two dressers, and a nightstand. I stood back to inspect our work. The master bedroom was a good size with two rectangular windows on either side of the bed, a skylight, and an adjoining bathroom with a claw-foot tub and a basin sink.

"What do you think?" Lance brushed dust from his hands.

"I love it." The four-poster bed had a romantic vibe with

its white finish, raised panel detailing on the head and footboards, and tapered legs. I had painted the bedroom a bright slate gray. The contrast of the white bed with the oak floors and gray walls gave the room an almost coastal feel. I planned to drape sheer fabric across the posters and accent the walls with art from my global travels.

"It feels like you," Lance agreed. "You need a large floor rug though, and you should replace that light fixture with a romantic chandelier." He pointed to the basic light fixture above the bed. "Something black with candles to add a touch of drama, yes?"

"Yeah. That's a good idea."

"And, plants, darling. For the love of God, please get yourself some plants."

"Deal." I piled up the cardboard boxes to recycle. "Are you ready for a dinner break?"

"I thought you would never ask."

I punched him in the shoulder. "Just for that I'm going to make you take this stack of recycling down."

Lance hauled the cardboard outside while I went to finish dinner. I ladled the hearty meatball soup into bowls and removed the rolls from the oven. Then I poured us each a glass of white wine and tossed the salad in a garlic vinaigrette.

"Thanks for your help. I couldn't have done that without you." I set our dinner on the island.

Lance raised his wineglass to me. "Don't sell yourself short. There's nothing you can't do, Juliet. We both know that. But, here's to new beginnings."

"To new beginnings." We clinked our glasses.

"This house suits you," Lance noted, glancing around the warm kitchen with cheery yellow accents. "In that comfy yet impressively stylish outfit with your dewy cheeks and this marvelous kitchen I feel like I'm in a spread for *Sunset* magazine."

"Stop." I rolled my eyes and blew on my soup. "Although I do agree about the house. I thought it might be weird at first. You know, coming home literally, but I love it. It feels right."

"What are you going to do with the rest of the empty rooms upstairs?"

"No idea. Do you know anyone looking for a room to rent? I've been thinking about renting out a couple rooms to SOU students." The truth was that the house was too big for me. The main floor had a living room, dining room, kitchen, half bath, and office. Upstairs was the master, plus two additional bedrooms, and there was a full unfinished basement. My former apartment could probably fit in the kitchen and dining room alone.

"Don't do that yet. Who knows what will happen with your talk, dark, and devilishly handsome husband. Wasn't there talk at the holidays of him coming to Ashland for a more permanent trial?"

"Permanent" and "trial" seemed to be in opposition to me. In some ways, that summed up my relationship with Carlos. We had been living apart for two years. When I had left him on the ship, I didn't look back. I had thought that my decision to leave was likely the end for us. But, Carlos hadn't given up that easily. He had been trying to convince me that we weren't star-crossed lovers. We had spent a magical holiday season together when he and Ramiro showed up on my doorstep (or rather Mom's doorstep) on Christmas Eve. They had stayed through the New Year, taking in all that Ashland had to offer, from ice-skating at the seasonal rink in Lithia Park to snow-shoeing on Mt. A and long lazy days spent in front of a roaring fire playing board games and drinking cups of Carlos's signature dark hot chocolate with a hint of cinnamon and spice. Being from Spain, Ramiro had never experienced a white Christmas. His joy was contagious. I couldn't contain a grin watching him engage in epic snowball battles with Andy and Sterling and dressing in so many layers that he could barely move. Having them in town had been easy, seamless, as if that's how our life had always been. But before I knew it, the week was over and they were packing their bags to catch a flight back to Spain. Carlos left me with a parting kiss and a promise that he would return soon.

"Mi querida, do not cry. I will be here with you soon. Everything has been arranged. I will take a six-week leave from the ship and come be with you. Our future is the only thing that matters to me, si?"

I had kissed him goodbye and promised to work out the details.

As to our future? I still wasn't sure. There was one thing that I knew—Ashland was home for me. I had put down roots and had no intention of leaving. I loved Carlos too. So much so, that being apart from him had left a lingering ache that I wasn't sure would ever fully heal.

I knew that we couldn't drag things out forever. It was time for us to make a decision about our future, and the only way to do that was for him to come to Ashland and stay. I desperately wanted things to work with us. Having Carlos and his son Ramiro in Ashland would be perfection. But was it nothing more than a fantasy?

My inner voice had been nagging me for a while now. I

wasn't sure that Carlos was meant to be somewhere small. He was made for the world. Maybe it was one of the reasons I had been living in limbo. If Carlos was away at sea I could pretend like he still belonged to me. If he came to Ashland and didn't love it then I was opening my heart to breaking all over again.

Mom had told me once that love was always worth the risk. I had a feeling I was soon going to learn the depths of that risk.

Chapter Two

After Lance left, I made quick work of the dishes. Then I returned upstairs to finish decorating my new bedroom. A fluffy tangerine down comforter and matching feather pillows softened the gray tones. Prints from my global travels framed the far wall. Mom had mentioned that she had left a few boxes of assorted vases, some artwork, and a set of lamps in the basement, so I went downstairs to see what I might be able to salvage. Otherwise, I had agreed to donate whatever I couldn't use.

I squeezed my thick cabin socks into a pair of slippers and headed downstairs. The basement was accessed through a door off of the entryway. Unlike the rest of the house, where the old floors had been resurfaced and stained, the basement stairs were rickety with open slats at a steep angle.

I yanked a string that clicked on a dim yellow light to illuminate my way. Maybe at some point I would have to tackle a basement remodel. For the moment, I ducked my head to avoid smacking it on the beams and made my descent into the cool space.

The basement was partially unfinished. Half of the dark

and musty space had dirt floors and exposed ductwork. Linoleum covered the remaining half of the floor. This section had also been sheetrocked and painted. The basement had been a great hiding spot for childhood games of hide-and-seek. Two large wooden shelves stood near the washer and dryer. I dug through boxes of old Christmas and Halloween decorations and tubs with dishes, towels, and silverware and found the two bedside lamps that Mom had left for me. They had dark walnut bases and cloth craft shades in a creamy off-white. With a little dusting, they would work perfectly in my new bedroom. At this rate, I might not have to go furniture shopping at all.

I set aside the things I wanted and began to restack the boxes. The last box wouldn't fit back on the shelf. I tried shoving it harder. No luck.

"Get in there," I said aloud, trying to force the box into the narrow space. It was futile, so I tried a new tactic. I made space on either side to try and squeeze the box back into place. It still wouldn't fit.

There was only one solution, I was going to have to restack the entire shelf. I carefully removed box after dusty box and set them on the dirt floor. Each box was labeled with old yellowed masking tape. There were boxes labeled, JULIET BALLET, THANKSGIVING DECORATIONS, and TORTE. It was a walk down memory lane to see faded cardboard boxes containing trinkets from my childhood and stacks of family photos. Mom had promised to come spend a weekend sorting through the memorabilia with me. She had teared up when offering her services.

"I'm sorry to leave you with this project, honey. After Dad died, I couldn't face the basement alone. It's become a wasteland down there. I promise, I'll come help you look through everything."

At the time, I had told her not to worry about it. She and the Professor had gifted me the house, the least I could do was take a few boxes to the Goodwill and organize the rest. And, there was no time like the present to get started.

Once I had taken all of the boxes down, I realized why the box wouldn't fit back in. A broken piece of wood had fallen from the shelf above and gotten lodged at the back of the rickety shelving unit. I tossed the wood on the dirt floor. Dust tickled my throat. I coughed and waved the tiny particles of debris from my face.

If I was already this far into reorganization I might as well give the entire shelves a good dusting. Thick empty patches where the boxes had been revealed deep layers of dust. It reminded me of an archaeological dig site, where years of evolution were apparent in each striation.

I went upstairs to grab a rag and cleaning supplies. Then I proceeded to remove every cardboard box and plastic tub. Mom had labeled most of them, but some of the labels were faded and hard to read, so I sorted through each box and placed new labels on them. A wave of nostalgia washed over me as I discovered pictures from Torte's early beginnings, family vacations, and even some of my baby clothes. Mom had mentioned that she was leaving some token of my childhood for me, but I hadn't seen many of the pictures in years. Tears welled in my eyes as I leafed through photos of my mom, dad, and me at the beach and Lake of the Woods. My favorite photo was of my parents in front of Torte on the day they opened the doors to the public for the first time. They were holding hands and beaming. My dad was tall and thin with light hair like mine. A trace of a mustache graced his upper lip. Mom looked much the same. She came to my dad's shoulder and leaned into his body. Her hair was longer in the picture and her honey highlights looked as if they'd been kissed by the sun.

I squinted to get a better look at the grainy picture. Torte's cherry red and teal blue logo was etched in the front window of the bakeshop. A vinyl sign hung above the front door announcing: ASHLAND'S FIRST ESPRESSO MACHINE!

I'll have to frame this one and put it on my nightstand, I thought, adding it to my "keep" pile and returning the tub of memories to the shelf. I was about to call it a night when another box caught my eye. It was stuffed at the very back of the shelves and covered in a half inch of dust. This box clearly hadn't been touched in years.

In order to free it, I had to move the shelving unit a few inches from the wall. The thin cardboard box dropped to the ground. I picked it up and peeled off yellowing masking tape. It wasn't labeled, or if it had been the label had completely faded. At first glance, there didn't appear to be anything in the box other than some old newspaper clippings, but when I removed the newsprint, I found a leather-bound journal inside.

My heart rate quickened as I unwound the leather string on the journal and let it fall open. I recognized my father's handwriting immediately. It had been years since I had seen his cursive scroll. Seeing it made my eyes well again. I ran my finger over the words as if the touch of the ink on my skin would connect us again.

"Miss you, Dad," I whispered, flipping through the pages of the journal. He had practically written a book.

Every page was filled in completely. Were these his personal thoughts? Should I read it?

I didn't want to violate his privacy, but he'd been gone for so many years now that the thought of reading his words in his voice was too enticing to pass up. Losing him in my formative years had forever changed me. Grief had defined and shaped my adolescence and set me on a course to see the world. Dad had always talked about traveling. He made up bedtime stories about Kathmandu and remote islands in the middle of the Bering Sea. His visions of wanderlust ignited my yearning for adventure. In part, I had decided to go to culinary school in New York because of him. He and Mom had never really traveled, since they were tethered to Torte and Ashland. Setting sail for tropical ports of call made me feel like I was paying homage to him.

I finished organizing the boxes and took my newfound treasures and Dad's journal upstairs. It wasn't terribly late, so I made myself a steaming-hot mug of apple cinnamon tea, put on my pajamas, and tucked myself into my new cozy bed with my father's journal. Was it a bad idea to venture into his past?

What if the journal contained details about my parents' relationship? What if he had intentionally hidden it in the basement? Maybe it contained a long-forgotten secret. Was it fair to dredge up the past?

In the same breath, I knew had to read it. Because my dad had died in my teen years, there were so many things I wished I could have asked him. So many questions left unanswered. Like, how did he silence the voice of worry in his head? Or what was his recipe for the perfect sourdough starter?

I had never questioned the big things. I knew that he

loved me—deeply, unconditionally. I knew that he loved Mom too. Their story could have graced the pages of Shakespeare. On the rare occasion that they had fought, they quickly mended things with a love note left at the coffee bar or a bouquet of wildflowers on the dining room table. They had been steadfast supporters of each other. At least through my eyes.

What if my memories weren't true?

There's only way to find out, Jules.

I took a long sip of my tea and opened the journal to the first page. The leather felt heavy in my hands.

It was dated March 14, 1988.

Some quick math informed me that I would have been five at the time.

Beneath the date were the words "*Feeling conflicted.*"

I almost flipped the journal shut, but I couldn't stop myself, so I read on.

What should I do? I should have told Doug no when he asked for my help, but he's a trusted friend and I never would have imagined that a small favor would lead us here.

My heart thudded in my chest. Doug, as in the Professor, Doug? As in Mom's new husband?

I had known that Doug was good friends with both my parents. He had said as much himself when he asked for my permission to marry Mom. I'll never forget our conversation, when he had confessed that he had loved her from afar for many years. He had barely admitted it to himself at the time because he and my father were best friends. His revelation had made me admire him even more. To have never acted on his desires and stand by

Mom in the years after Dad's death, offering support and a comforting shoulder for her grief, was the true test of enduring love, in my opinion.

I took another deep breath and read on.

"The Pastry Case," as Doug and I have agreed to refer to it, has spun out of my control. I fear for Helen, for Torte, and for Juliet. Yesterday when I returned to the bakeshop a man was seated in a booth at the front window. He wore a baseball cap to shroud his face from view. I asked Helen how long he'd been there. She said he'd been drinking the same cold cup of coffee for at least forty-five minutes. I knew right away something was off about him. He didn't meet my eyes when I offered him a refill. I could barely hear what he said. I think he mumbled something about being done anyway. He vanished minutes later. I had made my rounds in the dining room and when I walked past the booth again, he was gone. Thank goodness Helen was in the kitchen. When I picked up his coffee cup I noticed that he had written something on his napkin. I thought maybe it was a tip at first, but the words on that napkin have shaken me to my core. "Mind your own business. Stay out of it before someone else gets hurt." What have I done? How could I have put Helen and Juliet at risk? I'm going to talk to Doug tomorrow and tell him that I have to get out of this—now.

The phone rang. I was so startled that I dropped the journal on the floor and let out a scream.

"Hello?" I answered the phone.

"Oh, hi, honey. It's not too late to call is it?" Mom's voice greeted me on the other end of the line.

"No. Not at all. I was just reading." I glanced down at the journal on the floor. Suddenly it felt like a bomb that was about to explode. The tips of my fingers were white. It wasn't particularly cold in the bedroom, especially since I was wearing pajamas and under my fluffy down comforter. I reached for my tea to try and warm my fingers.

"Are you okay? You sound kind of shaky. You haven't been knocking back late-night espressos again have you?"

I chuckled. "Nope. As a matter of fact I'm drinking a nice cup of calming cinnamon tea as we speak."

"Good." I could hear relief in her voice. She worried too much. "I won't keep you, but I wanted to check in on tomorrow's schedule. Doug has an early morning meeting, so I thought I would come in with him and that way you don't have to open. You could actually sleep in."

"Thanks, Mom, but you know me. I'll be up anyway. However, I'd love to spend the morning with you and I could use an extra set of hands on the specialty wedding cake I've been working on."

"It's a date. See you then and sleep tight, Juliet."

She hung up. How was I going to face her in the morning? Mom and I didn't keep secrets from one another. And she had an uncanny knack for being able to read my emotions.

What had Dad and the Professor gotten mixed up in? The Pastry Case. What did it mean?

I thought about reading on but decided that if I was going to spend the morning under Mom's watchful and all-knowing eye, it would have to wait. The less I knew about whatever my dad and the Professor had been involved in the better—at least for the short-term.

Somehow, I managed to fall asleep, but my dreams were riddled with images of threatening notes on napkins and my dad running around Ashland wearing a deerstalker cap and a trench coat.

The next morning I woke up groggy and even more confused. I took a shower, pulled on a pair of jeans and my red Torte hoodie, tied my long blond hair into a ponytail, tucked the journal into my bag, and headed for the bakeshop. Maybe my normal daily routine would help push the thoughts of my dad's journal to the back of my mind. I didn't want to read another word until I had had a chance to talk to the Professor.

Ashland in the early morning is always sleepy no matter the season. I loved the quiet calm of the plaza dimly lit by the antique streetlamps and the soft orange halo of a waking sun. The first signs of spring had started to appear. Hundreds of pale pink buds waiting to burst to life dangled in the trees. Trickling water had returned to the Lithia bubblers now that we were past the season of hard freezes. I had to stop on Main Street to wait for a flock of wild turkeys to pass. I smiled at them as they squawked and puffed out their tail feathers.

The front of the bakeshop was dark, but the large bay windows were lit with the pale yellow overhead lights we leave on at night. Our holiday display had been replaced by a tribute to the Bard. The Oregon Shakespeare Festival, or OSF, had launched its new season early in the month and every shop in the plaza had decked out our storefronts to celebrate. Bethany and Rosa had partnered for Torte's homage to the theater by creating ribbons out of parchment paper. They had written sonnets on each piece of parchment and hung them from the ceiling. The twirling strings of antique paper and golden twinkle lights gave the front of the bakeshop a lovely amber glow.

We would need to swap out the display soon. I was leaning toward something for St. Patrick's Day and made a mental note to ask Rosa about ideas when she arrived. Then I rounded the corner that led to the Calle Guanajuato and Ashland Creek. Torte sat at the corner of the busy pedestrian walkway. I took a moment to drink in the sound of the gushing creek before heading down the side stairwell to the basement.

Mom was already at the bakeshop when I arrived. She and the Professor were sharing a cup of coffee in the kitchen. The bread ovens warmed the basement and the scent of rising dough and strong coffee brought a smile to my face.

"Morning," I called, tugging off my coat and looping my bag over my shoulder. We used the basement entrance that led directly to our newly remodeled kitchen in the mornings. Once we were ready to open the doors to the public, we would turn on the lights and unlock the front door upstairs.

"There she is." Mom waved. She wore a fire-engine red Torte apron. Her short bob was tucked behind her ears, revealing a simple pair of emerald stud earrings. "You'll be happy that I've already made the coffee."

"That's for sure." I greeted them both with a kiss and went to pour myself a mug. "When you said you were going to be here early, you meant *really* early."

The Professor cleared his throat. "I'm to blame. I agreed to speak at the chamber's breakfast meeting and it seemed a shame to drive two cars into town from the lake."

"We're so far away now." Mom winked.

Their new house on the hillside above Emigrant Lake was less than a ten-minute drive from Torte, but in Ashland anything longer than five minutes is considered a "commute." Just as "traffic" usually referred to having to wait for a herd of deer or a flock of turkeys to cross the street.

The Professor glanced at the gold watch on his wrist. He was dressed in his typical style: a pair of slacks, a crisp button-up shirt, a tweed jacket, and loafers. "I should probably be on my way." He went to kiss Mom goodbye. "I shall return for you sometime after lunch, milady." He gave her a bow.

Mom blushed. "No rush. I'm having lunch and a spa day with Janet and Wendy." Janet was my friend Thomas's mom who owned the flower shop A Rose by Any Other Name. She and Mom had been friends for as long as I could remember. Thomas and I had grown up together. Mom and Janet loved to show us photos from our preschool days. I don't think they were surprised in the slightest when Thomas and I dated in high school, but our breakup came as a shock to everyone and sent us in entirely different directions. Since I had returned home, Thomas and I had rekindled our friendship and put memories of our romantic past behind us.

"I'll walk you out," I offered. "I want to get the espresso machine warmed up for Andy and Sequoia." That was only half true. What I really wanted was a chance to ask him about the Pastry Case.

The Professor and I went upstairs together. "Do you have a minute?" I asked in a low whisper. Mom's hearing wasn't great anyway.

"For you, Juliet. Always." He clasped his hands together and waited for me to speak.

I motioned for him to move toward the dimly lit dining room. I didn't bother turning on the overhead lights. "I

found something last night." I unzipped my bag and removed the well-worn leather journal. "This involves you."

"Ah, most intriguing." His brow creased ever so slightly.
"What is it?"

"My dad's old journal." I watched his expression. If he
was concerned by this news, there was no hint of it on his
face.

"How wonderful for you. I didn't know that Will kept
a journal. What a gift. To be able to connect with your
father's words and writings."

"That's what I thought at first, but I'm afraid nothing
about his words brought me any comfort last night."

The Professor frowned. He reached out to touch my arm
in act of caring concern. "Why? I knew your father better
than anyone. I can't imagine what he possibly could have
said that would be disturbing."

He sounded genuinely surprised.

"I didn't get very far in here last night because I wanted
to talk to you first." I ran my index finger along the smooth
binding. "What I read last night was about the Pastry Case."

The Professor's face bleached white. He grabbed the
edge of the booth to steady himself. "The Pastry Case?
Will wrote about the Pastry Case?"

I nodded, expecting him to say more.

He looked over his shoulder as if someone might be
listening. "Please don't mention anything about this to
your mother. I have an appointment to keep, but let's have
lunch later and I'll tell you as much as I can."

He left before I could ask anything else. I didn't want
to keep a secret from Mom. I was starting to feel like I
had unearthed a long-forgotten mystery that should have
stayed in the past.

Chapter Three

Concentrating on baking took every ounce of self-control. My only saving grace was that the wedding cake that I had been working on required complete concentration. The bride had requested a five-tier lemon rosemary cake with hundreds of sugar flowers. The delicate work of transforming gum paste into gorgeous and dainty pastel flowers involved rolling out the paste into thin sheets and using cutters to fray the edges and shape each petal. Once we had thin petals, we glided a ball tool over them gently to create a wavy, leafy effect. It was slow going because the petals could easily crack and break. Some pastry chefs use wire to hold sugar flowers together, but at Torte we believed that everything on the cake should be edible, including any decorations or embellishments. It made the task more challenging, but the reward of seeing a happy bride's face was always worth it.

"How are your fingers holding up?" Mom asked around mid-morning. She set a pale pink flower on the drying rack in front of her and shook out her hands. "Mine are starting to cramp."

"You know what that means then?" I brushed lemon

juice between the layers of petals I was adhering together. "Coffee break."

Mom dipped her paintbrush into a bowl of shimmer dust. Applying a tiny dusting of the shimmer powder on the edges of the petals would give them a hint of a shine, as if they were being kissed by the sun. "I was telling Sterling earlier that it might be time for a coffee intervention for you."

"Me?" I pointed to my chest. "A coffeeholic? Never." To prove my point I took a sip of the half-full mug next to me.

Around us the kitchen was in the full rhythm of the morning swing. Stephanie and Bethany, our team of pastry designers, were working on piping dozens of individual cupcakes with beautiful pastel buttercream. Marty, our jovial bread maker, had his sleeves rolled up as he kneaded dough like he was trying to breathe life into it.

"Are you kneading dough, Marty, or performing CPR?" I teased.

Marty grinned. His thick, bulky arm muscles massaged the dough with tender care. "I like that. Breathing life into this challah for sure. That's what we do here. Breathe life into baked goods and build some arm muscles in the process."

"Or, some of us spend our days drinking copious amounts of coffee." Mom shot me a playful wink. "I warned your father that raising you in a bakeshop could have long-term consequences. If he were here now, you would be the living proof."

The mention of my dad made my back stiffen. "Or, you could thank him for introducing me to the wonderful world of artisan coffee. Torte is all the better for it."

Sterling interrupted us. "Can you guys taste this and let me know what you think?" He wore his Torte apron tied halfway around his waist and held a tray of miniature deep-dish pizzas.

Mom picked up a slice. "It smells divine."

"It's barbecue chicken with red onions, cilantro, and a three-cheese blend. Normally we do flat crusts in the pizza oven but Marty introduced me to his deep-dish crust yesterday and it's a winner. If you like it, we were thinking we could bake each pizza in an individual six-inch cast iron and serve them straight from the pan." His dark locks fell across the right side of his forehead.

The crust was two-inches thick with nicely crisped brown edges. I took a bite. The bubbly crust was dense without being heavy. Sterling had balanced the spice combination in the barbecue sauce with a hint of heat and a tangy, sweet finish. The cilantro and red onions gave the pizza extra texture and, like everything that we made in the brick oven, the touch of smoked applewood flavor gave the pizza a rustic taste that couldn't be achieved in a standard oven.

"Delish," I said through a mouthful.

"Amazing." Mom agreed, taking another bite.

"Glad you like it. That crust is something special, isn't it?" Sterling, in a true chef move, tapped the golden brown edge of one of the pieces. "I've got two more tests in the oven. A veggie option with peppers, tomatoes, olives, and goat cheese, and a meat combo with salami, pepperoni, and Canadian bacon. A pizza trio for our lunch special today. Does that work?"

"All of those sound great. I can't wait to sample the rest. In the meantime, I'll take like a dozen of these," I said.

Sterling smiled, but I could tell from the brightness in his blue eyes that he was pleased that Mom and I were raving about his pizza combinations. "We're also experimenting with a cauliflower crust for a gluten-free option. You basically separate the florets and pulse them in a food grinder until they resemble rice. Then you boil the rice-like mixture, let it cool, squeeze out any excess moisture, and press it into a crust. I'll let you know how it goes."

"I'll be excited to try it," I replied.

Sterling had taken a larger role in menu testing over the past few months. I rarely had to give him feedback. He had a naturally discerning palate and was inventive when it came to flavor profiles and new pairings. I couldn't ask for anything more in a chef.

He left to check on his other pizzas. A dish towel was slung over his left shoulder. It was a move he had learned from Carlos. For a moment I could almost see Carlos in the kitchen and hear him teaching Sterling the tools of the trade. "A chef must always have a towel at the ready, si? You do not need fancy oven mitts or silicone tools; a good chef needs only a handy kitchen towel. You use it to remove things from the oven, to dab a splash of sauce from the side of a plate. Many, many uses for a simple towel."

Mom wiped barbecue sauce from her cheek with a napkin. "He's really becoming a great chef. His instincts are spot-on."

"I was just thinking the same thing." I finished my tasting slice, wishing for another.

"Watching him and Marty together this morning makes my heart happy." Mom savored the last bite of her crust. "They are quite the pair but get along so well, and at least from an outward perspective seem to really appreciate each other and build on their individual skill sets."

Marty was old enough to be Sterling's dad or even grandfather. He had moved to the Rogue Valley a few years ago to care for his wife. When she died, he decided that he wanted to return to baking. He had worked as a bread maker in a famed San Francisco bakery. We were thrilled to tap into his experience, and I had known from the first minute I had met him that his jovial attitude and humor would be a good match for Torte's vibe. What I hadn't expected was that he and Sterling would become such fast friends. It was telling that both men felt confident in their abilities and unique roles at the bakeshop. When my parents had started Torte, they had set out with a goal of creating a space where everyone who came through the front doors, staff included, were family. I was glad to be upholding their values and continuing that tradition.

"So, coffee break?" I asked Mom, walking to place our dishes in the sink.

"Juliet, you are incorrigible." She shook her head. Then she glanced at the clock hanging above the line of industrial mixers. "I'll have to pass. Janet, Wendy, and I have a long day planned. Lunch, the spa, maybe a glass of wine at Uva later."

Uva was a boutique winery on the outskirts of town that I had recently become a partial owner of, along with Carlos, Lance, and the dreaded Richard Lord. I knew that sometime in the not so far future, we were all going to have to sit down and hash out a plan. Owing any share of a business with Richard Lord filled my stomach with dread. My strategy of late had been doing everything I could to avoid interacting with him. However, I knew that wasn't going to be a viable long-term strategy.

"That sounds wonderful," I said to Mom. "Tell Wendy and Janet hi for me. Where are you going for lunch?" I grabbed my ceramic Torte mug. "Admit it. I could have much worse habits than my daily dose of caffeine."

"Never." She swiped her hands in front of her petite frame, then she laughed. "Janet, Wendy, and I are trying the new falafel shop."

Mom having lunch and a spa day with her girlfriends would give me a chance to talk to the Professor alone. "That's right. You'll have to let me know what you think. I've heard good things."

I went upstairs to check in with my staff and top off my coffee. The only drawback to our redesign is having to run up and down the stairs throughout the day. Although, I suppose on the plus side it was good burning more calories.

"How's it going?" I asked Rosa, who was coming down the stairs with two empty pastry trays.

"Good. We sold out of croissants and breakfast sandwiches. It's been steady all morning." She wore her long curls in two braids. A warm smile graced her face. Rosa was closer to my age with a calm demeanor and a naturally easygoing spirit. Customers loved her. She had quickly built connections and relationships with our regulars. I often spotted her listening carefully to our guests as she refilled their coffees and delivered their pastry orders.

"That's what I like to hear."

Rosa went to restock the trays while I continued upstairs to the main floor. The pastry case was sparse. A handful of cookies and cupcakes were left, but otherwise the first round of morning baked goods had vanished. Sequoia spiraled foam onto the top of a latte while Andy manned the espresso machine, pulling shots of liquid gold in the form of rich espresso.

"Hey, boss. You ready for a refill or can I tempt you with our special for the day?" He poured the shots into a waiting ceramic mug and handed it off to Sequoia who finished the drink by adding steaming milk and thick layer of foam.

They had found a working routine and (fingers crossed) had developed a professional relationship. I wasn't sure that they would ever be best friends, given their very different personalities and lifestyles, but they didn't have to be. I was perfectly happy with the fact that they weren't killing each other behind the coffee bar.

"I know this will shock you, but it doesn't take much to tempt me, especially if there's coffee involved."

Andy laughed. Sequoia handed the coffee drinks to two waiting customers. "Okay, let's make her our special."

While they made my drink, I did a quick spin through the dining room to refill coffee, pick up any empty plates, and say hello to familiar faces. It was fun to watch generations of families come back to the bakeshop. Over the years, families brought in their kids, and now those kids had begun to bring in *their* babies and toddlers. It was a testament to my parents' original vision for the bakeshop that Torte had become a gathering spot for people of all ages.

We reserved a section of our chalkboard menu for our youngest guests. I paused for a minute and watched as two preschoolers drew stars and balloons on the bottom of the menu with colorful chalk. A tiny tug of longing came over me. Many of my friends and colleagues had begun to have families of their own. I was starting to feel like that ship might have sailed for me. Carlos and I had talked about having kids, but it was always "someday," as in way in the future. Then of course, I learned that he already had a son, Ramiro. Spending time with Ramiro had given me a taste of motherhood and I wanted more. Not that I didn't have time. I was still in my thirties and these days women have babies well into their forties, but for the first time I was experiencing the old adage of my biological clock beginning to tick.

I smiled at the budding young artists and returned to the coffee bar.

"Here you go, boss." Andy handed me a creamy pink latte with the shape of a heart cut in the foam and a dusting of green powder.

"What is it? It's almost too pretty to drink."

"It's a joint creation. Sequoia suggested a rose latte, so we made a rose-petal infused simple syrup."

"That's where you get the pink color," Sequoia added. Her dreadlocks were bundled on top of her head in a circular weave.

Andy's freckles were more pronounced than usual. He was a snowboarding junkie and spent every waking minute that he wasn't at Torte up on Mt. A. I could tell by the goggle rings around his eyes that he had been on the mountain this weekend. "Then we added milk, espresso, and the signature ingredient—house-made pistachio paste."

"Oh, these are pistachios on the top?" I pointed to the green flakes.

He nodded. "That's some extra-finely ground nuts for

effect, but the paste is mixed in with the shots of espresso. Try it. You should get floral notes and—"

Sequoia interrupted him. "Nuttiness. You know, a little salt from the pistachios."

"Wow. It's beautiful and so romantic. Lance would want to serve this at a performance of *Cymbeline*." I tasted the unique latte and was surprised to find it light and refreshing. The rose syrup wasn't too sweet or too floral. And, the pistachio paste added not only a balance of salt, but also a rich earthiness. "This is incredible."

"I told you she would love it," Andy said to Sequoia in a pretend mocking tone. "We took a chance and already put it on the specials board because we were pretty sure it was solid."

I looked to the specials board where we posted a weekly rotating Shakespeare quote in tribute to my dad. He had started the tradition when he and Mom first opened the bakeshop's doors. Now the bottom of the chalkboard had a colorful display of stick figures, flowers, balloons, hearts, and a game of tic-tac-toe provided by our hot-chocolate preschool crowd.

"You don't have to ask for permission every time," I said to Andy. "Like we talked about, you have full reign of the coffee counter. As long as you don't invite Richard Lord over as a special guest barista you can do whatever you want."

Mom and I had given Andy a raise and made him head barista. Like Sterling and the rest of our team, he didn't need much guidance. I loved that we had created a space for our staff to thrive and grow. Many chefs before me had paved a path forward. I was glad to be able to mentor my young staff and do the same for them. Eventually I knew that Andy and Sterling would likely want to strike out on their own. It's the nature of the business, but for the moment I was happy to have them in "leading roles," as Lance would say.

The bell above the front door jingled as the Professor came in. He caught my eye and pointed to an empty booth near the window. "Can you make another one of these and bring it over?" I asked Andy. Then I went to retrieve the journal and join the Professor.

"You're early." I sat across from him. My hands trembled with nervous anticipation as I placed the leather book on the table.

He removed his tweed jacket and hung it on the back of the booth. "I had intended to go to the office after the chamber meeting, but to be completely honest your mention of the Pastry Case rattled me. I figured if I was feeling out of sorts that you must be feeling the same and I owed it to you to offer what explanation I can."

I cradled the pistachio rose latte. "What about Mom?"

The Professor rubbed his temples. "That, fair Juliet, is the conundrum, isn't it? I do hope that after I share what I'm about to tell you, that you'll help me determine how best to proceed with Helen."

"Okay." My stomach gurgled, but not from the latte.

Andy delivered the Professor's drink and asked if he could get us anything else. I wondered if he picked up on the tension in the air because he made a fast exit when we declined his offer.

"I think it best if I start from the beginning." He thumbed through the first few page. "Do you have anywhere you need to be?" The Professor's astute eyes held my gaze.

"No. Why?"

"It's probably best to settle in, as this might take a while and I can't get to the crux of my dilemma with your dear, sweet mother unless you understand how it all started. We can review Will's account of the Pastry Case together and then I will attempt to fill in any missing gaps."

My stomach churned so much that I placed my hand over it in an attempt to silence my jittery nerves. Whatever I was about to learn about my dad's past didn't sound good.

Chapter Four

The Professor pressed his spine against the booth before he spoke. Was he trying to summon the courage to share what he knew?

I felt the need to brace myself for whatever he was about to say.

He cleared his throat and began to speak in a steady, slow tone. Then he placed his finger on the journal. "Before we look through this, I think a brief backstory would be helpful." His voice had a nostalgic quality as he leaned closer and began to speak. "In order to understand what transpired between your father and me, we have to go back to the very beginning. It was the 1980s and Ashland as we know it now was not the same charming, inviting tourist mecca that it is today. Yes, the Festival drew visitors to town, but the season was much shorter, and the Rogue Valley was in a desperate state." The Professor's voice was almost soothing as he began by giving me a brief history of Ashland. "The logging industry had vanished almost overnight and times were hard. This entire region depended on timber. The drop in timber receipts here in Oregon and across the border in California impacted everything. Libraries had to cut staff and hours, there was no money to keep up the city pool, the little funding that was left had to go to major services—police and fire—but everything else took a huge hit. There was a deep recession in the early eighties compounded with new federal regulations on logging. Unemployment here in the valley skyrocketed."

"Really?" I asked. I had a vague memory of picket lines and protests in Medford from childhood.

"Yes. This was true in other parts of the country as well, but here in Oregon we had the added issue of the spotted owl. The owl was added to the endangered species list as an indicator species, meaning that if it went extinct, countless other animals in the region would be at risk to follow."

The spotted owl was something I was more familiar with. We had studied it in school. The chocolate brown owl was native to forests along the West Coast and its decline had made national headlines. Huge debates and protests ensued. One of my most distinct memories was of protesters who climbed thirty feet into a tree and refused to come down until logging efforts were curbed.

The Professor sighed. "It was a trying time. I empathized with both sides of the argument. People were losing their jobs and the only livelihood they'd ever known. That's a scary proposition, especially in remote southern Oregon where there weren't many other opportunities for employment. Yet, at the same time an entire species was being threatened. How could we ethically allow that to happen when there was clear path to saving the owl by stopping the clear-cutting of our forests?"

He didn't wait for an answer. "The college was one of the biggest employers, but in those days it was much smaller too. It hadn't reached university status, and despite having students in town, they were always broke. None of them had extra income to help bolster the local economy. It's hard to describe what Ashland was like at the time, but certainly it was a far cry from what we see today. Many of the buildings along upper Main Street were abandoned and left in disrepair. You wouldn't recognize the plaza as we know it now. Buildings were boarded up with broken windows and crumbling exteriors. There were dozens of pawnshops in town, but very few restaurants. However, it was also a time of renaissance. Young families were moving in. Housing and commercial space was cheap—unbelievably cheap. Your parents bought Torte for eight thousand dollars. I was new to the police force and was able to buy my cottage in the railroad district for seventeen thousand dollars. Granted, it was in desperate need of repair, but nonetheless, can you imagine that price point?"

I shook my head.

"Even a new house on acreage in Ashland at the time would go for thirty to forty thousand at most. The railroad district was predominately made up of working-class folks who could afford the small cottages. What money there was in Ashland was all above the boulevard—mainly professors and doctors. Otherwise, the rest of the valley was pretty depressed, economically speaking. Lots of hippy communes scattered around. It was like the Wild West. Aside from some outdoor-adventure rafting companies and fishing-tour guides, there wasn't any other industry to speak of. Ashland was 'civilization.'"

"That's funny to think about."

His eyes twinkled. "Times have changed dramatically. I saw a sign for a two-bedroom cottage in the railroad district yesterday that was listed at half a million dollars."

I nodded and sipped my pistachio rose latte. "I was just having a conversation with Lance about that very thing last night."

"Your parents and I were good friends. Ashland was a younger town then too. Most of the business owners starting the revival in the plaza were in their twenties. None of us knew what we were doing, but it was worth the risk. There was an abundance of opportunity and we became a tight-knit community because we all needed one another to survive."

Much of what the Professor was saying I had heard from Mom over the years. She and my dad had never owned a business before they opened Torte. They had graduated from college in the Bay Area and worked a variety of odd jobs—waiting tables, bartending, and working at bakeries while my dad got some smaller roles in community theater and my mom contemplated going back to get her master's degree in family therapy. But even back then, the thought of buying a house in San Francisco was unobtainable. My parents had driven to Ashland in their VW van for an audition at OSF. My dad didn't get the role, but they fell in love with Ashland, and decided to move there on the spot.

"Your parents opened Torte," the Professor continued. "Janet and Mike were opening A Rose by Any Other Name, the Winchester was just opening, the Cabaret was getting started, there were jazz clubs in town bringing in big-name acts—some of the greats like Ella Fitzgerald, Ray Charles, and Tony Bennett to name a few played right here in our little hamlet. It was an exciting time to be here. It was also a scary time because there wasn't the tourist population to support the business community. The off-season as we know it now was dead. I mean deceased.

Ashland was a ghost town in the winter. We all knew we had to band together to make a go of things in order for any one of us to survive."

I appreciated hearing the Professor's perspective of Ashland, but I wanted him to get to the point. What did any of this have to do with my father and the mysterious Pastry Case he had journaled about?

"To set a gloss on faint deeds, hollow welcomes, Recanting goodness, sorry ere 'tis shown; But where there is true friendship, there needs none." He quoted Shakespeare.

"Shakespeare, right?"

"The Bard himself. *Timon of Athens* to be exact. A truer passage there is not to summarize what those early days in Ashland were like. We needed nothing because we had each other." A sad smile tugged on his jawline.

I couldn't help but try to move the Professor along. "I think it's wonderful that you all supported one another, but how does that connect to the Pastry Case?"

"Ah, yes." He sat up straighter. "Touché my dear. I suppose I wanted you to understand the smallness of our burgeoning town as a way to ease my guilt for involving your father, perhaps." He opened the journal and looked to me. "Shall we?"

MARCH 15, 1988
Beware the ides of March. Julius Caesar's warning has never rung truer. If I had heeded that advice and listened to my own internal guidance, I might never have found myself mixed up in this mess. This case feels as if it's beginning to crash down upon me. I think it's best that I start from the beginning. I'll use these pages to recount every detail of what has

transpired thus far, in hopes that the process of writing might trigger a new revelation. If nothing else, I'm hopeful that the kinesthetic act of putting pen to page may help silence my ever-growing anxiety and paranoia.

"Helen, where's Juliet?" I removed my raincoat and hung it on the wobbly hook near Torte's front door. Note to self—add a new coat rack to our ever-growing list of purchases for the bakeshop. Had we made a mistake? Perhaps we should have listened to our parents' advice when they told us that running a small business with a small child was the worst decision we could possibly make.

"She's here with me," Helen called from the kitchen. "We're making you a special treat for after dinner."

I walked through the empty dining room and into the open kitchen to find my wife and daughter at the butcher-block island (our first purchase for Torte and the most expensive piece of furniture we had ever owned). Juliet's pale blond pigtails were askew. Her tiny fingers were covered in flour as were her rosy pink cheeks. She was a miniature version of my wife. Helen was a true beauty. She was the kind of woman who Shakespeare wrote sonnets about. I'd known that from the minute I'd seen her on campus, and she'd only become more beautiful in motherhood.

"William, you're back. We wondered what happened to you, didn't we, Juliet?" Helen brushed flour from her hands.

"I brought you both a surprise." I pulled a large

paper shopping bag from behind my back and cradled the bottom of it.

"We said no presents, remember? Every penny we own is invested in the bakeshop." Helen's brow furrowed as she nodded toward Juliet.

"It's our anniversary, though, darling. Of course I had to get you a little something." I handed her the bag and watched as she removed a ceramic vase with a low cut bouquet of pale purple and ivy roses. "That which we call a rose, by any other name would smell as sweet."

"Will, they're beautiful." She walked around the island and stood on her tiptoes to kiss me. "You shouldn't have though."

"It's nothing. I did a little trade with Janet. Anniversary roses in exchange for a batch of your double-chocolate cookies tomorrow. That's acceptable, isn't it?"

Helen smelled the fragrant bouquet. I had asked Janet to create something romantic and ethereal. "There's something in the bag for you too, my little pea blossom."

Juliet's eyes widened as she dug her head into the bag and came out holding a flower crown. "It's beautiful. Thank you, Daddy."

"Put it on. Every heroine needs a crown now and then, doesn't she?"

Helen caught my eye and blew me a kiss. "We were just putting the finishing touches on Daddy's surprise. You want to help me with it?"

Juliet nodded. Helen helped her place the flower crown on her head. It was a simple string of *baby's breath, dotted with rose petals, but at five, to Juliet I was sure it seemed like a crown fit for a princess. Her light eyes sparkled with delight when Helen lifted her up to see her reflection in the mirror behind the pastry counter. She had started kindergarten this fall, and Helen and I were constantly in awe of how bright and curious our young daughter had become. Not a day went by when she didn't have at least a dozen questions for me, everything from how to make peanut butter cookies to wanting to understand why the stars disappeared behind the clouds sometimes.*

Helen set Juliet back on the floor. "Okay, close your eyes, William. No peeking."

I obliged, listening to their giggles.

"Okay, go ahead, open them."

I opened my eyes to see a spectacular cake shaped to resemble Shakespeare's scroll sitting on the edge of the countertop. "Did you bake this?"

"Mommy did it!" Juliet blurted out.

Helen beamed.

"It's amazing." I stepped closer to get a better look at the cake. It had been frosted meticulously with buttercream. The perfectly exact cake edges looked like they had been carved from tile. An antique scroll with bloodred tassels filled in the center of the cake and my favorite quote from Romeo and Juliet had been piped with chocolate frosting. It read:

"My bounty is as boundless as the sea,
  My love as deep; the more I give to thee,
  The more I have, for both are infinite."

I had recited those words to Helen on our wedding day.

"I knew you could bake, but when did you learn how to design like this?" I looked to Juliet and raised one eyebrow. "Have you two Capshaw women been keeping secrets from me?"

Juliet bit her bottom lip and nodded.

"It's nothing. The community center in Medford offered a weekend class on cake designing. Remember how I told you that I've been helping Janet set up the flower shop on Sunday afternoons? Well, really, I've been taking a design class. I've learned so much and the instructor said I have real promise. Your anniversary cake was my first attempt at something not in our class manual. Be honest, what do you think?"

"What do I think? I think that Torte is about to become the best-known bakeshop on the West Coast. Imagine, Helen, if you can do this for our customers. We can offer special birthday and holiday cakes like this? Maybe OSF will even hire us to do their opening shows. Wow. I'm almost speechless."

"You're never speechless, William." Helen reached for a stack of plates on the shelf next to the mirror.

"True, but this is going to be a game changer. My beautiful and talented wife is going to outshine all the professional pastry chefs."

"Don't get ahead of yourself, you haven't tasted it yet," Helen teased.

We cut into the cake and shared a slice around the kitchen island. Juliet relayed her big day in

*school and Helen told me that she had some even
more exciting news.*

*"Stewart Anderson called while you were gone.
He wants you to stop by the Cabaret first thing tomorrow morning. Apparently he doesn't think they're
going to be ready for dinner or dessert service for
the grand opening and is wondering if we might
cater it. Can you imagine? That would be a huge
client."*

*"That is great news," I agreed, savoring the
chocolate, raspberry fudge cake. "Catering live theater would be a big job, but that could mean some
serious cash. And, lord knows we need cash."*

*"Exactly." Helen wiped chocolate from Juliet's
cheek. "I can call one of my girlfriends to come
help me if you decide to do it. I'm sure Wendy would
gladly fill in for a little while, and Janet and I already agreed to do a kindergarten carpool. Thomas
and Juliet can take turns being here and at the
flower shop. We can make it work, if you want to
do it." She paused. I could see the slightest hint of
worry behind her walnut eyes.*

*"I mean it is a great opportunity and would mean
steady cash for the run of the show."*

*I scooped Juliet up in my arms and spun her in
a circle. "Let's see how the meeting goes tomorrow
and then we can make plans accordingly."*

*Later that night I couldn't sleep. The burden of
the bakeshop's finances and Juliet's future had been
weighing heavy on my mind. I knew that Helen was
equally concerned, so I'd been doing my best to stay
upbeat about our finances.*

"William, you're up again?" Helen's voice sounded groggy as she massaged my shoulder. "You worry too much. Your brain won't shut off, will it?"

She knew me too well. I reached for her hand. "Don't give it a thought. Go back to sleep and I will 'dream on, dream on, of bloody deeds and death.'"

I figured that quoting Shakespeare might get me a punch in the arm or a soft kick in the shin, but instead Helen whispered something under her breath, rolled over, and went back to sleep. At least one of us could sleep. She'd been working so hard, I would do anything to spare her any additional concern over our budget. Perhaps I was blowing things out of proportion. We were doing well for a new business, but sooner rather than later we were going to need to hire some part-time counter help.

Helen and I had chosen Ashland for its lifestyle. The entire motive for our move here was to give Juliet a better life. I didn't want to watch my daughter's life speed by and miss major milestones because we were tethered to the bakeshop. My friend Doug had been instrumental in helping me sort out a three-year financial plan for Torte. Everyone we had spoken with in the restaurant business had told us that the first three years were make-or-break. If we could survive these first years, the odds of growing and maintaining the business after the three-year mark skyrocketed. One of the biggest hurdles was the amount of time and sweat equity required to grow the business. Most new business owners didn't account for the fact that if they wanted to pull in a profit, hiring a huge staff (or any staff for that matter) wasn't feasible.

Helen and I knew that going into this endeavor, but what we hadn't counted on was public demand. Our loyal customer base was growing every day and requesting that we open earlier and stay open longer. It was a good problem to have. Extending our hours meant that we could sell more, but it also meant having to juggle our personal schedules and less free time to spend with Juliet.

If we could bring in extra money by partnering with the Cabaret and put together new pricing for specialty cake designs, we might be able to hire a part-time staffer. We were about to get the first espresso machine in the Rogue Valley. Espresso drinks like cappuccinos and lattes had caught on in San Francisco but hadn't made their way north yet. Helen and I had agonized over the hefty price point of the imported Italian machine, but it should make Torte stand out as the premier spot for coffee in all of southern Oregon. The machine was due to arrive tomorrow, and I couldn't wait to take it for a test drive.

Go to sleep, William. You won't be any good to Juliet or Helen if you're a zombie. I tossed and turned for another couple of hours, plagued by bad dreams and intrusive thoughts of my daughter and wife left out begging in the cold. If I couldn't find a way to get my emotions in check, I was personally going to be responsible for tanking our fledgling business before it even had a chance to get off the ground.

Chapter Five

The Professor clasped his hands together. "It is quite evident how deeply attached Will was to you and your mother, isn't it?"

"Yes, that's for sure." I turned to the next section in the journal, buying myself some time to gain control of my emotions. "You know, I have a vague memory of that cake." So many of my memories were tied to food. The pink raspberry angel food cake my parents made every year for my birthday, Sunday soups and stews served family style around our kitchen table, and gooey warm cinnamon rolls slathered with cream-cheese frosting. My father's descriptions of the early days of Torte brought a flood of food memories to the surface.

"Shall we read on?" The Professor nodded to the journal.

I dressed in a hurry the next morning, putting on my best pair of black slacks, and a collared shirt and sweater. Helen used to tease me when we were in college that I dressed like a professor, not a coed. It was a fair assessment. I had always felt

*like I was ahead of my time. It hadn't been until my
college years that I had found like-minded friends.*

*As I stared in the mirror, I found something else,
a single gray hair in my mustache—a sure sign that
stress was already getting to me. At twenty-eight
I shouldn't be going prematurely gray. Hopefully,
this partnership with the Cabaret would prove lu-
crative and start bringing in more cash flow.*

*Helen and Juliet were in the kitchen drinking
coffee and a vanilla steamer when I came downstairs. Juliet was dressed in a pair of overalls with a
rainbow-striped shirt. She wore the flower crown I
had given her last night.*

*"I'm wearing this for show-and-tell today, Daddy."
She pointed to her blond head.*

*"Great idea. It's perfect for my pea blossom
princess." I kissed her on the cheek and went to
pour myself a coffee.*

*"Do you have time for breakfast?" Helen asked,
motioning toward the counter where she had sliced
a loaf of sourdough for toast.*

*"Not this morning. I'll get Torte open and we can
trade off once you've dropped Juliet at school." I
ruffled the top of her golden blond hair. "Have fun
today. I want a full report after school, okay? And,
don't forget our magic espresso machine is coming
later. You will get to help Mommy and me test it out."*

*Juliet sipped her steamer and grinned. "Okay,
today is art so I'll draw a picture for you."*

*"Most excellent." I left with a wave. It was still
dark outside as I drove down Mountain Ave past*

Southern Oregon College and turned onto Sis-kiyou Boulevard. Ashland was the perfect-size town to raise a family. In the few years Helen and I had been here we had made lasting friend-ships with parents at Juliet's preschool, fellow shop owners, and people like Doug, who I had met in my midnight actor's group. Once a month we met at the Black Swan Theatre to do readings of Shake-speare's work or provide feedback on new plays that members were writing, producing, or auditioning for. Ashland's small size didn't diminish its thriving underground artistic community.

The group had nicknamed Doug and me "the Bard brothers" because we both enjoyed reciting sonnets and soliloquies. I had found my people here, which was yet another reason that Torte had to be successful.

When I pulled into a parking space across the street from the bakeshop, I spotted a familiar face, Chuck Faraday, an actor with the Festival as we locals referred to the Oregon Shakespeare Festival and its company members. Helen had once told me that all of the women in town thought that Chuck was Ashland's version of a young Burt Reynolds. This morning I could see the resemblance as he strutted toward me wearing a white turtleneck, blazer, and skintight white pants.

"Morning, Chuck. You're out and about early."

Chuck stopped and looked from me to my VW van and then to me again. "Hey, Will. What are you doing?" His skittish body movements reminded me of the hummingbirds that hovered around the feeders Helen had hung on our deck.

"Opening the bakeshop." I pointed across the street to the pristine red and blue awning with the Torte logo Helen had designed.

"Oh yeah, yeah, sure, right. How's the bakery doing?" He stroked his thick handlebar mustache with jittery hands. "I've heard pretty good things. I need to come by and get a slice of that pineapple upside-down cake I hear everyone talking about."

"We haven't seen you at the Midnight Group for a while. Too busy with the season at the Festival?" I asked.

Chuck's eyes were bloodshot. I wondered if he was ending his night as I was starting my day. "Yeah, I need to come back to the group. It's a cool vibe there. Pretty rad. You must not have heard. I'm not in the company this season. I'm performing at the new theater that's about to open—up on Hargadine Street in the converted old pink church—the Cabaret. Have you heard of it?"

"Yes. As a matter of fact, I'm heading up that way later this morning. We've been asked to potentially help with desserts for the opening show."

"Rad. Rad. That's a relief. Have you met Chef Ronald? He's a nutjob. The guy thinks he's working at the Ritz. I totally don't know how Shelley and Stewart are keeping a handle on him. Glad to hear that you're getting on board, Will." He clapped me on the back. "The premiere show is going to be great. We're doing Dames at Sea. *Do you know it?"*

I shook my head. "Can't say that I do."

"It's a throwback to the 1930s. Musical. Big production value. Huge! Like super-retro stuff. It's going to bring down the house. Mark my words right now. The Festival is going to be shaking in their boots once they see what we're doing up at the Cabaret."

I had been under the impression that the two theaters were symbiotic. Everything I had heard about the Cabaret's opening from our friends at the Festival had been nothing but positive. It was wonderful to have another venue in town and Ashland and the surrounding valley would certainly support more artistic endeavors. In fact, Stewart, the owner, was a set designer for the Festival, and Shelly, the artistic director, had been a guest director at Shakespeare for many years. As far as I knew the Cabaret's vision was unique—the intimate theater would offer traditional Cabaret dinner and dessert service along with each musical. There was room for more than one theater in town in my opinion.

"Look, I should jet." Chuck pulled his jacket sleeve back to reveal a neon green Swatch watch on his wrist. The colorful plastic watches had become all the rage with teenagers in town, but I was surprised that Chuck was following the trend. He was younger than me, but only by a couple years, which if my estimate was right would put him in his mid-twenties. "It's been a late night if you catch my drift. See you at the theater, maybe." He started up Main Street toward the Mark Antony Hotel, then stopped, turned around, and came back. "You *don't happen to have a quarter on you, do you, man? I think I'll call a friend for a ride."*

I reached into my pocket and handed him a quarter for the pay phone. "Enjoy the day." I crossed the street and unlocked Torte. Chuck's description of the Cabaret seemed off, but I could assess the situation for myself later this morning. I've never pretended to be a perfect man, but one thing I had always known about myself was my ability to read people. If things were in bad shape at the Cabaret, I would bow out gracefully. We had enough to focus on at the bakeshop without getting sucked into someone else's drama.

Starting my mornings in a quiet kitchen had been one of the best things about opening Torte. Helen claimed that I could charm my way into the heart of a rabid dog. I did enjoy chatting with customers and introducing them to our handcrafted style of baking. It wasn't always easy. Just last week I had a guy come in asking if we served Wonder Bread. Helen and I had made a pact that we would only serve the freshest, locally sourced products. Our philosophy was baking with love. Luckily, I had been able to convince the customer to try a loaf of our white bread and he came back two days later for more.

Due to the design of our small bakeshop, Helen and I were able to talk to customers in the open-concept kitchen, while kneading bread dough or frosting cupcakes. I took great pride in seeing friends' faces across the counter and catching up on the news about town. But I equally appreciated the early

Nothing that involved. What I'm hoping is that you and Helen can create a simple dessert menu. Maybe two or three choices. You can prepare everything at the bakery and then bring them here the night of the show."

I thought through logistics. "How would we plate everything and get it out to the tables?"

Stewart snapped like he was keeping time to music I couldn't hear. "I have a plan for that. We might not have the permits to finish the kitchen and get it functioning yet, but I can have my crew get it cleaned and patched up enough. If you can bring the desserts up in boxes, we can plate them in here."

I hesitated. "Here?"

Before I had a chance to answer, Ronald stomped into the kitchen from downstairs. His heavy combat boots thudded with each step. He looked like he belonged on the set of M*A*S*H* with his camouflaged chef's coat and dog tags hanging on a chain around his neck. "What's this all about, Stew? I heard a rumor you're trying to replace me." He locked his dark eyes on me.

I was going to assure him that I had no intention of taking over the disastrous kitchen when Chuck Faraday appeared behind him in the damp stairwell. Had they been at Rumors together?

Chuck's eyes were bloodshot. There was a slight slur to his words as he spoke. It made me wonder if he was on something. "If you want my advice, I say hire Will and cut this dirt bag loose."

Ronald lunged at Chuck. Stewart stepped in between them to break up the fight.

I watched as both men tried to get out of Stewart's grasp. There had been a number of rumors around town about some of the nightclubs and chefs having a coke problem. I didn't run in those circles, so couldn't attest to whether or not there was any truth to the rumors. Doug had once told me to pay attention to how quickly bartenders at some of the clubs would serve drinks or why there were so many hundred-dollar bills floating around town. Was Chuck on something?

If this was indicative of how the Cabaret was being run—I was making a break for it. No amount of extra money was worth getting myself mixed up with this motley crew.

Chapter Six

"Jules, Jules." Sterling's voice brought me back to the present.

The Professor caught my eye from across the table as if acknowledging that he too had been caught up in his recollections of the past.

I blinked twice, flipped the journal shut, and turned to Sterling, who stood balancing a tray of pan pizzas and salads on one arm. "Sorry, what's up?"

His astute eyes transferred from me to the Professor. "Your mom asked me to bring you two some lunch." He set a tray with pan pizzas and chopped salads on the table. "She wanted me to tell you that she took off with her friends and she'll call you when she's done," he said to the Professor.

"Many thanks." The Professor smiled.

"I brought you a sample of the cauliflower crust too. Marty and I feel pretty good about it, but we'd like your opinion." Sterling shifted the empty tray into his other arm and brushed a lock of hair from his eye. "Need anything else?"

"No, we're fine." The fragrant aroma of the wood-fired pizzas brought me into my body. I sat up. "How's everything going in the kitchen?" I felt terrible for abandoning my staff, and yet I knew that there was no way I was going to stop my conversation with the Professor.

"We're good." Sterling tucked the dish towel into his apron. "Everything's under control. No worries."

I shot him a grateful smile as he walked away. "So did my dad end up taking the job at the Cabaret?" I asked the Professor, helping myself to a taste of Sterling's cauliflower crust. He had topped it with pesto, Parmesan, and fresh basil and tomatoes. The crust had a nice crunch and a delicate almost buttery finish. I made a mental note to give him my approval later. Then I reached for a slice of barbecue chicken pizza.

"He did." The Professor reached for a napkin and unfolded it on his lap. "He and your mother came to an agreement with Stewart that they would provide desserts for opening week as a test. William was smart enough to know that Stewart's goal of having the kitchen open anytime soon was lofty at best. He and your mom figured that they could handle a week. If it turned out to be too much work or too much drama, they would gracefully bow out. They didn't want to be locked into a contract with Cabaret until they had a better sense of whether it was even doable."

I bit into my slice of deep-dish pizza. How long had the Professor and I been chatting? And how had Mom known to send up lunch?

The Professor placed his folded napkin next to his plate and stood up. "Would you like a glass of water?"

"Sure, thanks." I realized that during the time I'd been

listening to his story I had managed to drain my pistachio rose latte.

I watched as the Professor filled two water glasses. Andy and Sequoia were managing the line of customers waiting for coffee drinks and Rosa was ringing up orders at the pastry counter. It appeared as if my staff had everything under control. That was a relief.

When the Professor returned with our water, he paused and held my gaze for a moment. "Shall we continue? I don't want to keep you from your work."

"No, please. I won't be able to concentrate on pastries until we finish."

"Very well, then." The Professor picked at his slice of pizza while he leafed through the journal. "Like Will says here, opening night was the talk of Ashland. Everyone was invited to the Cabaret and everyone came. It was a great night until things took a deadly turn."

"Helen, the babysitter is here," I called from the bottom of the staircase.

"Coming, Will. Give me two minutes."

I opened the door to welcome our neighbors' daughter who had arrived to babysit Juliet. Juliet beat me to it. She scooted around me and ran to the door.

"Guess what?" she said to the sitter. "We get to make stove-top popcorn and Mommy said we can have ice cream after dinner. And there's an Alvin and the Chipmunks special on TV tonight."

I loved that Juliet was so enthusiastic. Some of our friend's kids threw tantrums when they had babysitters. Not Juliet. She adored having older teenager girls who would paint her nails neon pink and dance to UB40 in our living room. They were off to the kitchen in a flash without so much as a hug goodbye or a backward glance.

Helen descended the staircase wearing a flowing cream skirt and matching sweater. She was a vision. Her hair reminded me of spun honey. It caught the light, making her appear to have a halo. "You look gorgeous." I held out my hand.

"You look quite dashing yourself, William Capshaw. It's not often you wear a suit." She squeezed my hand. "Navy blue is your color. I'd forgotten you still had that suit."

"Not bad, eh?" I pressed my hands on my navy blazer. It had been a college graduation present from my parents.

We pulled Juliet away from the stove-top popcorn long enough to give her a kiss and say good night and left for the Cabaret. I had delivered boxes of pastries earlier in the day. Helen quizzed me on the ride. "Did you remember to bring aprons?"

"Yes, dear." I turned the headlights on. March had roared in like a lion. The first two weeks of the month had been a deluge of thunderstorms and cold rain. As we neared the ides of March it was as if the weather gods had opened up the skies above. I wondered if it was a cruel trick. We'd been in a stretch of long, warm sunny afternoons that had begun to linger into the evening. Dusk had just started to creep in as we drove downtown.

"What about the extra bags of frosting and my

piping tools just in case I need to touch anything up?" Helen asked.

"I got everything. I promise. Worst-case scenario, I'll run down to Torte if we need anything." We were scheduled to arrive an hour before the show started to plate the desserts. Stewart had recruited a small army of community volunteers who would serve as ushers and waitstaff for the theater. It was a smart business model. In exchange for a complimentary ticket and dessert, the volunteers would be responsible for table service and post-show clean up. Once Helen and I oversaw dessert prep, Stewart had reserved us front-row seats for the Rogue Valley premier of Dames at Sea.

I had always been superstitious. It seemed like it should be a relatively easy evening, but then again, the best laid plans could go haywire and unless things had changed dramatically since earlier in the day, I had a bad feeling that tonight's show might be less than harmonic.

When we arrived at the old church, it was a mob scene. It didn't look much improved from when I had first met Stewart to discuss the possibility of Torte providing desserts.

"William, did we get the wrong date?" Helen whispered. "The theater can't be opening tonight." She pointed to the tiered tables. "Half of the tables don't even have tops."

"I know." I watched crews heave tabletops into place and screw them together as if a hurricane was impending.

"This is chaos." Helen looked worried. Helen rarely looked worried. At least not outwardly so. It took a lot to rattle my wife.

Shelly Howell, the artistic director, stood at the base of the stage shouting out commands to the work crew in one direction and actors in the other. She was a striking woman with angular features and a towering presence. She must have been at least six feet tall, but she appeared even taller in her black high heels and sweeping purple cape.

The cast huddled onstage in full makeup and sailor suit costumes. They reminded me of sacrificial lambs awaiting slaughter. No one spoke. They simply stood shoulder to shoulder onstage, staring out into the theater as if they'd forgotten their lines. I'd been involved in enough small productions to know this was odd behavior for a cast before opening curtain. Why weren't they going over last-minute blocking or warming up their vocal cords?

"Chuck! Chuck? Where are you?" Shelly's shrill voice cut through the silence. "Chuck Faraday, I need you onstage now! Everyone's waiting for you."

I followed one of the sailor's eyes to stage left where Chuck was nuzzling a scantily clad woman.

Shelly yanked a clipboard from a stagehand and slammed it on a nearby table. "Chuck! Now!"

Chuck was deep in conversation with the woman. He tried to kiss her again, but the woman pulled back and slapped him on the cheek with such force that he stumbled into a half-assembled table.

"Is that Jeri?" Helen asked. The surprise in her voice mimicked mine. Jeri Heyward was the *membership director at the Festival and at least ten if not fifteen years our senior. She and Chuck were an unlikely couple.*

"Chuck!" Shelly's shrill voice cut through the sound of hammers and drills. "Chuck Faraday—center stage now!"

Her screams forced Chuck into action. He had moved closer to Jeri and reached for her arm. She flung his hand away from her chest and shot him a stare that would make even the lightest soufflé sink, pivoted, and stalked away. Chuck blew her a kiss behind her back. Then he followed Shelly's orders and joined the rest of the cast. It was like he had flipped a switch. The next thing I knew the cast kicked off a tap-dance number.

"What have we gotten ourselves into?" Helen moved closer to me to avoid being trampled by a stagehand wheeling in what appeared to be crates of champagne.

"My thoughts exactly." I shielded her from a two-man crew trying to lift another tabletop into place.

Shelly headed toward the balcony, calling Stewart's name.

"Shall we divide and conquer?" I asked Helen. "You head to the kitchen and I'll follow after Shelly to see if I can have a quick word with Stewart." What I didn't tell Helen was my intention of quitting this side gig before it even started.

"It's a plan." Helen followed the champagne delivery, while I navigated the maze of half-constructed tables.

Upstairs the mood was equally disorganized. At

least all of the balcony tables appeared to be finished. Volunteer ushers were unpacking boxes of dishes, silverware, and napkins and were racing around like Juliet and her friends during outdoor recess trying to get each table set. Shelly had gotten distracted with her search for Stewart by the lighting crew who were having issues with the wiring in the sound and lighting booth.

"Can anything else go wrong tonight?" Shelly wailed. She reminded me of one of the witches in The Wizard of Oz *with her nasal tone and long royal cape. Her bleached hair had been crimped, tousled, and sprayed with a can of Aqua Net. Not a strand moved as she spoke.*

I knew that Stewart and Shelly's office was behind the director's box, so I headed that way. When I knocked on the door it swung open. Stewart and a short gentleman wearing a sport coat two sizes too big stood with their backs to me. I recognized the other man—it was Pat, the owner of Rumors. He was one of the founding members of what we referred to as Ashland's "old boys club." Pat owned a number of businesses in the plaza. He had served as president of the chamber and was on the city council. I had never had any issues with him, but Helen wasn't a fan. Understandably so. Pat's views on women in business were dated.

"Listen, Stew, the deal is off. Faraday has to go. That's the deal. Faraday is gone—got it. I want him destroyed. If you don't do it, I will."

I cleared my throat to announce my presence. Both men turned around.

"*Oh William, great to see you. So glad you're with us tonight. It's electric out there, isn't it? I love the pre-opening energy in the theater. I've been missing this.*" Stewart seemed relieved to see me. He stood and twisted a thin black scarf around his neck.

He walked over to shake my hand. "*Pat, you know William Capshaw, right? He and his wife Helen opened that great bakery, Torte, on the plaza.*"

Pat attempted civility by extending his hand, but his focus remained on Stewart. "*Nice to see you again. I hear good things about your little bakery.*"

Internally I flinched at the not-so-subtle dig at Torte, but I shook his hand.

To me Stewart said, "*As I told you, Will. Pat's been kind enough to allow us to share Rumors' kitchen space this week and I'm forever indebted to him, right, Pat?*" Stewart bowed to Pat.

"*I'm serious about what I said, Stewart.*" Pat gave me a curt nod and left without another word.

"*How's everything downstairs for you?*" Stewart pretended like nothing had happened. "*Do you have everything you need? Tell the volunteers what needs to be done and put them to work. They have to earn their free tickets, if you know what I mean. Show them how to plate the desserts now and they'll work on it during the first act. I reserved you and Helen the best table in the house, and Doug is going to join you. I figured you would want him at your table.*"

"*Of course.*"

"*You may want to sneak back into the kitchen*"

*before intermission just to make sure that every-
thing is plated to your standards,"* Stewart continued. *"We only want the best for the Cabaret and for
Torte. I made sure that the programs reflect the fact
that we've partnered with you. It should be some
great advertising for the bakery. The entire first
week is already sold out."*

He had inched closer and closer to the door as
he spoke. *"Listen, I have about a million fires to put
out, but if you need anything tonight, you come find
me, okay?"*

I started to tell him that I wasn't sure this was
a good match, but Shelly swept in with her cape
billowing behind her.

*"Stew, come with me now, we have a major issue
with Faraday."* She yanked him from the room.

I stared at them in disbelief. This was no way to
operate a professional theater company. Stewart
had been in the business for years. He was well re-
spected and was a revered arts professor at Southern
Oregon College. Shelly had been a guest director at
the Festival multiple times. I couldn't believe they
were all over the place tonight.

My conversation would have to wait, so I went
to the kitchen to check on Helen. She had plated
our three signature desserts. A crew of volunteer
waiters dressed in black slacks and matching black
Polos watched with rapt attention as Helen show-
cased her pastry skills.

Coming up with the menu had been a challenge,
but we were always up to the task. We wanted to create elegant and decadent desserts for the Cabaret's

inaugural audiences, but had to take into account that we wouldn't have any way to heat things up. The good news was that Stewart had informed us that the kitchen's industrial refrigerators were operable, so we could store cold items until just before intermission.

After experimenting with a variety of recipes, we landed on a devil's food cake with Helen's famous chocolate buttercream icing. That we would serve with a scoop of vanilla bean ice cream on the side and a drizzle of dark chocolate sauce. For a fruiter option we had created berry parfaits with blackberries, raspberries, and strawberries. The parfaits were layered with a rich almond custard and topped with a crisp butter cookie. Lastly, we had made individual banana toffee pies with caramel crusts. Those we would complete with a generous piping of whipped cream and chocolate shavings.

Helen was demonstrating how to pipe the whipped cream onto the pies when I came into the kitchen. "It's simple. Hold the piping bag like this," she said, positioning her thin arm in the air. "Start from one side of the pie and work your way in a circle. Repeat the pattern until the entire pie is covered in whipped cream." Everyone leaned closer to watch her pipe perfect spirals on the toffee pie. "Next take a bar of dark chocolate and shave it on the top." She completed the artistic decorating to applause. Her cheeks warmed with color. I smiled, knowing that the praise embarrassed her, but it was well deserved.

"Why don't you each get a piping bag and give it

a try," Helen suggested. She could have been a culinary instructor with her gentle nature and innate ability to bring out the best in everyone around her.

"It looks like this is the only place in the entire building that's under control. Well done, Chef Capshaw," I said in her ear.

She turned and raised her brow in the direction of the theater. "How's it going out there?"

"It's better not to know. Sometimes denial is a wonderful thing."

"Excellent piping," Helen commented to one of the volunteers.

"How did you get that peak in the center of your pie?" the woman asked.

Helen picked up a piping bag and expertly demonstrated her technique again. "When you get to the end, give the bag a little flip of your wrist." A perfect ring of fluffy peaks formed a neat mountain of whipped cream on Helen's test pie.

The volunteers practiced again.

"It's not only the physical state of things, but I've witnessed a number of arguments amongst staff and the acting company. I supposed it's normal for tempers to be running high on opening night, but the mood is uncomfortable."

"Were you able to talk to Stewart?"

I shook my head.

The calm of Helen's kitchen was disrupted by Chuck. He ran into me, literally. He was breathless. His stage makeup glistened and was beginning to streak with sweat. "Did Pat go down there?" He *pointed to the off-limits stairwell that led down-stairs to Rumors.*

I shrugged. "Not since I've been here."

"Ah. I don't have time for this." Chuck braced the base of the door with one foot. He used his full body weight with the other to force the door open. It looked odd to see the actor in his sailor costume battling with a door. He took the stairs two at a time and disappeared out of sight.

Minutes later he reappeared at the bottom of the stairwell. Pat's voice echoed up the stairs. "If you dare set foot in here again, Faraday, you're dead. Understand? You're a dead man. I never want to see your face around here again."

Helen looked to me.

"No idea," I mouthed.

The volunteer waitstaff had gone silent. It was impossible not to overhear the fight.

"You're going to regret this, Pat."

"Not as much as you are, Faraday. You're a dead man."

Chapter Seven

"I have a bad feeling about where this is going," I said to the Professor.

He, like me, had his head bent forward to read my dad's perfect penmanship. "Indeed." He shifted his shoulders and cut into a second slice of pizza. "As I mentioned, Ashland in the eighties was a different place. None of us were flush with cash. We had to create our own destiny, and that meant long, arduous hours and plenty of resourcefulness when it came to launching new endeavors like the Cabaret. Let me assure you that the Cabaret wasn't the only business in town that struggled. I suppose that's one of the reasons Will agreed to help, despite his reservations. It was that community attitude and spirit that pulled us through the difficult times, but in reading these passages, I'm also reminded how young we were. We might have been wise to be a bit more skeptical."

The Professor sighed and read on.

In a miracle of all miracles the show opened on time. I got swept up into the clever choreography and staging. The acoustics in the old church were nothing short of stunning. Helen clutched my hand under the table as we were sucked into the happy, vibrant sounds of tap dancing and the beautiful harmonies of the chorus. The musical production was on par with shows I had seen on Broadway. Even Chef Ronald's appetizers were better than expected. I especially enjoyed his beer-battered mozzarella sticks with marinara dipping sauce.

Helen, Doug, and his date laughed along with the rest of the audience through the first half. The musical was fast-paced, zany, and upbeat. It was a total departure from most of the shows I'd seen at the Festival. I was floored by Shelly's use of the small space and her deliberate staging. Actors swapped out costumes right in front of our eyes. Props and set changes were worked into the choreography. The entire show felt intimate. Actors traversed through the rows of tables and stopped every so often to engage the audience. It was like nothing I'd ever experienced before.

I excused myself a few minutes before intermission to check on progress in the kitchen. Helen's crash course in plating had paid off. The volunteers had followed her instructions to the letter. I was pleased to see how sophisticated each dessert looked.

Ronald kept a watchful eye from the corner of the kitchen. His twitchy demeanor put me on guard. He tapped a pack of cigarettes on the counter like he was in need of a smoke, and bounced his foot on the cement floor. "Lovely job on the appetizers," I said to him as the waitstaff readied trays of desserts. As soon as the applause sounded and the house lights came on they would begin serving. There was a narrow fifteen-minute window during intermission to serve each table, refill coffee, tea, and cocktails, and settle the dining bills. "I especially enjoyed the breaded mozzarella with marinara sauce."

He tugged a single cigarette from the pack and held it beneath his nose. "That's garbage compared to my original menu. Stewart thinks everything is too expensive. He's constantly on me about sticking to the budget. I keep telling him this place is going to bomb if he doesn't spend time and money investing in the restaurant. It's dinner and a show. It's not a dinner show."

"Is there a difference?"

"Is there a difference? Yes, there's a difference. A dinner show is all one-ticket price. You get a song-and-dance number, a rubber piece of chicken, and a stale cookie. That's not what he sold me on when he hired me. The audience pays for the show. If they want dinner and dessert, it's separate. That way we can focus on the food. Ashland needs another fine dining establishment and we have a chance right now to be that, but Stewart won't listen. He has Chuck in his ear. What does Chuck know about running a restaurant?" *His face blotched with color. I wanted to reach out and put my hand on his leg to stop it from bouncing on the floor. Like when I had witnessed him and Chuck get into it, I wondered if he was on something or in need of a fix.*

"Chuck is advising Stewart on the menu?" *I was confused.*

"On everything." Ronald *breathed in the smell of the unlit cigarette and returned it to the pack. "Chuck is basically running this place and no one understands why. The guy has to go. If he doesn't, the cast and crew are going to walk."*

"Why?" I moved to make way for the waitstaff as applause and cheers sounded in the theater. The audience had obviously enjoyed the first act.

"Don't ask me. I'm the chef." Ronald stuffed the pack of cigarettes in his camo chef's coat. "I need a smoke."

He left, and I helped scoop vanilla ice cream on the already plated slices of devil's food cake.

Applause erupted in the theater. That was our cue to start sending out the dessert course. Helen hurried into the kitchen and immediately tied her Torte apron around her waist. "What can I do?"

She dotted the pastel parfaits with butter cookies and handed a tray to a volunteer. We refilled coffee carafes and made sure that no table went without dessert. Intermission went by in a mad dash of desserts and drinks. In what felt like mere minutes the lights flashed and audience members were asked to return to their seats.

The volunteers returned with empty plates—a good sign that people had enjoyed the desserts. Helen and I went back to our table for the second act. It was as delightful as the first. Despite the last-minute rush to get the theater show-ready, the evening appeared to be a huge success. The audience gave the actors a standing ovation at the end of the show. People mingled and chatted about how wonderful it was to have another theater in town. I overheard quite a few comments about wanting to return again for another slice of devil's food cake.

We circled the room together, talking with friends and fellow business owners. Sometime close to eleven, I looked over to see Helen trying to stifle a yawn.

"Why don't you head home?" I said, handing her the keys to the VW. "I'll check in with Stewart about tomorrow and do one last kitchen walk-through."

"How will you get home?"

Doug came up behind us. He wore a pair of khaki slacks, matching oversized blazer, and a Hawaiian shirt straight from a scene out of *Magnum, P.I.* "I'll take him home, Helen. I might have to take him out for a beer first."

"What about your date?" Helen glanced around us.

"Ah, she had an early morning meeting, so she already took off." Doug shrugged. I knew that he had been unlucky in love lately. I wasn't sure why. He was a great guy. Intelligent, attractive, funny. But finding a woman of equal caliber had been a challenge.

"Uh-oh." Helen gave me a knowing look. "Not a keeper then?"

Doug winked. "You know me, I like to keep my options open."

"The eternal bachelor," I teased my friend.

He nudged me. "Will, you scored Ashland's best woman, why should I even bother?"

Helen batted at both of us. "Just for that I am going home." She winked. "Don't stay out too late, boys."

"What do you say?" Doug asked. "Can you make it up for a pint or are you too old now?"

"You jest, dear friend. A drink? I'm in."

"I'll go bid adieu to our Midnight pals and meet you out front in a few?"

The Midnight Group Doug was referring to was our late-night troupe, many of whom had come to support the cast on opening night. I couldn't find Stewart anywhere. Maybe he and the cast were already out celebrating. I did check on the kitchen and was impressed to find it in immaculate condition. Three small boxes of leftover desserts had been boxed up and stored in the fridge. Our Torte aprons were hanging from an exposed nail on the wall, and Helen's extra supplies were carefully arranged in a shopping tote.

Knowing that dessert service had gone smoothly gave me confidence. Maybe this could become a beneficial partnership for us. I found my coat and went to meet Doug outside.

The evening air had a bite to it. I pulled up the collar on my coat. Two streetlights cast a faint glow on Hargadine Street where a row of cute houses lined the sidewalk. Across the street was the parking lot for Ashland's one and only "skyscraper," the Mark Antony Hotel that sat at the bottom of the hill. I could hear music from Rumors reverberating in the nightclub next door.

Doug stood waiting for me on the corner. Across

the street I could make out the silhouette of someone standing underneath the streetlight smoking.
Was it Ronald? Had he been outside since intermission?

I buttoned my coat. "Where to, Doug?"

Doug wrapped a wool scarf around his neck.
"I'd say that the world is our oyster, Will, but sadly
there are what—maybe two places—in town still
open. You want to walk down to the Mark Antony?"

"Maybe we should open a nightclub."

"You think Helen will go for that? Don't you
have enough on your plate with the bakeshop, Juliet, and now dessert at the Cabaret?"

"Doug, you're such a realist." I stuffed my hands
into my coat pockets.

"It comes with the territory." He patted his chest
pocket. I knew that he was referring to the fact that
his shiny new police badge was tucked inside.

We were about to head down the hill to the
vintage hotel, when Chuck Faraday stumbled out
of the theater belting the words to "Broadway
Baby," one of the songs from the musical. He saw
us and proceeded to tap-dance right into the middle
of the street. The guy was definitely not in his
right mind.

"Careful there, Chuck," Doug cautioned.

Chuck tapped on the top of a storm drain, his
legs moving like an ostrich learning how to walk.

"He's done for," Doug said to me.

"I couldn't have said it better myself. Either he
started drinking right after close of the show, or he's
on something strong."

"I'd put my money on a combination of drugs and alcohol."

"Where are you heading, friend?" Doug asked Chuck, who continued to sing and dance in the middle of the street. "Can we give you a lift home?"

Chuck ignored him and started a new number from Dames at Sea—"There's Something About You."

"What should we do?" I asked Doug.

"I think we might need to offer him a formal escort home."

We were about to cross the street when the sound of a revving engine made us both turn around. Out of nowhere a sports car barreled down the street.

My heart thudded. Doug waved and shouted, trying to signal the car, but it was too dark. "Chuck, move!" Doug yelled.

He started toward him just as the car sped up and slammed into Chuck's body.

Chuck went flying through the air and landed ten feet away with the most horrific thud I had ever heard. The car didn't stop. It squealed as it made a sharp turn down Second Street and disappeared out of sight.

"Go call nine-one-one," Doug commanded. He was already halfway to Chuck.

I ran back into the theater. The front lobby doors were still unlocked, thankfully. No one was in sight, so I raced behind the ticket counter and dialed 9-1-1. "A man's been hit by a car. We need an ambulance."

The operator remained calm while I explained what I had witnessed. She stayed on the line until *the sound of sirens rang out nearby. I returned to the scene of the crime to find three police cars, an ambulance, and fire truck blocking the street. The glare of their lights dancing off the trees made me dizzy.*

I hung back, not wanting to get in anyone's way. Paramedics tended to Chuck while two of the police cars sped off. I assumed they were likely trying to track down the driver of the car. Was it a hit-and-run? Had the driver been drunk and not seen Chuck standing in the middle of the road? Even if the driver was drunk, they must have realized they'd hit something—or in this case someone. I couldn't imagine fleeing the scene.

"What's all the commotion?" A man's voice made me startle.

I turned to see Ronald behind me. He wore his camo chef's coat and puffed on a cigarette.

I coughed and waved smoke from my face.

He realized that the smoke was bothering me and moved his head so that the smoke wafted the other direction.

"There's been a hit-and-run. Weren't you over there when it happened?" I pointed across the street where I had seen someone smoking when Doug and I had first come outside.

"Nope. I've been at Rumors. Heard the sirens and came up to see what was going on."

I could have sworn that Ronald had been across the street.

He buttoned the top button on his chef's coat. "Looks like Chuck got mowed down."

"What?" I hadn't mentioned Chuck's name. How did Ronald know that Chuck had been hit?

"That's Chuck, right?" He took a drag off the cigarette and stared toward the emergency vehicles. The jumpiness I'd seen in him earlier had disappeared.

"It is." I stared down the street. The ambulance blocked most of our view, as did the team of first responders gathered around Chuck. There was no way Ronald could know that Chuck was the victim from this distance, not unless he had some sort of superpower that allowed him to see through cars.

Ronald took another puff from the cigarette, dropped it on the sidewalk, and smashed it with his tennis shoe. "Doesn't look like he's going to make it."

"Why do you say that?"

He pointed to the cart and body bag being wheeled off the ambulance.

I thought I might be sick. I'd never seen anyone die before. Poor Chuck.

Ronald didn't appear to share my angst over witnessing something so horrific. "I'm not surprised to see this happen. He made a lot of enemies around town. I can't say that there are going to be many people mourning Chuck's death."

His callous attitude made the already surreal turn of events that much more disturbing. "I can't agree with you on that," I said, defending Ashland. "Things like this don't happen here. I think the opposite will be true—if Chuck is dead. Our

*community will mourn his death and rally around
one another."*

"You didn't know him well, did you?"

*"I knew him well enough. And I know Ashland
well enough to say with conviction that no one is
going to take his death lightly."*

*"We'll see about that." Ronald took another cig-
arette from the pack. "We could wager a bet since
it looks like I'm right."*

*I looked down the street to see the EMS work-
ers zipping the body bag. Nerves sent my stomach
twirling. I tried to calm it by placing my hand on my
solar plexus. There was not a chance that I would
wager a bet on a man's death. "I need to go check
on my ride." I walked away from Ronald. His attitude and complete lack of compassion for Chuck
gave me the creeps.*

*Could he have done it? I replayed what I had
seen. There had been a man smoking across the
street who had disappeared. If that had been Ronald, how much time would he have needed to slip
away and get his car? Five minutes? Ten?*

*It was possible. The car had come out of no-
where and Doug and I had been chatting and
watching Chuck prance around the street. It was
definitely plausible that Ronald could have had
his car parked around the corner, run over Chuck,
sped off, and then casually strolled up to me in an
attempt to provide an alibi. It was also possible
that he hadn't been the person I'd seen smoking,
which made him even more of a suspect. He could*

*have been waiting in his car for the right moment
and seized the opportunity when he saw Chuck.*

*I didn't like the vibe I had gotten from him and
intended to fill Doug in about our strange and uncomfortable conversation.*

Chapter Eight

"What happened next?" I asked the Professor when he paused in reading my dad's account of the night of Chuck's accident. "Was it a hit-and-run? Did you find whoever did it?"

The Professor took a drink of water and dabbed his chin with a napkin. "Chuck Faraday's death turned out to be my first official solo case. The lead detective at the time sent me off on my own. He claimed it was because he thought I was ready, but the truth of the matter was that he was well aware of the fact that hit-and-runs are extremely hard to solve. That remains true today. We have the luxury of more cameras today, but without photographic evidence or witnesses who are able to clearly identify the make, model, and even license plate, hit-and-run fatalities often go unsolved."

"Really?" I took a drink of my water. The bakeshop was alive with the scent of wood-fired pizza and baking bread.

"I'm afraid so. The first forty-eight hours are critical. Sometimes we'll get a break if the driver attempts to repair any damage by taking the vehicle to an auto body shop. Unlike in other crimes, with a hit-and-run the primary evidence is gone. The only thing you're left with is the actual body. It's maddening for those of us in the field and absolutely heart wrenching for the families of the victims."

Torte's front doorbell jingled as a group of middle-schoolers on a field trip to OSF walked inside. They giggled and chatted happily as they went up to the counter to place their orders. Their upbeat energy was in direct contrast to the Professor's story.

"Your father helped me with the investigation. He didn't want Helen to know. I knew that your parents had poured everything they had into Torte. I offered Will some extra cash on the side if he would accompany me and help be another set of eyes. You have to understand this was a deal between the two of us. It was unique in that there wasn't other physical evidence to examine, so having him come along while I interviewed auto body shops and canvassed the neighborhood and businesses around the Cabaret wouldn't have jeopardized my investigation. I couldn't pay him as an official consultant, but I could pay him out of my own pocket." He folded his napkin into a neat square and placed it on top of his empty plate.

"Did you really want his help or were you just trying to find a way to give my parents some extra cash?" I too had polished every last crumb of Sterling's delectable panned pizza.

"No, I was desperate for his wisdom and insight. Remember, we were in our late twenties. This was my first opportunity to investigate a fatality on my own and I wanted to impress my boss and the powers that be. In hindsight, I should have considered the risk I was putting your father in, but we were young and naive."

"I can't imagine that you were ever naive." I wrinkled my forehead.

He wavered. "Perhaps not in the textbook definition, but I made more than my fair share of mistakes early in my career and involving your father in this case was certainly my worst."

"But he must have wanted to be involved. He wouldn't have agreed otherwise." I hoped that was true. Learning that my father had witnessed a fatality and had been active in trying to track down who had done it gave me new insight and understanding into my past. Maybe my desire to see justice was in my genes.

"Oh yes. Will was eager to provide assistance, but he was nervous about what Helen would think. It was the one and only time he kept a secret from her, and I know that he took that regret to the grave." The Professor sighed and rubbed his temples.

I reached across the table and placed my hand over his. "It's okay. My dad was an adult. He made his own choices."

"Thank you for that, Juliet." The Professor tried to smile. "Shall we continue?"

"If you're up for it?"

"Certainly." He leaned forward and rested his elbows on the booth as he continued to read.

The next morning, I awoke to a throbbing headache. I had waited for Doug last night. It took a couple hours for the police to clear the scene. I had offered to walk or call a cab, but Doug had said he wanted to talk to me about something in private if I didn't mind waiting. On the ride home, he had informed me that he was going to be the lead in Chuck Faraday's hit-and-run investigation and he wanted my help. I was happy for him, and I agreed. It had seemed like the right thing to do last night. Maybe it had been due to the fact of witnessing the crime—that I felt responsible to bring Chuck's killer to justice somehow. Or maybe it had been triggered by my conversation with Ronald. In the light of day I wondered if I had made a mistake. If Helen found out that Doug and I were working a case together, she would kill both of us.

I didn't like the thought of keeping a secret from her, but I couldn't stop seeing Chuck's body flying through the air or silence the sound of the car's screeches. What harm could there be in tagging along with Doug for a couple days? He told me that the next two days were the most critical. If we could get a solid lead on the driver in forty-eight hours our odds of catching who did this would go up exponentially.

Helen was brushing Juliet's hair when I dragged myself downstairs. "Late night? You and Doug must have really hit the town."

"Something like that." I poured myself a cup of coffee.

In true Helen form, I could tell by the line creasing her brow she knew something was amiss. "Juliet, run upstairs and get your library books. Today is library day at school."

"Library day!" Juliet jumped from her chair and ran upstairs.

"What is it, William? Are you hungover? Is something wrong with Doug?"

I nursed my coffee. *"Nothing gets by you, does it?"*

She picked up Juliet's breakfast dishes and walked them to the sink. *"No, and you better remember that,"* she teased. *"Plus you have no poker face and you're as white as Juliet's hair. What happened last night?"*

"I'm not hungover, but I feel like I am. Doug and I never made it out for that beer." I proceeded to fill her in on Chuck's death, leaving out one important detail—that I had been invited to be on the case.

"Will, that's horrible." Helen came and embraced me. Her hair smelled like honey. *"Are you okay? What can I do? I mean, first of all you are not coming into Torte today. Drink your coffee and then go back to bed."*

"Helen, no I'll be fine. You can't manage the bakery on your own. We have another round of desserts to make for tonight's performance. Assuming tonight's performance goes on." I hadn't considered whether or not the show would continue without Chuck.

"Nope. I'm putting my foot down on this, Will Capshaw. You didn't get home until after two. I heard you come in, and you look miserable. You're the one who is always saying that everything we bake is made with love. You can't bake with love after what you witnessed last night."

I tried to protest, but she stopped me.

"Not another word. I'm going to call Wendy right now. She already offered to help. Plus we were going to pop over to Small Change later this morning anyway. They're having a big sale on girls' dresses. You rest this morning. I don't want to see you anywhere near the bakeshop."

She had given me the perfect out to go with Doug, which made me feel even worse. However there was no arguing with my wife when she set her mind to an idea. She shooed me back to bed with a fresh cup of coffee and a cinnamon raisin bagel. "Get some sleep. Come in if you're feeling better later or take the entire day."

I waited until I heard the door shut and the van pull out of the driveway, before I took a hot shower and got dressed. Then I called Doug, who agreed to swing by to pick me up within the hour. Helen's coffee and the shower revived my senses. I started thinking through everything leading up to Chuck's death. While I didn't agree with Ronald's tone, he was right about one thing—Chuck had appeared to have gotten into disagreements with a number of people. There was Shelly, the artistic director. I had seen them arguing off stage right before the show. I had overheard Pat, the owner of Rumors, telling Stewart that Chuck was banned from his night-club. Chuck and Ronald had almost come to blows, and Stewart had alluded to the fact that he wasn't thrilled with the star's behavior.

The beep of Doug's vintage 1965 red convertible

mustang stopped my train of thought. Hopefully we would uncover something this morning.

"How are you feeling? That was a rough night." Doug opened the passenger door for me.

"I know. Helen banned me from Torte." I hopped into the passenger seat. Last night's chill had given way to a warm morning. The sun beat down on the pavement. A Steller's jay with a black mohawk hopped on our front picket fence, begging for peanuts. Everything about the day from the bright sky to the kiss of the wind in the glossy oak trees felt wrong. I had witnessed a man's death last night. Would I ever feel the same again?

"That's good news. She didn't ban you from coming along with me, did she?" Doug reached into the glove box and pulled out a cassette tape.

"I didn't tell her. We agreed to keep this between the two of us, right?"

"You have my word, Will. I swear upon the Bard." He maneuvered the car out of our driveway. "We need a code name though. Something that won't alert Helen."

I thought for a moment as he steered the car down the hill. "What about the Pastry Case? That way if anyone hears us talking, they'll assume I'm telling you about whatever is currently in the actual pastry case."

"The Pastry Case, yes. That's perfect." He chuckled and then popped the tape into the cassette player. "How do you feel about a little CCR to start our drive?"

"Sure." I turned up the volume as "Bad Moon Rising" started to play. "Where are we going first?"

"If you reach into the glove box, I highlighted every auto body shop from Yreka to Grants Pass. I figured we'd start south and work our way north. Does that work for you?" Doug flipped a pair of John Lennon sunglasses over his eyes.

"Sure."

The California border was only sixteen miles south. We drove along Old Highway 99 past Kelly green hills to the east. While Doug drove, we talked through each possible suspect. "There is one other possibility," he said as he took the first exit in Yreka.

"What's that?"

"That Chuck's death was a random accident. The driver could have been intoxicated or high. There's an outside chance that the driver didn't realize they'd hit someone."

"Is that what you think?"

Doug steered us to Ray's Auto Body, the first X on our map. "No. If I was a betting man, I would put my money on it being intentional. Everything about it felt off. The way the engine revved. The speed. The fact that the driver didn't slow for one minute. Is that the way you remember it?"

I nodded. "To the letter."

The wind on my face as we sped along the highway felt oddly refreshing. "Do you think it could have something to do with drugs?" I asked, then I told him about the fight I'd seen between Ronald and Chuck. "What if Ronald was Chuck's supplier or vice versa?"

"It's possible. The nightclub scene is notorious for drug problems. I should have toxicology reports soon, so that will at least tell us what Chuck had in his system."

Accompanying Doug on his interviews was eye opening. He didn't rush. Rather he took his time, asking deliberate questions and studying each response. We struck out in Yreka, Ashland, Medford, and Talent. Our luck changed when we pulled into a run-down shop in White City. The rural town was well off the beaten path and not much more than a few run-down buildings and one small diner.

The owner of the repair shop looked as if he was as old as the building. He wiped grease on his coveralls as we approached him.

"Morning, sir. I'm wondering if you've had any cars in for repair this morning." Doug placed his sunglasses on the top of his head. He removed a leather notebook from the breast pocket of his Hawaiian shirt.

"This is a repair shop, yeah. I've had cars in."

Doug filled him in on the details along with a description of the car.

"Nope. Nothing matching that has come in today, but I did get a call this morning from a guy asking for a price on front body damage. I told him he had to bring the car in so I could see it. Asked for his name and number. He got cagey and hung up right after that."

"You're sure it was a man?"

"Yep. Unless it was a woman with a voice as deep as James Earl Jones."

Doug looked to me and then made a note. "Excellent. Thank you for your help. If you think of anything else or if this guy calls again or comes in, please call me right away." He handed him a business card.

"How does that help us?" I asked once we were in the car again.

"I can pull phone records. If we can try to trace where the call came from, we might be able to make an arrest. That would be amazing, Will. Can you imagine if we solve this in the first day?"

"How long will it take to pull phone records?"

"I'll call my secretary at our next stop and get that going. This has to be our guy. It would make sense that he would put some feelers out, and White City is far out of town. I say we hit the remaining spots on the map and then head back to Ashland."

The rest of the auto shops were dead ends. We received good news when we returned to Ashland shortly after lunchtime. The call to the shop in White City had come in and been traced to a payphone on the plaza in Ashland.

Doug left to check the phone for prints, and I returned to the bakeshop. For the first time since last night, I felt hopeful. If we could catch Chuck's killer, maybe things would start to feel normal again.

Chapter Nine

"Things must have been much harder back then," I said to the Professor.

"Very true. Yes, without a doubt. Had I had access to today's technology I'm quite confident we would have made a prompt arrest." He smoothed the napkin that rested on his empty plate.

"You must have suspected someone though?" I asked, noting that the lunchtime rush around us had begun to thin. A small line remained at the pastry counter and espresso bar. The sound of foaming milk and customers chatting filled the space. Rosa expertly navigated past the line, balancing a tray of caramel and chocolate shortbread squares, custard tarts, and pecan hand pies.

"I did. I suspected many, but without proof—ah, that's the rub." His tone was somber. "Chuck's death is the one case that has lingered in my mind. I wouldn't go as far as to say that it's haunted me. I've had long stretches where I've not thought of that fateful evening, but every so often that night will flash in my mind and fill me with trouble."

It was strange to see the Professor so downtrodden. He had always been one of the wisest men I knew. It felt like

I was reopening an old wound and dragging him into the past with me. "Do you want to stop?" I asked. "I can finish reading on my own."

"No, no. Not at all." He waved me off. "Please, let's press on."

When I returned to Torte, things were buzzing. Helen and our good friend Wendy had made a huge dent in the Cabaret desserts. The pastry case was stocked and every table in the dining area had a collection of happy customers sharing plates of pineapple upside-down cake and bread-and-butter pudding.

"Ladies, you've outdone yourselves." I went to the sink to wash my hands.

"You look better," Helen noted. "Did you sleep?"

"No." If I was going to be successful in keep my investigating from my wife, I intended to keep the lies to a minimum. "I got some fresh air, had a coffee or two, and now I'm at your mercy. Put me to work."

Wendy grinned. She was our age with a young daughter, Amanda, who went to school with Juliet. The girls, like Helen and Wendy, had become fast friends. "I told Helen, I don't think I can work here any longer. It's too tempting. I've been nibbling on bites of everything all morning." She dipped her pinky into a vat of buttercream to prove her point.

"No, you can't desert us." Helen pretended to collapse. "Tell her, Will. She'll get over the tasting, right? We did."

"'Tis true." I folded my hands together in a meditation. "The siren song of pastry is difficult to resist,

but rest assured her sweet, sweet, calls will be silenced after a few days, and the stomachache that
comes with sampling." I rested my arm next to a tray
of mini lemon meringue pies. "As the Bard says,
'The fiend is at mine elbow and tempts me.'"

Helen and Wendy cracked up. I picked up a pot
of coffee. "I'll take over refill duty." With that, I
swept into the dining room. As usual there were
a number of familiar faces in the room. Everyone
was talking about the hit-and-run. I tried not to
eavesdrop but couldn't help getting drawn into the
discussion when I stopped to top off coffees at one
of the window booths.

"William, you were at the Cabaret last night,
weren't you?" a woman asked. I looked up from
the coffeepot to see Jeri Heyward, the membership
director for the Oregon Shakespeare Festival. She
was sitting with a friend, whom I didn't recognize.

"Good to see you, Jeri. Yes, I was there. You
were too, right? I thought I saw you talking to
Chuck." I didn't say anything about seeing her and
Chuck locked in an embrace or the fact that she
had subsequently slapped him.

She didn't respond to my question as she rifled
through a stack of carbon-copy receipts in a file
folder. "Sorry, this is such a mess. I've taken over
your bakery with my donation forms." She pushed
the paper receipts toward the woman seated across
from her. "Can you take these back to the office?
We can continue our conversation there. I want a
word with William."

The woman acquiesced to her request. Once

she had left, Jeri pointed to the empty seat. "Sit, please."

Jeri was a commanding woman, not in size but in personality. She was short and petite with long, black feathered hair, styled like Joan Collins in Dynasty. *The bulky shoulder pads in her gray suit jacket gave her an imposing stance.*

"How are things at the Festival?" I asked, sitting across from her and resting the nearly empty coffeepot on the table.

"Don't ask."

"Really? I thought I had read in the paper that ticket sales and patron donations were up this year?"

"Not anymore thanks to Chuck Faraday." She strummed her long, fake nails on the tabletop. They were painted bright neon orange.

I wondered if she knew about Chuck's accident. Then again, I didn't know how she couldn't. It was the only thing customers were talking about.

"I can't say I'm sorry he's dead," Jeri continued, answering my question for me. "He's been poaching OSF's best actors, actresses, and patrons. I had a meeting with our executive team last week to tell them they had better find a way to put a stop to whatever Chuck's been up to at the Cabaret or else we might have to start cutting back shows and trimming staff."

This news shocked me. The long-running repertory theater had been gaining popularity and bringing in well-received talent and productions. I couldn't fathom how the Cabaret would threaten that. If anything, having another theater in town would help strengthen Ashland's artistic reputation.

"There are ways to go about building recipro-cal relationships and Chuck obviously did not understand the importance of that." She tapped her fingernails on the tabletop.

"What did you think of last night's opening?" I asked. "The production was so different than anything the Festival is doing. They don't seem competitive to me. If anything, they're complimen-tary."

"I didn't see the show. I refused. Imagine the message that would have sent. Seeing my face there would have been the same as giving that farce of a theater my blessing. I did stop by after the show to watch audience reaction on their way out and I have to say it wasn't good. I heard many comments about how junior high the production felt."

That hadn't been my experience, and I knew that Jeri was lying. Helen and I had both seen her fighting with Chuck before the show. "I could have sworn I saw you there."

Jeri twisted a fake gaudy gold ring on her pinky. "Well, yes. I mean it was my duty to get a read on how things went, but I wasn't about to sit front and center and give that fake theater my stamp of approval. After the show I asked a few questions, that's all. Rest assured, I didn't overstep my bounds. I didn't directly ask anyone their opinion."

Was she openly admitting to being at the scene of the crime? And why was she lying about being *at the theater before curtain? I decided to test the waters. "Did you see the hit-and-run?"*

She lost her swagger. Her pinky ring dropped on the table and went spinning. "No. No. I wasn't there." She tried to grab the ring, but it fell to the floor.

I reached under the table to retrieve it for her.

"Thank you." Her hand trembled as I placed the ring in it.

"Was there something you wanted to ask me?"

Jeri paused for a moment, appearing flustered. Billy Joel played on the speakers overhead. A couple customers lined up near the counter. I needed to get back to work.

"As someone well versed in the theater, I wanted to get your honest opinion on the show, William. Don't hold back. Tell me what you really thought."

"I enjoyed it. I thought it was quite fun and lively. Everyone around us seemed to share that sentiment."

Jeri's hands squeezed into tight fists. "I see. Well, excellent. Good for you. I need to get back to my office. Paperwork calls."

She didn't seem pleased with my response, but it was the truth. I made a mental note to share my conversation with Doug later.

The next few hours passed quickly. We sold out of my handmade Ding Dongs, and Helen's chicken-and-rice soup was a huge hit for lunch. Wendy prepped the Cabaret desserts, and I waited tables. It was a welcome distraction to steep pots of Earl Gray tea and wipe down tables.

Our imported espresso machine arrived about an hour after we closed for the afternoon. We were worse than Juliet on Christmas morning as we watched the shiny stainless steel machine get unloaded from a truck and waited with eager anticipation for it to be installed. Helen snapped dozens of pictures while our coffee rep installed it on the far edge of the pastry counter. We had gone over multiple ideas of where to place the espresso machine and finally landed on what I hoped would be the perfect spot.

One of our goals at the bakeshop was to build lasting relationships with our customers, and placing the espresso machine at the end of the counter would allow us to chat and maintain eye contact with people while pulling shots of strong Italian coffee.

"You've gone through two rolls of film, Helen," I said pouring a thick fragrant shot of espresso into a clear glass mug, while our coffee rep critiqued my technique.

"It's so exciting. I can't believe we're the first restaurant or bakery in the Rogue Valley to have a real espresso machine. Can you make a layered latte, like the ones we've seen in the coffee culture magazines?"

Our rep and I practiced the technique of steaming milk and adding a generous layer of foam on the top of the coffee. Most of our customers were used to drinking Folgers at home. It would be interesting to see how our Italian-style line of new espresso drinks would be received. The latte looked

*sophisticated with three unique layers and colors—
dark espresso on the bottom, a layer of creamy milk
in the middle, and two inches of foam on the top.*

*"I don't think we can drink it," Helen said to
Wendy. "It's too pretty."*

*Specialty coffee would be a small part of our bak-
ery offerings. We would continue to brew house drip
coffees, and offer customers three selections: lattes,
cappuccinos, and straight shots of espresso served
at the bar, just like in Italy. While our customers
might savor a latte, straight espresso was meant to
be drunk very quickly while the crema, a creamy
emulsion of the coffee's oils, was still on the top.*

*Our coffee rep pulled espressos for each of us
and showed us how to knock it back like a strong
shot of whiskey. Neither Helen nor I had ever been
to Italy, but we had spent many hours looking
through magazines and catalogs, as well as sampling coffee shops up and down the West Coast.
We had tasted a number of similar espresso drinks
in San Francisco and in Seattle where a relatively
new coffee company, Starbucks, was starting to
make a name for itself. It was a risk to introduce
European coffees to Ashland, but a well-calculated
one. Helen and I had modeled Torte to match Ashland's Elizabethan aesthetic. We felt confident that
even if our local customer base turned their noses
down at "fancy" coffee, we would be able to gain a
following with the tourist crowd.*

"This is delicious," Wendy said finishing her shot.

*Helen set her empty glass on the counter. "I'll
have another. Or maybe a dozen."*

"Pace yourself," I cautioned.

We took turns practicing on the machine and sharing complimentary samples with customers. Perhaps our loyal base was being kind, but the feedback seemed positive; every mug and shot glass was returned empty. Hopefully that was a sign of things to come. Once Helen and Wendy had both familiarized themselves with pulling creamy espresso shots, they took a break to go check out the sale at Small Change, a clothing store nearby in the plaza. I had thought that having a moment of reprieve would be good for me, but the opposite was true. The quiet lull of the afternoon and the absence of Helen's laughter brought memories of Chuck's death to the forefront of my mind. I replayed every detail of the night. What if I had run out to grab him? Maybe I could have stopped him. I should have reacted faster, but everything had happened in a strange, dream-like blur.

Fortunately, I didn't have too much time alone with my thoughts. Helen and Wendy returned shortly with bags full of dresses for Juliet and Amanda. I had to resist racing over to hug Helen. She definitely would have suspected that something was wrong. Instead I took solace in listening to them describe the great deals they had found and nodded approval when they showed me their haul.

Late in the afternoon Doug came into the bakery. His cheeks had a touch of color, I guessed from driving around with the top down all afternoon.

"Doug, you're just in time to try a cappuccino," Helen said, handing him a coffee. *"This is my tenth*

attempt, and I think I'm getting better, but promise you'll be honest."

"Helen, everything you make is next to godliness." Doug took the drink.

"Stop, you'll make me blush." She waved him off.

"Then my work here is done." He winked. "Will, do you have a minute? I want to run something by you."

"Sure." I wiped my hands on a dish towel and went to join him at a two-person table.

Helen and Wendy were so busy boxing up the Cabaret desserts that they didn't take notice.

"Any news on the pay phone?"

Doug shook his head. "Another dead end. Wiped clean."

"What does that mean?"

"I'm not sure." He took a sip of the cappuccino. "This is really good."

"I know. I think we might be onto something with specialty coffees."

"Agreed." He took another drink, then continued. "I don't know if it officially means anything, but my instincts are telling me that this has to be our guy. They're also telling me that he knew he had hit someone and now is trying to clean up his tracks."

"Do you think that it means that the hit-and-run was intentional?"

He removed his notebook from his short-sleeve black shirt with tropical white flowers. "That's the crux of the issue isn't it? I don't know, Will. Am I in over my head?" He ran his fingers through his reddish hair.

"Why do you say that?" I glanced out the window where a group of high-schoolers skateboarded in the plaza. It would be time to pick up Juliet from school soon. If Doug was worried, should I be too?

"I want to make a good impression and I'd been so hopeful after our lead this morning, and now I feel like all those clues have evaporated and I'm back at square one with nothing." He doodled on his notebook as he spoke.

"Isn't that how investigations go?"

"I don't know. That's why I feel like I'm in over my head. Maybe I shouldn't have offered to take this one on." He let out a low sigh and took another drink of his coffee.

"It's way too soon to start thinking that. It hasn't even been twenty-four hours. You said yourself that the first forty-eight hours are the most critical. We're not even halfway through that window."

He shifted his body weight. "You're right. Thanks, Will. I needed a pep talk. What do you think? The more time I spend replaying everything, the more I'm convinced that this was intentional."

I glanced behind us to make sure Helen wasn't watching. *"Me too."* I told him about my conversation with Jeri. *"Why would she lie to me? She was definitely there before opening, and she and Chuck were making out. Then out of nowhere she slapped him and stormed off."*

"Hmm." Doug strummed his amber beard. *"A lover's spat? This is good intel. I'll add her to my list. I've made it through about half of the neighborhood*

*surrounding the Cabaret, but I'm going to continue
to canvass."*

"What can I do?"

*"You're sure you still want to be involved?"
Doug raised an eyebrow in Helen's direction. "If
our instincts are right, it means we're looking for
a killer."*

*"I know." I intentionally kept my focus on my
friend.*

*"In that case, you're delivering desserts to the
Cabaret again tonight. Can you stick around for a
while? Keep an ear and eye open. I suspect that
the killer is tied to the theater. It's probably someone involved or maybe even a fellow cast member.
I interviewed Chuck's understudy on the off chance
that he was seeking the limelight. No luck. He had
an air-tight alibi."*

"I'm on it."

*"Let's meet for that beer later and regroup." He
finished his cappuccino and left.*

*I sent Wendy and Helen home, claiming that I
would take care of the rest of the cleaning, lock up,
and deliver pastries to the Cabaret. A feeling of guilt
came over me when Helen kissed me and thanked
me for being the best husband on the planet. If she
knew what I was really up to, she might not feel the
same.*

Chapter Ten

With every new detail that the journal revealed, I found myself feeling more connected to my father. I didn't fault him for not telling Mom, although I did appreciate that he was torn over the decision.

"You were really thinking about giving up the case?" I asked the Professor.

"I was considering walking off the case and walking away from detective life."

"Really? I can't imagine."

"But remember, as I said before, we were young. The Pastry Case, as your father and I referred to it, has haunted me for years, but it taught me many things. One of the most important things I've learned over the course of my career, in fact."

"What's that?"

"To always trust your instincts." His golden-flecked eyes met mine. "Always. Your instincts will never lead you astray. That's a lesson for work, for love, for life."

The Professor's words struck a chord. He was right. I wished I had a clear instinct on what was next for me and Carlos. I had been intentionally trying to sit with the distance between us. To allow myself space and time. I had thought that an answer or a sense of knowing might magically appear, but it hadn't yet.

"What did your instincts tell you about the case?"

"That we were looking for a cold-blooded killer. The crime-scene analysts came in to examine any potential skid marks—the only physical evidence possibly left on the scene—aside from some broken pieces of headlights. Remember, this was before the kind of digital technology we have today. We were shooting photos on my old Nikon camera, and I would have to run it up the street to the drug store to have them process the film. The team was able to determine that the car had intentionally sped up before coming in contact with Chuck. There were no signs of skid marks that would have indicated an attempt to brake or stop. The only trace they found was when the car took a sharp right turn."

"You mean as in when the driver was making his or her getaway?"

"Exactly." His kind eyes held a hint of nostalgia. Or was it regret? "You are your father's daughter. If the driver had attempted to stop, there would have been marks in the street from the impact of slamming on his brakes quickly. The analysts found no evidence of that. Quite frankly it confirmed my suspicion. Since your father and I were witnesses, we would have heard and seen the car attempting to brake. Vehicles in the eighties didn't have the same safety standards we have today. It's likely that the car would have flipped. I certainly had plenty of learning to do, but we were right about Chuck being murdered."

I glanced up at the clock on the far wall. We had been talking for over an hour.

"Am I keeping you?" the Professor asked.

"No. And, even if you were, we can't stop now." I leafed through the journal. There were only twenty or thirty pages left labeled "The Pastry Case." The remaining pages were notes and some of my dad's poetry.

"I suppose that's true."

It was no wonder that the Professor had been drawn to Ashland. My father's words made our town come to life. I could almost hear his calming, baritone voice through the pages of his journal. It made me feel like I had been transported to the 1980s. I craved more. I had become completely immersed in the past. So much so that I knew there was no hope of being productive in the kitchen or with my staff until I had learned every detail about my dad's involvement in the Pastry Case.

I kept my promise to Doug and arrived an hour early to deliver desserts to the Cabaret. The mood was improved from opening night in terms of the frantic rush to get the theater ready, but it was solemn.

Shelly was delivering a speech to the cast when I walked inside. She wore another cape. This time, black with silver trimming. "I know everyone is shaken about what happened to Chuck, but we're professionals and as they say in the biz, 'The show must go on.' I want you to do another walk-through of the choreography before the doors open for dinner service."

I felt sorry for Chuck's understudy—he looked like a deer in headlights as he fumbled his way through the first dance routine.

"William, glad you are here. Would you mind heading downstairs to Rumors and checking on Chef Ronald?" Stewart asked. He looked the part of a theater owner in his black slacks and matching black turtleneck with the Cabaret logo. A pair of wire-rim glasses hung from the tip of his nose.

"Let me get these into the kitchen first." I nodded to the box of pastries.

He scribbled something on his clipboard. "Do what you need to do. I could use another set of eyes on Ronald. He's trying to go off script with the menu again."

I wasn't sure what I was supposed to do about that. Nor was I sure why suddenly everyone in town wanted my "eyes" on the lookout. Although, checking on Ronald would give me another chance to see if I could learn anything about his whereabouts last night, so I dropped off the dessert boxes and headed down the steep kitchen stairwell to Rumors.

The nightclub had an underground vibe that wasn't merely due to its location. Dark wood paneling lined every wall. There were red vinyl booths and black leather chairs arranged around barstools, each offering a customer an unobstructed view of the stage. The smell of stale cigarettes hung heavy in the cavernous space. It made me appreciate our decision to make Torte a non-smoking bakeshop.

A jazz trio warmed up on the small stage while a handful of people listened at the bar. The light fixtures throughout the basement bar had been crafted from recycled musical instruments. Small

*advertising tents sat at each table, proclaiming that
Mel Brown had signed on as the house band. I had
heard mention that he was moving to Ashland for
a six-month gig. That had to be a big coup for Pat.*

*Rumors had a blend of Ashland's countercul-
ture, with a smattering of hippies, plenty of actors
who frequented the nightclub, and college students
who would line up on the street for Flash Dance
Night. The event kicked off at midnight on Sundays,
offering one-dollar drinks and a chance to party
to disco music with the lead choreographer at the
Festival. Helen had jokingly threatened to get a
babysitter and drag me to the disco. Fortunately,
she agreed that Mel Brown was more our speed.*

*The popular underground bar was known for its
late-night scene and for bringing big-name musicians to town. Ashland wasn't exactly on the beaten
path for headliners, but Pat, the owner of Rumors,
had come up with a masterful plan. He invited jazz
greats like Mel Brown, Anthony Davis, and Henry
Threadgill to stop in Ashland on their way north
to Portland and Seattle or south to San Francisco.
Ashland was a perfect halfway point, and the musicians could pull in some good cash for a mid-week
show.*

*I asked the bartender where the kitchen was. He
pointed behind him.*

*It turned out that I didn't need to ask for di-
rections because as the trio ended their set, the
sound of angry voices filled the bar. Pat and Ronald were nose to nose in the kitchen.*

"Enough. I've told you a dozen times I don't have

space for you down here." Pat puffed out his chest to make himself appear bigger. His head was level with Ronald's shoulders.

Ronald mimicked his body movement. "You have tons of space, man. You just don't want to give it up because you know my food is better than this bar crap."

Pat's face ballooned. "Look, I'm doing Stewart a favor. I don't owe you a thing. You can try to lie and cover all you want, but I know that you and Chuck had something shady going on. I might not have proof but I don't trust you for one second."

I cleared my throat. The men stepped away from each other.

"Sorry to interrupt. Stewart asked me to come offer my services. He thought you might need another set of hands."

The galley kitchen wasn't more than fifteen to twenty feet long with stainless steel counters and a cement floor. From the looks of the well-used fryers and massive freezer, I had a feeling everything on Rumors' menu was processed and deep-fried. Not exactly in the spirit of what Helen and I were going for at Torte.

"There's no room for any more help." Ronald tossed a dish towel next to the sink.

Pat got called away to help the bartender with a broken tap handle.

I was glad to have a moment alone with Ronald. What had Pat meant that he was sure Ronald and Chuck were scheming together?

"Are you sure there's nothing I can do?" I asked.

"Pastry is my muse, but you can put me to work chopping, shredding, whatever you need."

"I don't need your help." Ronald's tone was icy.

Since he wasn't going to take me up on my offer, I decided I might as well see if I could get any info out of him. "I overheard Pat say something about you and Chuck working together? I was under the impression that you two weren't exactly friends."

"We weren't. Like I told you, I'm not sorry he's dead." Ronald removed boxes of frozen fries from the cooler.

"What did Pat mean then?"

He banged the box on the counter. It was as hard as Rumors' brick exterior. "Why you asking me?"

How should I proceed? I was in uncharted territory. Doug had asked me to be discreet, and yet I knew that beating around the bush with someone like Ronald wasn't going to get me anywhere. I took a risk. "It sounds like the police are treating Chuck's death as intentional. They're going to be asking a lot of questions, and I have to warn you that your attitude about the hit-and-run isn't going to look good."

Ronald's demeanor shifted. His left eye twitched and his leg starting shaking so violently it made the floor feel as if we were experiencing a minor earthquake. "What? What are you saying?"

"I'm trying to give you fair warning that you could be on the top of their list right now."

My tactic was working. He pushed the frozen fry box aside and moved closer to me. "You think so?"

"Well, you're hardly being discreet about how

much you disliked him, and you were on the scene last night so, yes, I think there's a good chance that you'll be getting a visit from a detective soon."

"Crap." Ronald began pacing. "What do you think they're going to ask me?"

"I don't know. That's not my domain."

"You're friends with that new guy, what's his name?"

"Doug."

"Right. Doug. Can you talk to him? Put in a good word for me?"

"I'm not sure I feel comfortable doing that. To be honest, your reaction to Chuck's death is disturbing."

Ronald's face slacked. "No, no, man, you've got it all wrong." He stopped pacing for a minute. "Wait, you think I killed him?"

"I didn't say that."

"No, but I can see it on your face. That's why you're telling me the police are coming. They think I did it, don't they?"

His tone had changed. He almost sounded manic. Was that because he really was the killer?

Maybe I should have thought my approach through a bit more.

"No, it wasn't me. I didn't like the guy, that's the truth, but I didn't kill him. If you want to know who had motive to run Chuck down, then you're talking to the wrong guy." He patted his camo chef's coat frantically as if searching for something.

"What do you mean?" I studied his face.

Ronald nodded toward the bar. "You should talk to Pat. Pat was fuming mad at Chuck. I overheard them having a blowup. Pat actually said something like, 'I'm going to kill you for this.'" He finally found what he was looking for, a pack of cigarettes. He ripped it open and stuffed a cigarette in his mouth without lighting it.

"For what?"

Ronald shrugged. "I don't know. I think it had something to do with an unpaid bar bill. Chuck liked to bring all of his actor friends to Rumors. They would drink like crazy and order plate after plate of food. He never paid. He always said to put it on his tab. Claimed that he and Pat had some sort of deal worked out. No one questioned him."

This was new information.

"Last week Pat came down on him hard. Told him that he owed every penny he had spent and charged to the bar. Chuck freaked out."

I nodded in response, hoping that if I didn't say anything Ronald would say more.

"You have to talk to your friend, okay? Tell him this. Tell him what I said. If anyone is a suspect around here, it's Pat. Not me." He yanked the unlit cigarette from his mouth and stared at it with longing. "I need a smoke break. See you later."

He took off before I could pepper him with more questions. Was he telling the truth? It was hard to say. His attitude about Chuck's death had certainly changed once I had revealed that the police were investigating. Had he told me about Chuck and

Pat's fight just to shift suspicion away from him, or was there any truth to his story? If Chuck had run up an enormous tab, could that give Pat a motive for murder? I wasn't sure, but at least I had something to report to Doug.

Chapter Eleven

"Did you suspect Pat?" I asked the Professor.

Before he could answer, Andy stopped by our booth with a fresh pot of coffee. "Can I top you off, boss?"

I declined. As did the Professor. Andy cleared our plates and moved on to the next table. We made it our mission to keep our customer's coffee cups filled to the brim. While there were tubs located near the espresso bar for guests to bus their own dishes, we also tried to do consistent sweeps through the dining rooms to pick up any used plates and cups and to wipe down tables. During the height of the morning and lunch rushes it was nearly impossible, but whenever there was a lull we made sure the dining room sparkled. I was glad that my staff took the initiative and I didn't need to remind them to make sure the bakeshop was clean and welcoming.

After Andy was out of earshot, the Professor nodded. "I suspected everyone at one point. Pat certainly had motive, but Jeri, Shelly, Stewart, and Ronald did as well. Everyone connected to the Cabaret had a motive to kill Chuck. It was most vexing." He massaged his ginger and gray beard for a moment. "The burden of proof was my responsibility. My boss reminded me of that fact almost daily, when I would walk into his office with the latest theory that Will and I had concocted. 'Doug, you must find proof,' he would say. 'Theories are nothing more than speculation. Follow the evidence.' That was the problem. There was no evidence." He turned to the next page in the journal. "You'll see our dilemma."

I didn't have a chance to speak to Pat before the show. It was another busy night in the Cabaret's kitchen, prepping dessert plates and ensuring that patrons had fresh cups of coffee and tea. The show lost some of its luster without Chuck in the lead. He might have amassed a list of enemies, but the man was a talented actor.

Shelly and Stewart took the stage before opening curtain and asked the audience to join them in a moment of silence in memory of Chuck. It was a nice gesture, but it felt forced. Shelly pretended to dab tears from her eyes. I doubted that her tears were real. After the moment of silence she practically danced off stage and proceeded to greet one of the front-row tables with kisses and hugs. It was strange behavior for an artistic director who had lost the star of her show.

Stewart wasn't much different. He worked the room, stopping to mingle at tables and talk up the renovations. Maybe that was show biz. If it was, I was glad that I had opted for pastry.

Dessert service went smoother than it had the night before. That was a plus in an otherwise strange evening. I trained a new crew of volunteers, who picked up our signature techniques with ease. By the time the dishes had been cleared after intermission, I was beat. All I wanted was to be home with Helen and Juliet. However I had promised Doug that I would meet him for a beer to go over what I had learned, and Juliet had gone to bed hours ago. Hopefully Doug had uncovered enough evidence to make an arrest and we could put Chuck's murder behind us and get back to our normal routine.

We had agreed to meet at the Mark Antony after the show—I needed a break from the Cabaret. As soon as the last plate had been cleared, I snuck out the rear exit. An ice-cold beer and one of the Mark Antony's world-famous cheeseburgers sounded like the antidote to my troubles. When I arrived at the vintage hotel, Doug had beaten me there. He was sitting near the fireplace reviewing his notes.

"Will, you made it." He looked up as I approached the table. "I took the liberty of ordering you a beer and a burger."

"You are a true friend."

"It's the least I can offer." He folded the Moleskine notebook shut as a waiter delivered our beers. "To discerning the truth."

We raised our glasses.

"Did your evening at the Cabaret unveil anything?" Doug asked.

I drank the light beer. "As a matter of fact, it did." I went on to tell him about my conversation with Ronald and what Ronald had told me about Pat.

"Indeed." Doug made more notes as I relayed

everything. "I didn't have Pat on my interviewee list. I'm adding him now."

"Is a bar tab a reasonable motive for murder?"

Doug tapped his pencil on the notepad. "Depends on the bar tab. Our burgers and beer set me back a whopping twelve bucks." He laughed. "Jesting aside, it's definitely something to consider. If Chuck had charged a sustainable amount of money to his tab without Pat's approval, that could be cause, especially if the nightclub is in any sort of financial trouble. I'll be sure to follow up on that as well. Good work."

"Thanks." Our burgers arrived with a platter of thick-cut fries to share. "What about you? Any new developments in the case?"

"Not enough to make an arrest as of yet, but I did get the toxicology report back. Chuck had a mixture of gin and cocaine in his system."

The news didn't surprise me, but I did wonder if Ronald shared Chuck's recreational pastimes.

Doug continued. "I was able to piece together a few more low-hanging fruits that might lead us in the right direction."

"Such as." I bit into the juicy burger. It was pink in the center with a nice char on the outside. Topped with Oregon cheddar, lettuce, red onions, pickles, a thick tomato slice, and the Mark Antony secret sauce. Their cheeseburgers and their eggplant burgers were the reason locals return again and again to the dining room.

"I had a long chat with Jeri at the Festival. She tried to gloss over this, but the truth is that ticket

sales are down with the opening of the Cabaret and she let it slip more than once that she thinks Chuck was the root cause. Hang on a sec." He flipped through his notebook. "Here it is. Her exact words were that Chuck was 'poaching patrons and single-handedly trying to ruin the Festival.' What do you make of that?"

"Seems like she's giving Chuck ample credit. Why would Chuck be responsible? Wouldn't she be upset with Shelly and Stewart? They started the theater." I took a long drink of my beer.

"My thoughts exactly. When I pressed her on that line of questioning, she claimed that Chuck had worked out an exaggerated scheme involving kick-backs from audience members. She believes that he was selling tickets to the Cabaret directly and keeping a portion of the proceeds for himself."

"Interesting. I wonder if there's a connection with whatever he was involved in at Rumors?"

"It's going on my follow-up list for first thing to-morrow. If Chuck had pulled off something of this magnitude it would definitely give a number of people motive for murder. We'd be talking about much more than four-dollar burgers." He pointed to our plates.

"That could open a number of people up as suspects, couldn't it?" I dipped a fry in Thousand Island dressing.

Doug nursed his beer. "I could spin out on that angle all night. What if Stewart or Shelly were in on it? Maybe Chuck threatened to come clean—developed a conscience—and one of them took him out. The same could be true for Pat, Jeri, even

Ronald. It's potentially far-fetched, but it's not impossible."

"How do you pursue that line of thinking?"

"We try to get them talking. I go to the bank. I
see what I can dig up in Chuck's financial records.
I'm going to request recent statements for the Festival and the Cabaret too. Maybe there's a paper
trail of big deposits."

"That would be lucky."

He yawned. "Alas, it's not very likely. If Chuck
was astute enough to set up a scheme like this, he
probably was smart enough to pay in cash to avoid
any trace. That's one thing you can help with. Chuck
frequented the bakeshop, didn't he? Did he pay in
cash?"

I tried to remember. Our customers paid with
cash, check, or net-30 terms for our wholesale customers. Helen and I had discussed the possibility of
getting a credit card machine, but for the short-term
our price points weren't high enough to justify the
percentage the credit card companies would take off
the top. We needed every cent of our profit margin.
"I'm not sure, but I can take a look at the books in
the morning and see if I have any cleared checks
under his name."

"Maybe you could ask some of your fellow shop
owners on the plaza? See if anyone remembers
Chuck carrying around a wad of cash."

"No problem. I can ask around. That should be
easy enough. Anything else I can help with?"

"You're at the Cabaret for the rest of the week,
right?"

I nodded.

"More of the same would be good. People trust you, Will. You have an earnest face."

I choked on a fry. "I don't know about that."

"It's true. You don't buy into the trend of needing to be cool. You're comfortable in your own skin, which makes you naturally cool."

"Thanks." I leaned back in my chair and gave him my best attempt at a James Dean snarl.

"I'm serious, Will. You are a rare breed. A true Renaissance man."

"Ha! I could say the same for you."

Doug pretended to bow. "A compliment I would gladly accept, but you have a gift, my friend. Your warm nature brings out the best in even the most jaded. Take Richard over there, for example." He pointed to a long bar where Richard Lord sat knocking back shots of tequila.

"What about Richard? I can't stand the guy." Richard Lord had recently acquired an old hotel that sat catty-corner to the bakery. He was new to Ashland and not a good fit. His idea of Shakespeare was trying to capitalize on the kitsch. He'd been walking around the plaza wearing a handmade signboard with the Bard's bust and the tagline: IF SHAKESPEARE MADE BREAKFAST, HE'D COOK A HAMLET. COME TO THE MERRY WINDSOR FOR THE BEST HAMLETS IN TOWN.

So far, the only takers had been desperate tourists who didn't want to wait in line at Torte for one of our handmade omelets. I had it on good authority that Richard was using microwaved omelets at *the Merry Windsor. Helen was convinced the only reason he was in the plaza trying to drum up breakfast business was because of us. Richard had tried hitting on Helen when we first moved to Ashland. I hadn't needed to step in to defend my wife's honor. She had made it abundantly clear that she wasn't interested in his advances. Richard hadn't taken the rejection lightly. He stopped by the bakeshop at least once a day and lingered at the counter. It made me uncomfortable, but Helen insisted that we ignore him. "The only way to deal with a bully like Richard, is to completely ignore him, William. If we get upset, we're giving him exactly what he wants. Let him come sit at the counter and spend his money at Torte. He'll get tired of not getting the reaction he's hoping for after a while and forget about us, but in the meantime, I'll gladly take his cash."*

I hoped that Helen was right. Richard hadn't shown any signs of relenting.

Doug finished his burger and washed it down with his beer. "I understand that you're not a fan, but you've handled Richard beautifully. I've watched how he changes around you. He doesn't try to puff out his chest and pretend like he's the big man around Ashland with you."

"That's thanks to Helen, not me. If I had it my way, I'd like to deck the guy."

"I've had a few instances where the thought crossed my mind as well. My point is that you take the moral high ground. Not because you have to. Because that's who you are. People open up to you because of that fact."

I stared at Richard. He was my age, but his hairline had begun to recede prematurely and he had developed a bit of a beer gut. "You want me to ask about Chuck spending cash around town and continue to keep an ear open when I'm at the Cabaret. Anything else?"

Doug set his napkin on his empty plate. "Is there a chance you can sneak away from the bakeshop for a couple hours tomorrow? I mean, as long as you don't think it will raise any red flags with Helen. I don't want to get you in trouble with Helen."

"I can take off for a couple hours. Why?"

"I'd like to walk-through the crime scene one more time while things are still relatively fresh. And, I'd like to do it in broad daylight. In fact, I think I'll invite one of the Daily Tidings' reporters too."

"What are you hoping to accomplish with the press?"

"I want to keep whoever did this spooked. I think there's a solid chance that our killer is connected to the Cabaret, and I want the actors, company members, volunteers, staff—everyone involved with the show—to see our presence. I want Chuck's killer to be running scared. To know that I'm not giving up on this case. I want them to see that we're actively tracing every clue we can. If we can keep them worried, I think we'll have a better shot at flushing them out."

"That makes sense." I took a final sip of my beer. It had gone flat and warm.

"It could backfire, but it's worth a shot, right?" Doug paid the bill. "Honestly, Will, it's the only *shot I have at the moment, so cross your fingers that it works."*

I clapped him on the back on my way out the door. "I have confidence in you. We're going to close this case and bring Chuck's killer to justice."

As I walked to my van, I wished that I felt as confident as I had tried to sound for my friend. The truth was I was more confused than ever.

I had parked the van at the top of Hargadine. The street was dark and quiet. A cat ran past me as I trekked up the steep hill. It darted down the alley behind the Mark Antony and out of sight.

My mind ran through different scenarios related to Chuck's murder. I was so lost in my thoughts that at first, I didn't notice the sound of footsteps behind me. The footsteps got faster and closer.

I stopped and turned around, expecting to see Doug running up the hill to catch up with me.

When I turned, I spotted someone dressed in black from head to toe. They blended in with the pitch-black sky. "Who's there?"

I reached into my coat pocket, wishing I had some sort of weapon.

The person froze.

"What do you want?" I yelled as loud as I could. The street might be quiet, but I knew there were people around at Rumors, the Mark Antony, and the Cabaret.

My stalker stood as still as a statue.

"What do you want?" I repeated. I looked around me for anything I could use as a weapon. The only thing I spotted was a crushed Coke can nearby.

The person in black began walking backward away from me.

I should have run up the hill to the van and headed home to Helen and Juliet, but something compelled me forward. My legs moved like they were being controlled by a puppet master. "Stop! Who are you?"

The mystery person sprinted away before I could catch up. I ran down Second Street and turned onto Main. By the time I rounded the corner, they were gone. Vanished. Had they ducked into the hotel or disappeared down an alley?

I paused to catch my breath and collect my wits. Was I imagining things? Maybe working the case with Doug was bad for my imagination. I had always had a tendency to create stories in my head. Was I doing that now? Maybe I hadn't been followed. It could have been a teenager playing around, or someone on their way home like me. Maybe I had spooked them.

Go home, Will, I told myself, retracing my steps up Second Street. I paused every twenty or thirty feet to make sure I wasn't being followed. Whoever had been behind me was gone.

There were two possibilities. The first was that I was blowing things out of proportion. And the second was that I could be in danger.

Chapter Twelve

"Which was it?" I asked the Professor. "Was my dad imagining things or was he in danger?"

The Professor rested his chin in his hands. "The latter, I'm afraid."

"Really?"

"Things escalated from there. We continued to work the case together, but that night he was followed was just the beginning. There were threatening notes, phone calls, mysterious cars driving by your house at night. It was terrible, Juliet." He sounded distraught.

I tried to console him. "It's not like that was your fault."

"Oh, but it was. I never should have involved your father, and I felt awful that I was responsible for putting you and your mother at risk."

"We weren't really at risk, were we?" I reached for my water glass. It was empty.

"You were. I'll explain. Go ahead and get another drink."

I stood and stretched. My back was stiff from sitting in the booth for over two hours. "Can I get you anything while I'm up?"

He shook his head. "I'm fine. Thank you."

I took the opportunity to do a quick check-in with my staff. Andy was on break. Sequoia and Rosa were behind the coffee counter. "Everything good?"

Rosa's dimples pinched as she smiled. "Yes, the mini cakes have been a hit. We've nearly sold out. Bethany is making another batch."

"Excellent." The glass pastry case shined under the overhead light. Two single mini cakes remained on the top shelf. Bethany had suggested the idea of small, individual-sized cakes that were designed and decorated to resemble miniature wedding cakes. The trend of beautiful, dainty cakes had caught on. They made a sweet gift or simply a lovely afternoon treat.

Sequoia frothed oat milk. "We're running low on coconut and almond milk, FYI."

"Thanks for letting me know. I'll make sure they deliver both tomorrow." We had also expanded our milk offerings. From coconut to almond and oat to soy, we tried to have a variety of alternative nondairy options for all of our customers. My personal favorite was the chocolate milk we used in our mochas. It was made by a local dairy farmer with rich, delectable chocolate flavors that were a perfect accompaniment to our house-made chocolate sauce.

I went downstairs to see how the kitchen staff were faring. Steph, per usual, had earphones in and her head down as she piped tiny pink hearts onto miniature vanilla strawberry cakes. Bethany and Marty were staging bread photos next to the wood-fired oven, and Sterling was cleaning up at the sink.

"How's everything down here?"

He used a damp cloth to wipe a cast-iron skillet. "Good. How about you? You and the Professor have been"—he searched for the right word—"in deep thought for a while. Is everything okay?" One of the things I appreciated most about Sterling was his perceptiveness. I knew that he wasn't prying. He was genuinely concerned that something was wrong.

"It's a long story. I'll fill you in later. By the way, that cauliflower crust is incredible. I hope you opted to make more."

"We did." Sterling grinned. "And we're already sold out."

"Any sign of Mom?" I glanced toward the small seating area adjacent to the kitchen.

"No, but she said not to expect her for a few hours. Apparently, she and her friend are going to the spa. There was mention of pedicures. That's when I stopped listening." Sterling pointed to the tattoo on his forearm. "Now if they had said they were going to the tattoo shop, I might have paid more attention."

"I'd love to see Mom with a tattoo. Can you imagine?" I scrunched my forehead trying to picture her with one.

"Helen would rock a tattoo, preferably some sort of cake or cupcake. It could be our next team-building exercise. Group tattoos."

I winced at the thought of needles piercing my skin. "Nah, I say let's stick to staff feasts or maybe even a group hike, instead of sticking ourselves, cool?"

Sterling plunged a soup pot into soapy water. "Suit yourself, Jules. We could be onto something with Torte tattoos."

"I'll think on it. You're sure you're okay down here?"

I don't know why I was worried. My staff was extremely competent. Everyone we hired was a self-starter. Most of whom needed little to no direction. I guess more than anything I felt guilty for not working.

"We're fine. Go do what you need to do."

"Thanks. Come get me if you need anything, though."

"We won't, but okay."

I tried to fake disgust, but ended up laughing. "Fine. I'm going." I returned upstairs with a plate of Bethany's bittersweet chocolate brownies.

The Professor was gone. Had memories of the past overwhelmed him? I peered out the front windows and spotted him standing near the Lithia Fountains speaking with a woman I didn't recognize. While I waited for him to return, I nibbled on a brownie. Before we had convinced Bethany to come work with us, she had specialized in brownies, running a pop-up brownie delivery service from her home kitchen. The bittersweet chocolate and touch of sea salt in Bethany's chewy brownies made me want to polish off the entire plate.

When the Professor returned, his jaw was clenched tight and his brow was pinched. "Many apologies. Sorry to keep you waiting."

"No problem." I passed the plate to him. "Brownie?"

"Don't mind if I do." He picked one up. "In a strange twist of fate, you'll never guess who I was speaking with."

"Who?"

"Jeri Heyward. Former OSF membership director."

"I don't think I know her."

"You probably wouldn't. She moved to Talent about a decade ago and has been working for the Camelot Theater. When Lance was hired as artistic director, he brought in a number of new staff members, and Jeri made her exit. It was time. She'd been with the company for nearly twenty years. That tends to happen with changes at the top level."

"Right. What's she doing here?"

The Professor tore off a corner of the brownie. "An excellent question. I must say that the hairs on my arms and the back of my neck are standing at attention at this very moment. Don't you find it odd that we would be rehashing the past and Jeri would appear?"

"How could she know that we were talking about Chuck's case?"

"How could she, indeed?" He tasted the brownie. "Did you mention anything about this to Lance?"

"Yeah, I did. I mean, nothing specific."

"Hmm." The Professor rubbed his temples. "Interesting."

"You think Lance told Jeri?"

"It's quite a coincidence. I have no idea, but in my line of work things rarely line up with such synchronicity. It's certainly something to watch, don't you agree?"

"For sure." I couldn't argue with the Professor's logic, but I also couldn't understand why Lance would involve Jeri. I'd never heard him mention her.

"Shall we continue?" The Professor brushed flaked sea salt from his hands before opening the journal.

"Please."

The next morning, Helen gave me her signature look of disapproval over the breakfast table.

"What's going on with you William Capshaw?" She frowned as she stabbed her scrambled eggs. "You're not acting like yourself."

"I'm fine." I buttered a piece of toast.

"You are not." She lowered her voice and shielded her face with her hand for Juliet's sake. "It's because of Chuck's death, isn't it? I know you, Will. I know that you're replaying that night over and over in your head. I'm worried about you."

"It's not a pleasant memory, but I'll be fine." I smiled at Juliet, who was drawing in a Strawberry Shortcake coloring book.

"I disagree." She passed me a jar of homemade peach jam. "I'm worried about Doug too. Could you offer to help him with the case? I know you can't do much as an average citizen, but as his best friend maybe you could be a sounding board. It would do you both good."

I was glad that I hadn't taken a bite of toast yet. I probably would have choked on it with Helen's suggestion. "That's a good idea." I felt terrible lying to her.

"Good. Why don't you stop by the police station after the lunch rush?"

"I will, I promise."

We finished our breakfast. I left to open the bakeshop. Did Helen know I was already working with Doug? It was weird that she had broached the subject. I didn't have much time to dwell on what she might or might not suspect because we had a large bread order for a new wholesale client. The morning breezed by while I kneaded loaf after loaf of sourdough and whole wheat. Helen concentrated on our standard offerings and Wendy worked the counter. The novelty of the espresso machine drew in a steady line of customers.

I relieved Wendy late morning, taking a turn pulling shots and foaming milk. Customers loved watching the process of creating a layered latte and foamy cappuccino. By the time the lunch crowd had dispersed, I was ready for a break, so I made a latte to go and headed over to police head-quarters.

The plaza office was conveniently located right across the street from Torte. The secretary told me that Doug was up at the Cabaret. It was a nice after-noon for a walk. Main Street was humming with activity. I waved to friends as I strolled up the side-walk, taking in the sun. When Helen and I had left California for Oregon, we'd been nervous about the state's famed rain, but fortunately Ashland was blessed with long stretches of sun no matter the season.

Spring in Ashland was arguably the most gor-geous season. Cherry buds dotted the trees as I walked along Main Street past Giuseppi's New York Pizza and Rosie's Sweet Shop, two popular hangouts for the teenage crowds. Rosie's classic soda fountain and its made-from-scratch ice cream made it Juliet's favorite spot on summer nights. The three of us would share a banana split, complete with a cherry on top.

A group of high-schoolers zoomed past me on BMX bikes. They were headed for the video store. I watched as they propped their bikes against the *side of the building. Helen had recently read an article at the pediatrician's office recommending mandatory bike helmets for anyone under the age of eighteen. It sounded like a solid plan to me. We insisted that Juliet wore her pink helmet whenever she rode her bike.*

I turned at the Mark Antony with its deco façade. A wave of anxiety made my cheeks flush. Had I been imagining things last night? What were the odds that someone had actually tried to follow me?

I trekked onward and found Doug at the corner of Second and Hargadine. He was taking notes and reexamining the scene.

"Need a hit of caffeine?" I asked, handing him the latte.

"Will, you made it." He took the paper cup. "Thank you, my friend. I can use every extra edge for this case."

"Any new developments since last night?" I wondered if I should tell him about being followed.

"I spoke with the bank this morning. They should have a printout of Chuck's statements for us in the next few hours. You? Any gossip at the bakeshop?"

"Only about our fancy new espresso machine." I nodded to his latte. "It's the talk of the town."

"Understandably." Doug took a drink. "This beats the stale Folgers at the station any day. You're going to have a line of latte addicts within the week."

"That's the plan." I chuckled. "Actually, something did happen after we parted ways last night. Well, at least I think something may have happened,

it could be in my head." I proceeded to tell him about being followed and chasing the mysterious stalker in black.

"Will, I don't think that's in your head. I had a similar experience this morning. I could have sworn that someone was following me. You know when you get that feeling that you're being watched?"

I nodded.

"I had that when I was at the bank. I kept turning around. I never saw anyone in the bank, but when I left, there was a guy standing across the street at the vacuum store. He was smoking a cigarette and staring at the bank. When I crossed the street to confront him, he took off. I couldn't catch him because he hopped on a bus in front of the library. I think our plan is working. We're spooking whoever did this. I can feel it. We're close."

"I hope you're right. I don't want to put Helen or Juliet in any danger."

Doug's face went white. "Will, I don't either. If you want to stop, I understand. No hard feelings, understood."

"No. I don't want to stop, but I don't want to do anything stupid either. I made sure that no one followed me home last night. I drove all the way out to the other side of town and looped back around just in case."

"Did you see any cars? Headlights behind you?"

"Nothing. I wasn't followed home. I'm sure of that."

"Could you identify whoever followed you up to your van? Do you have a sense of height? Build?"

I tried to describe the person I had seen in black, but it had been dark, and we were on a hill. I thought it was a man, but it could have been a woman, and for all I knew they could have been taller than me. It was too hard to tell.

Doug jotted some notes in his journal. "This is good. Your description matches mine."

"Do you think it could be the same person I saw smoking over there the night of the accident?"

"Possibly. It's worth another look, don't you think?"

A car drove by. Once it was out of the way we crossed the street to the streetlamp where I'd seen the smoker. Doug crouched down on his knees and scanned the sidewalk and bushes. "The team already swept this area, but let's take one more look. If we could find a cigarette butt, there's a chance they could pull prints or even DNA from it."

We carefully scoured the area. I didn't see anything out of the ordinary. The sidewalk had a few pine needles, a broken pine cone, and dried leaves, but no sign of a cigarette butt. We expanded our perimeter to include the entire block. Doug was precise in his investigation, literally leaving no stone unturned. I found an old sock and a faded penny. Neither appeared to have any connection to our case, but Doug bagged them as a precaution. "You never know, Will. It's worth a shot."

I was about to give up when Doug whistled. "Jackpot!"

I went to see what he had found. He removed the butt of a cigarette from the edge of a storm drain with a pair of tweezers. "This could be it. This could be solid evidence." He dropped the used cigarette into a plastic bag and zipped it shut. "I'll take this to the lab in Medford and check in with the bank again. Do you want to come with me?"

As much as I wanted to join him, I didn't want to leave all of the cleanup to Helen and Wendy. "I should probably get back to work."

"Understood. I'll let you know what we hear from the lab."

I made it back to the bakeshop in time to help Wendy and Helen finish prepping the Cabaret desserts. Not long before closing I did a walk-through of the dining room, picking up any last plates and cups left at tables and letting the few customers who were lingering know that we would be locking the front door in about a half hour. A man who I didn't recognize sat at the window booth in the corner of the bakery. His baseball hat was pulled so low on his brow that I couldn't make out his face.

"Can I get you anything? Top off your coffee, perhaps?" I asked, pausing at the booth.

He didn't look up from his empty coffee cup. "No."

"Okay, just want to let you know that we're closing in about twenty minutes."

If he heard me, he made no notice of it. I returned to the kitchen. "Do you know that guy in the booth up front?" I asked Helen.

She wiped flour onto her apron and stood on her tiptoes. "No. I asked Wendy about him earlier. He's been sitting there for at least an hour. He ordered a black coffee and a chocolate chip cookie—which he finished in the first five minutes. Wendy's gone over a couple times to check on him and he hasn't wanted a refill or anything. We were wondering if maybe he's down on his luck and just needed a place to stay warm for a little while."

"That's probably it." I didn't want to alarm Helen, but a familiar churning feeling came over me. The guy was wearing a pair of expensive red-and-black Nike Air Jordans. After being followed last night, my nerves were running high. Could this be the guy I'd seen?

I didn't want to make a big deal of it in front of Helen, so I kept an eye on the guy as we went about boxing up the Cabaret desserts and cleaning. He must have snuck out at some point because when I went to lock the front door he was already gone.

Will, stop blowing things out of proportion, I told myself as I picked up the guy's coffee cup and plate. A one-dollar bill had been tucked into a folded paper napkin.

See. The guy left us a tip, and I was worried that he was casing the place.

I unfolded the napkin to take out the money and saw that he had written something on it with a black pen. Sweat beaded on my forehead as I read the note.

"Mind your own business. Stay out of it before someone else gets hurt."

I thought I might be sick. What had I done?

The note was tangible proof that I wasn't imagining things. And worse, it meant that whatever Doug and I had done, someone, most likely Chuck's

killer, had taken notice. They were threatening me
and my family. I had to put an end to this now.

Once we had finished cleaning, I sent Wendy
and Helen home early and went straight to the police station. Yet again, Doug's secretary told me he
was out and she wasn't sure when he would return.

I went back to the bakeshop, found a notebook
we used to sketch cake designs, and made as many
notes about the mystery guy's appearance as I
could while they were still fresh in my head. Who
was he? Was he an accomplice or was he the driver
of the car? I didn't recognize him from the Cabaret,
Rumors, the Festival, or anywhere else in town,
but that didn't necessarily mean anything. I didn't
know everyone in Ashland and certainly not in the
surrounding Rogue Valley.

Why warn me?

What had I done, other than tag along with Doug
to interview body shops and ask a few questions at
the Cabaret? It didn't make sense. If Chuck's killer
was a stranger, someone unknown around town,
then how was I being targeted? There had to be a
connection with one of the suspects Doug and I had
been in contact with the past two days. The question
was who? And why did they see me as a threat?

I thought through everyone on my potential list.
First there was Chef Ronald. Could the guy in the
baseball hat be a friend of his? Could he have hired
him to scare me? To throw us off the scent? I wouldn't
put it past the surly chef. But, then again, why?

Next there was Pat, the owner of Rumors. I
couldn't see Pat pulling a stunt like this. He was a

fellow small business owner after all. The same was true for Shelly and Stewart at the Cabaret. That left Jeri from the Festival. Would the membership director of the West Coast's most revered repertory theater send some goon out to threaten me? Doubtful.

 I ripped my page of notes from the notebook and tucked it into my pocket to share with Doug as soon as I could track him down. Then I loaded up the Cabaret desserts and double-checked that every door and window in the bakeshop was locked. I wasn't about to take any chances knowing that Torte was under threat.

Chapter Thirteen

"That's terrifying," I said to the Professor. "No wonder my dad was upset."

"Exactly. Imagine how I felt. I had involved Will in my feeble attempt at tracking a killer and put him and his family in harm's way." Deep lines etched in his brow as he spoke. "I made so many mistakes those days. Don't try to console me." He held up his hand to stop me as I tried to reassure him. "I know what you're likely to say. That mistakes are how we learn. But in hindsight, I see how ridiculously selfish it was of me to include Will."

"But you couldn't have known what was going to happen," I offered.

"Case in point, Juliet. Yet still." Without another word, he read on.

I couldn't stop looking over my shoulder on my way to the Cabaret. Every sound from birds chirping overhead to theatergoers laughing made me jump. I expected to see the guy in the baseball hat and Air Jordans every time I turned around. At the Cabaret I was even more jittery. I nearly dropped the

*entire box of devil's food cakes and couldn't steady
my hand when demonstrating piping the whipping
cream to a new crew of volunteers.*

Get it together, Will.

*Once I had the volunteers trained for dessert
service, I decided to go down to Rumors and get
a drink. Maybe a martini would help calm my
nerves. The smoky bar was packed. A well-known
jazz singer crooned from the stage. She wore a
skin-tight sequined dress. Her crimped red curls reminded me of a lion's mane. I found an empty seat
at the bar and ordered a martini.*

*The ice-cold drink took the edge off. I drank it
faster than usual and was taken aback when the
bartender pointed to my empty glass and asked if I
wanted another.*

"No. I'm fine."

*"He'll have another." A voice sounded behind
me. "On the house." Pat yanked out an empty bar-
stool. He struggled to climb up onto it.*

*"I'm glad to see you here, William. You are just
the guy I've been looking for. I was hoping for a
word."*

*I didn't know Pat well. He and I had bumped into
each other at the occasional chamber meeting and
around town at business events, but we were casual
acquaintances at best. Hearing that he wanted to
talk to me was a surprise. He was an Ashland leg-
end. Rumors was the fourth business he had opened
downtown in the past few years and I highly doubted
it would be his last. He was short and stocky with
a swath of white hair. He reminded me of a retired*

wrestler with his mammoth arm muscles and bowed legs. If you were on Pat's good side, he treated you well, but I wouldn't want to be on his bad side. I had heard stories about him starting vicious rumors, and sabotaging business owners who slighted him. Helen teased that the reason he named his nightclub Rumors was because he was the king of the rumor mill in Ashland.

The bartender handed Pat a double shot of whiskey and delivered me a fresh martini. I had to pace myself, otherwise I would have to call Doug and beg for a ride home.

"How are things, Pat?"

Pat took my question literally. He surveyed the lounge. "Nearly a packed house for the opener. I'd say we're going to have a good night."

"A packed house is always a good thing," I concurred.

"Especially these days. I don't know about the bakery business, but the bar business has been slow. Real slow."

"Yeah? Rumors seems like the place to be." Pat's remark didn't match up with the busy nightclub. I'd never seen Rumors on a weekend night without a line queuing down the block to get in. What made Rumors unique was the range of people it attracted, from college students to members of the acting company to music fans.

"It is. Don't get me wrong, kid. You'll learn as you're in the business longer never to complain about a packed house. I'm happy about the size of tonight's crowd but we have some serious cash to

make up thanks to one actor who tried to bleed me dry."

"Chuck?"

Pat tapped his empty shot glass on the walnut bar to signal the bartender. "Did you have problems with him too?"

"Problems?" I took a slow sip of my martini, hoping that my voice sounded casual and neutral.

"I shouldn't speak ill of the dead, but Chuck deserves a special place in hell if you ask me."

"What happened?"

"Did he run up a huge bill at the bakery?" Internally I cringed. I wanted to correct him. Helen and I had intentionally used the word "bakeshop" in all of our signage, marketing materials, and menus to differentiate ourselves. Not that we had anything against bakeries. It was more about perception. Bakeries were places to go to pick up a birthday cake or a box of donuts to share with the office. Helen and I wanted Torte to be a gathering place. A space where people lingered. Where neighbors came to talk and where strangers became friends.

On opening day, I had gotten into it with Richard Lord, who made fun of us. "Bakeshop, huh, Will? Sounds like pretentious Californian to me."

For some reason unbeknownst to me, I tried to reason with Richard, explaining that the term "bakeshop" was more encompassing. That we intended to serve simple soups and lunches in addition to our pastries. He had laughed in my face.

"No. To be honest, he never frequented the bakeshop much," I said to Pat, not bothering to correct him. "Helen and I probably would have welcomed having a local celebrity hanging around, but I didn't see much of Chuck."

Pat's puffy cheeks burned with color. I wasn't sure if it was from the whiskey or because he couldn't control his emotions. "Count yourself lucky. I made a huge mistake. Huge." He knocked back another shot. "I thought, like you, that having someone with Chuck's status at Rumors would be like free advertising. In fact, we were getting ready to shoot a commercial here at the bar with Chuck."

"Really?"

"That was the plan, but Chuck bailed on me. What happened to a man's handshake being his word? Have we lost those days, William? Take that as a lesson for your bakery. I gave Chuck my word and a hefty down payment for his endorsement of the jazz club. I shook the man's hand and he looked me in the eye. Then do you know what he did?"

From the bitter look in Pat's eyes and the way his thick fingers clutched the shot glass, it didn't take a genius to figure out that he and Chuck had fallen out.

"He took the money and ran."

"He ran?" I asked.

"Not physically speaking." Pat turned the glass over and slammed it upside down on the bar. "I made a deal with Chuck, like a gentleman and a business owner, and he screwed me in return."

I stirred my drink with the olive resting on the edge of a plastic toothpick. "I don't understand. What was your deal with Chuck?"

"It was twofold. I hired him to endorse Rumors. He was supposed to bring other members of the Festival here for dinner and drinks. He promised that he would bring in what he called his 'high-roller friends.' Tourists with dollars to spend from L.A., San Francisco, and Seattle. He brought them in all right. He brought them in and ran up huge bar tabs. I'm talking thousands of dollars in drinks, dinners, cover charges. For what? For nothing. None of his high rollers ever came back and none of them ever paid a single dime for anything. That wasn't the deal.

"I told Chuck I would comp him for a drink or dinner here or there, but he took advantage of me. Told my waiters and bartenders to put everything— the entire bill—every time on his tab. My staff didn't know better. I had told them that Chuck and I had an endorsement deal and to be sure that whenever he brought in friends that they got our best service." He pounded his fist on the bar. "Oh they got our best service all right. They got steak dinners, expensive bottles of French wine, and front-row seats to every show . . . for nothing. Nothing. Not a penny."

I wasn't sure how to respond. It turned out that I didn't need to formulate my thoughts. Pat was on a roll.

"That's not even the worst of it," he continued. "I gave Chuck a hefty check, a deposit for the commercial we were about to start shooting. He agreed to star in the commercial and promote it. The spot was going to air from Roseburg to Redding. I hired an advertising agency from Medford to shoot it. I had some big-name musicians coming up to do back-ground vocals. The works. It was going to be big, and then Chuck bailed. I paid him the deposit, and the balance would be due upon completion. Do you know what he did, William?"

I shook my head.

"He cashed the check, spent the money, and re-fused to be in the commercial."

"Why?" I was surprised at how forthcoming Pat was, and I was also making mental notes of every-thing he was telling me. Pat was clearly furious with Chuck. The more he told me, the more I wondered if he could be involved in Chuck's gruesome murder.

"Who knows? The man was an egotistical, con-niving liar. He said that he didn't feel like it was ethical for him to endorse a nightclub. Ethical? Ha!" Pat threw his hands up in disgust. "He had no issue with ethics when it came to spending my money, but suddenly he got a conscience and de-cided he wouldn't endorse a bar. No. He was play-ing me the whole time. He took advantage of the fact that I'm old school. A man's handshake used to be all you needed in this world. I didn't want to pay a lawyer in a suit to give me a bunch of carbon copies of legal contracts. I didn't think we needed it. I laid out the deal for Chuck, shook his hand, and paid him the deposit. That should be enough, don't you think?"

I didn't share Pat's perspective. While I agreed that it was important to be true to your word, I un-derstood that in business, having things in writing was key.

"I tried to get my money back when Chuck refused to start shooting, but he said it was the cost of 'considering' the deal. He considered it and decided it was a no." Pat flipped the shot glass over and over again. "Can you imagine the nerve? The guy used Rumors as his personal hot spot, brought his friends in to drink for free, cashed a large deposit for work he was never going to do, and then he had the nerve to tell me to back off?"

"How so?"

"He told me if I didn't stop pestering—that's the word he used—pestering him for my money he was going to go to the police and get a restraining order. Can you believe that?"

"No." I shook my head. "Have you talked to the police? To Doug? Could they help get your money returned?"

Pat hit the shot glass on the wood so hard I thought it might shatter. "I called them. They said there was nothing they could do if I didn't have anything in writing. They didn't even sound sympathetic."

That didn't sound like Doug.

"The only way to deal with Chuck was to give him a taste of his own medicine. Treat a bully like a bully. You know?"

Again, Pat and I had differing opinions. "Have you thought about talking to Doug now that Chuck is dead? They're going through his finances. They might be able to help you recover some of the deposit."

Pat's face dropped. "What do you mean they're going through his finances?"

"It's part of the investigation. Doug sounded like it was routine."

"Why? Why would they need to go through his finances if he was killed in a hit-and-run?"

I could tell by the way Pat's foot bounced up and down in rapid-fire movement that this news was making him nervous. Why? I decided to reveal a bit more about the investigation and watch his response.

"You must not have heard. The police are pretty sure it wasn't an accident. They think that Chuck was murdered."

Pat fiddled with the shot glass. "What? Murder?"

"That's right. They've studied the car tracks and determined that whoever ran over Chuck was intending to harm him."

"Oh no." Pat rested the glass on its side and sent it spinning like a top. "That's not good. They're going to look at me. They're going to think I did it."

"Why do you say that?"

"Everything I just told you." He looked to me. "Wait, you don't think I killed him, do you? I didn't. Listen, kid, I didn't kill him. I was furious at the guy, but I didn't kill him. Ask anyone. I was here all night. I didn't leave until well after closing. I have an alibi. My entire staff will tell you that I was here. I was here all night."

His frantic tone made me suspicious. Shakespeare's "The lady doth protest too much, methinks" rang in my head.

"No, listen. Why would I have told you all of this tonight if I killed him? That would be stupid. I *would never have told you any of this if I were the killer."*

He had a point.

"I told you this because I wondered if Chuck had done the same thing to you. I'm trying to look out for you. People did that for me in this town when I was young like you. I'm just trying to repay the favor. Wouldn't want you and your pretty wife bamboozled. I've heard some rumors about other business and restaurants in town that he was trying to swindle. I thought maybe the bakery had fallen trap to his games, that's all. You believe me, right?"

"It's not up to me. I don't have anything to do with the case."

"But you and Doug are good friends. You can talk to him for me. Won't you, Will? Tell him that I'm innocent. I have an alibi, okay?"

"You should really talk to Doug yourself. You know what Doug's like. He'll listen. He doesn't jump to conclusions or overreact."

Pat clutched my arm. *"Will, please. Promise me you'll talk to him, kid. Promise me that. Put in a good word for me. Tell him everything I told you. Tell him to come talk to me and I'll lay everything out for him. I'll tell him anything he wants to know."*

"Okay, relax."

"No, I can't have this now. I can't have any bad press for Rumors. Chuck put me in the hole. I need bodies in the dining room and lounge right now. I swear I didn't kill him. Not that I didn't want to." He let out an uncomfortable laugh. *"If someone*

really did kill him though, I'll tell Doug who he should be talking to."

"Who?"

"Jeri. Do you know her? She works for the Festival. She was in here with Chuck the night he was killed, and they were going at it. She threatened to kill him. Right over there." He pointed to a table near the stage. *"In front of about thirty people. If Chuck's death wasn't an accident, then I would bet good money that Jeri did it."*

Chapter Fourteen

"I can't believe my dad learned so much," I said to the Professor as he loosened his grip on the journal.

He pressed his hands together. "He was a natural. I asked him—well, he would tell you that I begged—on more than one occasion to reconsider a career in pastry and join the force. He declined." The Professor looked to the espresso bar where Andy was cleaning up for the day. How late was it?

"I can't blame him. Torte never would have been the same without his early influences."

I wondered if the same was true for me. I had always questioned why I was drawn to helping Thomas and the Professor. Why I was obsessed with piecing clues together and trying to puzzle through motives. Now it was beginning to make sense. I was my father's daughter. I had inherited his penchant for investigating. What would he think if he could see me now? Learning that he too had a deep-seated need to bring justice to the world made me feel better somehow.

As if reading my mind, the Professor cleared his throat. "You were your father's greatest achievement, you know.

Even if he had a desire to work as a detective, he never would have wanted to be pulled away from time here—with you and your mother. Torte was his happy place."

"I can relate." I smiled, letting my gaze linger on the chalkboard menu. Today's quote read: "No legacy is so rich as honesty."

Shakespeare's words rang especially true in light of the Professor's recounting of the past. Someone involved in Chuck's death had not been honest. How had they never figured out who?

"Was it Jeri?" I asked the Professor.

He gave a half shrug. "I wish I could say for certain. That was the most perplexing thing about the case. Everyone connected to Chuck had reason to do him in, so to speak. It would have been easier if he had been beloved, but at each turn your father and I discovered yet another person he had wronged. It began to feel as if all of Ashland had motive and opportunity. The burden of proof was the critical piece that we were missing. I kept hoping for a break. We got close a few times, like with Jeri. But to this day, there's a killer walking amongst us who has never been brought to justice. That's a thought that I still cannot stomach. I failed Chuck, I failed his family, and I failed our community."

I reached for his hand. "Don't be so hard on yourself. You did your best. Anyone would have struggled in the same situation."

He tried to smile. "Thank you, but I disagree. It was my duty to solve the case and find the killer. Not to allow someone who brutally ran down one of our citizens to live a life of freedom for these many years. Think about that, Juliet. There's a killer living amongst us right now."

The thought sent a shiver down my back. "What about Jeri? Do you think she did it?" I glanced at the clock, trying to keep his spirits up. It was almost closing time. The afternoon had vanished. Thankfully, from the looks of things my capable staff had managed without me. Rosa boxed up the few remaining pastries in the case, and Sequoia restocked the coffee grinders with aromatic beans. I felt like we were close to a conclusion. We couldn't stop now.

"Perhaps." He rubbed his temples then stared at the clock on the wall. "Your mother will be done with her lunch and spa afternoon soon. Shall we try to wrap this up before her return?"

There was a sense of urgency in his tone.

"As long as you're okay with continuing?" I flipped through the journal to see that only a few pages remained.

"We've come this far. It wouldn't be fair to leave you without a conclusion, now would it?" Once again he drifted back in time.

When I left Rumors I felt unsteady on my feet. It wasn't from the martinis. My second drink had gone untouched. Pat's confession had rattled me. It made me reconsider everything that Doug and I had learned thus far. Was Pat telling the truth? In some ways I couldn't understand why he would have possibly told me about his financial battles with Chuck if he had killed him. What purpose would that serve? It put more focus and suspicion on him. But, maybe that was his end goal. Perhaps he thought that if he was forthcoming and "honest" about his challenges with Chuck, the police would take his disclosure as a sign of good faith. I wondered what Doug would think. My intuition erred on the side of believing Pat, but this was a murder investigation. I knew all too well that we needed hard evidence and facts.

Where was Doug now? I kicked myself for not making firm plans to meet up. I ducked out the back exit and decided to head to the plaza on the off-chance that Doug was in his office. On my way down Main Street, I bumped into none other than Jeri. She was standing in front of the Mark Antony smoking a cigarette and shading herself from the drizzle with a large black golf umbrella.

There was something familiar about her stance. The way she leaned against the exterior wall puffing her cigarette. It reminded me of the person I had seen smoking the night Chuck was killed. Could I have been wrong? Could it have been a woman smoking?

"You coming in for a nightcap?" Jeri asked, reaching for the heavy iron door handle. "The Stage Door is the who's who of Ashland tonight."

Half the ground floor of the Mark Antony had been taken over by the Stage Door, a cocktail bar that was popular with locals and tourists.

"No. I'm on my way to the bakeshop. Just have to tidy up and make sure we're ready for the morning rush. What about you? Late-night fun or work?"

Jeri filled her lungs with the noxious smoke. "Lucky. I'm on the clock. What else is new? It's the story of my life these days."

"Yeah, you mentioned that membership sales are

down at the Festival. That's so surprising because the season has such an incredible lineup of productions and talent."

"You know who we have to thank for dropping ticket sales?" Jeri held the smoke in her lungs before slowly exhaling.

I stepped to the side to avoid breathing in her second-hand smoke. Why did everyone in Ashland smoke? I could only hold out hope that by the time Juliet was my age, the trend would be passé. "I have a guess." Riding the high from everything I had learned from Pat, I decided to employ the same tactic with Jeri. "It seems like Chuck had a number of run-ins with businesses in town."

"Run-ins?" Jeri scowled. "That's a very kind way of putting it, Will. What Chuck did to the Festival was unforgiveable."

"How so?" She had finished the cigarette, so I moved under the overhang to avoid the misty rain. The streetlamps along Main Street cast a golden glow on the sidewalk, illuminating puddles of water that had begun to pool. A few cars drove by, their wiper blades trying to keep up with the spray. Most of the shops were closed for the night. A block to the south, the coin-operated laundry mat still had its lights on, and a crowd of college students queued up for their turn at the rows of washing machines and dryers.

Across the street and a half block to the north, the Underground Deli had a sidewalk sign announcing special late-night hours for students studying for midterms. The basement restaurant was themed like the London Underground with a mural depicting the famous train station and tables designed to resemble train cars.

"Didn't you hear? We talked about this. Chuck was trying to ruin the Festival. Why? I have no idea? Why would he turn his back on the people who gave him his start? Without the Festival he would have been a nobody. Instead of thanking us for helping to build his career and fan base, he kicked us in the gut." She pressed a black go-go boot on her cigarette butt and squashed it into the sidewalk.

"By encouraging people to purchase tickets at the Cabaret? I don't understand. The Festival doesn't even open for another month. It seems like Ashland and the surrounding valley can certainly support more than one theater. You're doing totally different things after all, and from what I had been told it sounded like Stewart and Shelly are planning to continue to do some side projects for the Festival while running the Cabaret. If anything, the two venues seem symbiotic."

"Oh they are. Of course they are," Jeri agreed.

"Then where does Chuck come in?"

"You don't get it, Will. He wasn't just encouraging people to buy a ticket to the Cabaret. He was poaching our donors and patrons. I wish I knew why. It doesn't make sense at all. I told him that. He and I got into it. We had worked together for three years. Why did he suddenly decide to throw me under the bus?" She laughed. "Pardon the pun."

I didn't respond to that. "You mean, you personally?"

"Yes. He was wining and dining all of my big

*donors. He claimed that he could get them pre-
mier tickets, backstage passes, access to the cast.
You name it. It was all a lie. He was taking their
money directly as part of what he was calling an
'insider's package.' His fake scheme involved dinner and drinks—and who knows what other kind of
shady stuff—at Rumors, and tickets to our shows
and the Cabaret. I had even heard that he was trying to work out a dessert-and-coffee package with
you."* A bus sped past us, kicking up spray. We both
moved closer to the side of the hotel to avoid getting splashed.

"What?" If what Jeri was saying was true, I was
floored. Chuck really had been a master schemer.

"He didn't approach you, did he?"

"No." I shook my head.

"Probably because he was starting to get scared.
I confronted him. He tried to lie his way out of it.
That's the problem. He's a good actor, but I wasn't
having it. Maybe someone else would have believed
the load of crap he was dishing out, but not me. I've
been around actors long enough to know when someone is blowing smoke, if you know what I mean."
She rolled her eyes. "I told him that I was going to
the police. He freaked. He swore he would hand over
the money he had pulled in and promised he would
stop immediately. I didn't believe that either."

"Wait. Can we back up for a minute? What exactly was he selling?"

Jeri sighed and stared at me like I was an idiot. "I
told you. Fake packages. He stole my donor list out
of my filing cabinet and started combing through it

name by name, offering exclusive actor-led pack-ages. He probably wouldn't have gotten away with it if it wasn't for the fact that he had gained celeb-rity status. Our patrons recognized him by name and felt special—singled out—that someone of his notoriety was personally calling them. They sent checks and cash made out to him."

"How did you figure out what was going on?" I wished I had brought a warmer coat. The minute the sun set these early spring days, the temperature plummeted.

"It took a while. My job has been on the line for over a month now. I looked like the idiot for 'mis-placing' our patron list. I never misplace anything. I knew immediately when it was missing from my files that someone had taken it. I just didn't know who or why. I had to go through last year's sales ticket by ticket and re-create the list. Once I started making calls, it was evident that Chuck had pulled one over on us. Our patrons would say things like, 'Oh, I just purchased your special package.'" She twisted her umbrella.

"Did you tell anyone?"

"Of course." Jeri stared at me in disbelief. "I was about to get fired. I wasn't going to keep the information to myself. I finally put it all together opening night at the Cabaret. One of my top donors returned my call and told me she had purchased Chuck's package. I went straight to my boss. I called a meeting of the board and management team for the next morning. Not only was I going to set the record straight to protect my job, but I was *going to go to the police. Chuck wasn't going to get away with what he had done. Not on my watch."*

My opinion of Chuck was completely altered. Jeri's story matched Pat's. I was beginning to feel like everyone might have had a hand in his death.

"What about Doug? Have you told him this?"

Jeri nodded. "We had a long chat at my office this afternoon. I didn't spare him any of the gory details. I shared my insight about who might have run him down too. Not that the thought hadn't crossed my mind, but I'm not into blood."

Her words made the hair on my arms stand at attention.

"You think you know who killed him?"

"Absolutely. I told Doug he needed to interrogate Stewart and Shelly ASAP. They both put every dime they had into the Cabaret, and when I confronted Chuck, he admitted that I wasn't alone. It was stupid. I think he said it to make me feel better. Moron. All it did was give me more ammunition to go to the police. He had his own crime ring right here in Ashland."

"How was the Cabaret involved?" I wanted to ask her about her personal relationship with Chuck, but I wasn't sure how to broach the subject.

She moved to the side to make room for two men exiting the hotel lobby. "I don't know. He didn't give me details, but he alluded to the fact that he bled them dry."

What did that mean? "Can I ask you something personal?" I hoped that my tone wasn't too forward.

"What?"

"I noticed you and Chuck on opening night. You looked, well, like maybe there was more to your relationship."

Her nostrils flared. "No. Not at all. I don't know what you saw, but there was nothing between me and Chuck."

Jeri shook rain from her umbrella and closed it. "I should get back inside. There's a table full of board members and staff waiting to brainstorm how we move on from this. The board has already drafted a letter that we will be mailing to patrons, explaining Chuck's indiscretions and offering them discounted season-ticket packages. We're formulating language to ensure this doesn't happen again. It's a tricky situation, as we don't want any of our donors to feel like they got the wool pulled over their eyes, and yet we want to make it clear that ticket packages are only sold through the Festival."

"That sounds like a challenge. I'm sure you'll figure it out."

"I hope that Doug and his team figure out Chuck's finances, because I want every cent returned to our patrons. If this ruins our season, I don't know what I'll do."

Jeri went inside, and I continued down Main Street in what now had become a full-fledged Oregon rain. Chuck's killer remained elusive, but with each new thing I learned I felt like the pieces of a puzzle were starting to fall into place.

Chapter Fifteen

"Don't get your hopes up, Juliet," the Professor said, pausing briefly to take a few sips of water.

"What do you mean?"

"Like Will, your face reflects your every emotion. It's a thing of beauty, but it betrays you now."

"Or maybe you're a good detective who has mastered the art of reading people over the years," I bantered back.

"I appreciate the praise, but alas, I hate having to dash your hopes, as our story is shortly going to come to an end." He picked up the journal and continued.

Doug wasn't at the station when I stopped by. I knocked for a good five minutes before giving up and crossing the street to Torte. Once again I got the sense I was being watched. Was it time to start carrying a rolling pin with me wherever I went? The latest craze these days was pepper spray. What had once been a weapon reserved for the police had gone mainstream. I'd never considered carrying any kind of weapon, but maybe I needed a can for my own safety? I tried to laugh and make light of my current paranoia. If Helen had any idea what I'd been up to these last few days, she would probably come after me with a rolling pin. And rightfully so. I couldn't blame her. I was acting like I was a teenager, not a mature adult with a wife, young daughter, and budding baking business.

The case was getting the best of me.

I kept my shoulders square as I moved toward the bakeshop. It was hardly as if someone would try to attack me in the middle of the plaza. The second that thought crossed my mind an image of Chuck's body flying through the air replaced it.

If someone was following me, I didn't want to stop at Torte. Odds were good that whoever had killed Chuck knew I owned the bakeshop, but on the off chance they didn't, there was no point in drawing attention to the fact. I quickened my pace past Pucks Pub and continued down the sidewalk toward two dance clubs that had recently opened. The college crowd usually packed the clubs, so my best chance of shaking whoever was following me was to duck into one of the bars. The only problem was that both clubs were located on the third floor. And to access them I would have to pass through a dark alley and wait for a notoriously slow elevator.

Not a smart plan, William.

The sound of footsteps splattering through puddles made me want to break out into a full run, but I maintained as much control over my spiking adrenaline as possible.

Heavy breathing cut through the otherwise quiet sidewalk.

I wasn't imagining this. Someone was really after me.

Shop Oregon, a store that catered to tourists with displays of local wine, beef jerky, and smoked salmon, was completely dark. As was the Iron Buffalo, with its sheepskin slippers and custom leatherwork. Nothing else down this way was open.

The footsteps thudded closer.

I passed the alleyway leading to the Bohemian and considered my choices. I could make a break for it. My long legs had led me to be a four-year varsity athlete on my high school cross-country team. I figured I could probably outrun whoever was following me. But then I would be at the mercy of the elevator.

I couldn't chance it, so instead I switched directions and plowed across the street. I ran past the Lithia Fountains, the bus stop, and the pay phone. I thought about sprinting to the Mark Antony since Jeri and her group of board members would be there, but a chalkboard sign in front of the Merry Windsor hotel gave me another idea.

Richard Lord had been trying to take a cut of Ashland's youthful night scene. He'd recently been advertising MTV dance parties in the Windsor's ballroom on weekend nights. For once, I was actually thrilled to go into Richard's hotel. Never had I imagined hearing those words in my head.

The Windsor was dark and gaudy with plush, almost velvety, emerald green carpet, brass railings and accents, and a slew of cheap Shakespearean artwork. Richard liked to boast that the Windsor was

the closest thing to actually staying at the Bard's
residence in Stratford-upon-Avon. Helen and I joked
that my namesake would rise from his grave just to
pen a scene where Richard met an untimely death
for the hideous comparison.

I walked past the reception desk where a college student thumbed through a Sports Illustrated
magazine.

"The dance party is in the ballroom, right?" I
pointed to the hallway lit by fake yellow candles.

"Yeah. It's a five-dollar cover." His voice was
loud as he tried to speak over the sound of his Walkman. He didn't bother removing his headphones.

I felt sorry for the kid. Not only was Richard Lord
his boss, but all staff at the Merry Windsor were
required to wear pantaloons and puffy Elizabethan
shirts as their uniform. It was quite a contrast to
see his modern magazine and Walkman while he
wore an inexpensive and ill-fitting costume.

I checked behind me to see if whoever was following me had come inside. The lobby was empty,
so I followed the long hallway, flanked by styrofoam
busts of Shakespeare, to the ballroom.

There was a sign posted on the door about a cover
charge, but no bouncer waiting to take payment. I
wasn't about to hand any money over to Richard
Lord if I didn't have to, so after one more check to
make sure no one was watching me, I opened the
doors.

Inside was a sea of neon. Neon T-shirts, leg warm-
ers, jackets, and acid-washed jeans. A huge crystal
disco ball spun overhead, creating a sea of flashing

lights on the dance floor and walls. I felt fortunate for being on the other side of the MTV generation. Madonna blasted from two large speakers. The room was hot and humid from sweat and body heat. It didn't smell particularly great either.

A temporary bar had been set up to my left where a long line—if I could call it that, it was more of a mosh pit—pressed forward to order expensive neon cocktails like Kelly green Midori sours and aqua-colored blue lagoons. It was no wonder the college and early twentysomething crowd gravitated toward these drinks, as they were basically sugar bombs. I wouldn't put it past Richard to skimp on the alcohol content in the five-to eight-dollar cocktails.

I needed to blend in to avoid my stalker, so I squeezed past a group of young women jumping up and down to the beat. They wore their hair in matching side ponytails with colorful scrunchies. I had a flash of Juliet and her long pale blond hair. What would she be like in her twenties? She was already an old soul with a huge heart and a smile that lit up any room. It was hard to imagine that changing, but then again, we were a long way from the teen years. Maybe I would come to regret my words.

"Capshaw!"

I heard my name being called out.

"Capshaw, what are you doing here?"

I turned to find Richard Lord glaring at me. Was he auditioning for a role in a John Hughes movie? He wore a pair of white slacks that accentuated the slight paunch of beer belly. His pale pink Izod T-shirt had the collar popped and he had *tied a mint green sweater around his neck. A bulky beeper was secured to his belt.*

"Nice crowd, Richard."

"It's like this every night. Too bad you went into the bakery business. Can't pull in the kind of cash I am with donuts and chocolate cake, can you?" Sweat stains spread from his armpits and beads dampened his forehead.

Had he been dancing? Richard didn't strike me as the disco type.

"Nope." I didn't bother to elaborate on the fact that neither Helen nor I had any interest in catering to the dance party crowd.

"You should see how much I'm making on the cover alone. These kids like their cocktails," he shouted over the music. "You're missing out, Will. The good money is all in the bar tab."

"Glad to hear things are going well."

"Oh, things are going better than well." He loosened his sweater. "I'm making more money than anyone in town between the hotel rooms, which have been at a hundred percent occupancy since I took over, our dining room, special events, and now these dances. I'm going to be named number one in the Rogue Valley's Thirty under Thirty edition that comes out next month."

I didn't know a ton about the hotel business, but if Richard was telling the truth about having an occupancy rate at one hundred percent, I would have to guess that meant he had been offering deep discounts. There simply wasn't enough traffic through town when the theater was dark to support those numbers.

"You having a night off from the old ball and chain?" Richard nudged me. "There's some cute coeds around, if you know what I mean."

Describing Helen as a ball and chain was offensive at best. "No. I'm meeting a friend."

"Who?" Richard's beady eyes darted from side to side. "Someone from your bakery, or wait, it's a bakeshop, right? Ha! You know you're in Ashland, Oregon, not in some fancy San Francisco or New York village?"

I ignored his dig at Torte. It was nothing new. "No one you know."

"Why are you meeting here, at a dance party? Does this have anything to do with Chuck's death? I heard that you've been trying to play Hardy Boys with Doug. That's a bad idea, Will. You should listen to me as a friend."

A friend? Richard Lord? The old English proverb "With friends like these, who needs enemies?" rang through my head.

"You're in too deep. You might think that no one knows what you are up to, but they do, Will Capshaw. They do. You're putting Helen and Juliet in danger, you know."

"What are you talking about?" Was Richard up to his usual tricks, or did he actually know something?

"This is a small town and news travels fast. You're not a detective. Neither is Doug, technically *speaking. You two have been traipsing around like you're Don Johnson and Philip Michael Thomas. You're asking for trouble."*

"Richard, if you know something about the case, you need to tell Doug." I rubbed my ears as the loud music thumped in my head.

He brushed imaginary dust from his Izod. "I don't know anything. I'm giving you a warning, as a friend. That's all."

"Why would you warn me? You obviously aren't telling me something."

He tried to flirt with a group of women who walked by us with pink martinis. "Hey ladies, how are you enjoying the party?"

They gave him a sideways glance, sniggered, and returned to the dance floor

"Too bad you're tied down, Will. There's so much action here." He shot a lewd glance at a young coed and unclipped his beeper from his belt. No one else I knew in Ashland had a pager. Richard glanced at the electronic screen.

I wasn't going to let him off the hook that easy. "What do you know about Chuck's death?"

He looped the beeper back on his belt and narrowed his eyes. "You have it all, don't you Capshaw. A gorgeous wife, pretty daughter, a bakery—sorry, bakeshop—that everyone around here seems to love. Why? I don't know. I can do donuts, too. You watch, I will. But you're going to toss it all aside to play detective? You may be book smart and like to walk around quoting Shakespeare, but you're stupid, Capshaw. If I had Helen, I'd keep her under lock and key. I wouldn't let her out of my sight and I certainly wouldn't run all around town pretending to be a cop when there's a killer on the loose."

"I'm not pretending to be a cop, Richard. And are you threatening me?"

"You're so jumpy, Will. I'm not threatening you, I'm simply telling you that if you think you and Doug are the only ones who get information, then you're mistaken. I get information too. Maybe I don't have a best friend to run around playing Miami Vice *with, but I hear things. I know things." Richard wet his fingers and slicked back his hair.*

For the briefest moment I felt sorry for Richard. Was he envious of my friendship with Doug? Was his constant ribbing due the fact that he wished he had a family like I do? I saw him in a new light.

A bartender waved Richard over. "Duty calls. You should heed my advice, Will. I'd stop playing cop if I were you, and get back to baking."

He made sure his collar was completely popped, then strutted to the bar.

What did Richard know? Had I read him wrong? Was he looking out for me?

I exited the sweaty ballroom. Enough time had passed that I felt confident I could head for the van and go home. The looming question was if Richard knew something vital to the case, how could Doug get it out of him?

Chapter Sixteen

"Professor, sorry to bug you, but you have a phone call." Andy stood next to the booth, giving us an apologetic grin.

The Professor smoothed his shirt. I wondered if he was struggling, like me, to ground himself in present day.

"Excuse me a moment." He cleared his throat and tilted his head in a slight bow.

I marked our place in the journal with a napkin and then stretched my feet in small circles, up, down, side to side. Movement felt odd. I'd been sitting for way too long. It was as if I had been listening to a movie while the Professor read. Each time we'd been interrupted, it became harder and harder to shake free of the past. I hadn't felt this connected to my father, well, maybe ever. My memories of him blurred and morphed together. They weren't to be trusted. He'd been gone for so long that the memories I did have of him were amalgams of stories I'd heard over the years.

Not today. Today was different. I felt like I was sitting across from my dad. He felt alive and whole through the Professor, so much more than the rough sketch I'd created of him in my head. Flawed, confused, struggling, and yet also so clearly strong in his resolve to follow his inner guidance. I could see many pieces of myself in him.

I stared out at the plaza, which was so different now compared with the Professor's descriptions of Ashland in the 1980s. Where there had once been grass and oak trees, there was now a paved gathering space with an information kiosk, the bubbling Lithia Fountains, ceramic flowerpots overflowing with brilliant purple fuchsias, benches, and antique lamp posts with banners announcing the spring garden show. I could just make out the front porch of the Merry Windsor hotel, which was the only thing in town that sounded like it hadn't had a facelift or been updated in the past three decades.

The Professor returned shortly. "Many apologies. That was your mother. Apparently, I had silenced my cell phone and she was worried." He took his cell out of his tweed jacket and clicked on the sound.

"Do you need to go?"

"No. She was calling to tell me that she and her friends decided to follow up their spa afternoon with a glass of wine. I told her to order a bottle to share and I will gladly provide chauffeur services when they're done with their afternoon of pampering. No one deserves some respite as much as Helen."

I knew that the Professor would have told Mom the same thing, regardless of our conversation, but I was glad he had bought us some extra time.

"Shall we finish?"

"Please."

He picked up the journal. "I'm afraid I should warn you that as you can see from the few remaining pages, we're nearing the end of the story and I fear that the conclusion will not satisfy you."

"That's okay." I tried to keep my bottom lip from quivering as I proceeded. "I have to tell you that regardless of how things ended with the case, that you sharing this story has meant more than I can ever express. I feel like my dad is right here with us." Tears spilled from my eyes.

The Professor reached into his breast pocket and offered me his handkerchief. "He is."

That made me cry harder.

He waited for me to compose myself, then quietly read the final few pages.

The next morning, I went straight to the police station after getting Torte up and running for the day.

"Doug, am I crazy to think that Richard Lord might have my best interest at heart?" I asked, helping myself to a cinnamon-and-sugar donut hole from the box that I'd brought along.

Doug ate a powdered sugar donut, leaving white residue on his hands. "Will, you see the best in people. That's one of the reasons that I'm happy to be able to call you a friend."

"Let me translate that. I'm crazy."

"No." Doug wiped his hands on a paper napkin, then attempted to brush powdered sugar from his blue uniform. "I don't doubt that Richard has a multifaceted personality, but if you want my professional opinion, I think his interest lies elsewhere."

"What do you mean?"

"Helen." Doug raised one eyebrow.

"What about Helen?" I ate a plain donut. It had

the slightest hint of cardamom and cinnamon. When we made donuts at the bakeshop, we saved the holes to sell by the dozen. Helen had been using the same two-piece donut cutter that allowed us to cut the donut and hole at the same time, for as long as I could remember. The stainless steel tool had seen many years of use. I had asked her when we opened Torte if she wanted to upgrade. I'd seen a variety of rollers and cutters that could make do-nuts by the dozens, but Helen refused. She liked her method. And who was I to argue? Donut holes had become a popular favorite amongst our customers. It was a win/win. We were able to use dough that we would otherwise have to scrap, and our custom-ers could buy a box of assorted holes at half the cost of a traditional dozen.

"If Richard has any genuine concern about your family's well-being, I would bet that is due to the fact that he has a crush on your wife."

I nearly dropped the box of donuts. "Still? I thought he was over that."

Doug's face changed. I couldn't quite decipher the look. Was he irritated with me?

"Will, half of Ashland is in love with Helen. Not only because she's beautiful, but because she has a rare gift of really listening. There's no one else like her." He busied himself with a stack of napkins. "You're a lucky man."

I sensed a shift in energy between us. "You think Richard likes Helen?"

He threw his hands up in exasperation. "Yeah, I do. I'm telling you, Will, everyone in town has a little crush on Helen." Then he shook his head and laughed. "*Hand me a chocolate donut and come to my office with me. I can give you a cup of terrible station coffee to wash down the donuts while I show you what I learned from the bank.*"

I followed him to his office, which was more like a glorified broom closet. Doug had said everyone in town had a crush on Helen. Did that include him? I'd never considered the possibility. Helen and Doug were friends. We were all friends. If Doug did have feelings for Helen that would seriously complicate things.

I dropped it as we crammed into his office, where he had set out stacks of bank records. Despite the worn patches in the carpet, the rusting filing cabinet, and the olive green phone and intercom system on his desk, Doug had managed to make the office feel somewhat homey with posters and playbills taped to the walls.

"These are Chuck's statements?" I declined Doug's offer of stale coffee.

"Yes." He sat down at his desk and pointed to a folding chair in the corner. "Pull that up and take a look at this."

I unfolded the metal chair and sat across from him. Doug had highlighted sections of each bank statement.

"Look at these. These are large deposits that don't match his salary from the Festival or the Cabaret. Every deposit is in cash. They've been coming in steady for three months. The same amount every month. Take a look."

Doug handed me the first few pages for a closer look. "You're not kidding about large deposits. Two thousand dollars?"

"Exactly." Doug pointed to highlighted sections on more of the statements. "Where was Chuck getting that kind of cash?"

"His schemes? Drugs? Could he have been dealing?"

"Possibly. This is the first tangible proof we have in the case. Chuck was raking in the cash."

"Do you think this means that Pat and Jeri were telling the truth?" I handed him the computer printout pages with little holes perforated along the edges.

"I think it likely means that Chuck was indeed working under-the-table deals anywhere and everywhere that he could. It's also possible that he was dealing, but I don't have any proof of that at the moment."

"Where does that leave us in terms of suspects though?"

"And, there's the rub." Doug restacked the bank statements. "Unfortunately it means that everyone had a motive to kill him. As I learned in the academy, money is the motive in the vast majority of murders."

"Now what?"

Doug sighed. "I don't know, Will. I'm running out of ideas and time. My boss thinks the window has already closed. I've hit a dead end on hard evidence. These statements help support my theory, but they would never stand up in court on their own. The defense could simply say Chuck received cash from a rich aunt or side jobs."

"Do you think you should try to talk to Richard? He seemed like he knew something last night. Unless he was just trying to one-up me."

"I'll talk to him. He's first on my list this morning. And I'll circle back with Pat. If we could determine who had the most to lose financially, that could break open the case."

I thought for a minute. "Jeri is convinced that Shelly and Stewart are in financial trouble. She said they both cashed out retirement savings, took second mortgages. They got the old church for a steal because it was in such bad shape, but it sounds like they grossly underestimated how much renovations were going to cost."

Doug took a sip from a coffee cup on his desk that looked like it might have been sitting there for days. A thin film had formed on the top of the coffee. "Ah. This is terrible." He grimaced and set the mug down.

"Come over to the bakeshop. I'll make you a real coffee." I pointed to the chocolate donut hole that he hadn't touched yet. "You're starting out your career, Doug. This is the time to make a statement about the kind of detective you're going to be, and as your best friend I can't allow you to become a bad-coffee-and-donuts stereotype."

"Touché." He reached for the chocolate donut hole and ate it in one bite. "First rule of crime, get rid of the evidence."

Our normal banter had been restored. I felt

relieved. Maybe I had read more into what he had said about Helen than I should have. It was probably because Richard Lord had weaseled his way under my skin.

"Helen and I didn't have anywhere near the same kind of expenses to get the bakery up and running and even we had sticker shock with the final bills for plumbing, electricity, sheetrock. If Chuck was doing the same kind of thing to the Cabaret that he did to OSF and Rumors, it's possible that Shelly and Stewart have the most money to lose."

Doug nodded. "That's a good point. And with both of them we have opportunity covered. The hit-and-run occurred right in front of the Cabaret where they had both been seen minutes before. They're checking all three boxes on my list: motive, means, opportunity."

"What do you do next?"

He scribbled a note on a yellow legal pad. "That is the question."

"Anything you want me to help with?"

"No. I hate to say it, but Richard is right. You've done more than your fair share already, and I'm hoping that whoever has been following you around is trying to scare you. But with the note on the napkin and someone coming after you two nights in a row, it's not safe. It's time to back off, Will. For Helen and Juliet."

One part of me felt relieved. The other disappointed. I'd come this far with Doug that it would be nice to see the case through to the end and get some closure, but no amount of personal desire would outweigh the guilt I would feel if something did happen to Juliet or Helen.

"Fair enough. Promise me you'll let me know how it turns out, though."

"Of course. It will give me an excuse to up my detective game and establish myself as Ashland's latte-drinking sleuth."

"That I can most certainly help you with."

Doug stood and shook my hand. "Seriously, Will, I can't thank you enough for everything you've done the last few days. I wouldn't have a single lead in the case if it weren't for you."

"You know that's not true. It's been fun. I mean, not that it's fun that Chuck is dead or that his killer is running around free, but spending time with you and watching how you go about piecing together the clues. If I wasn't in the baking business, I might have to consider a career change."

"Will, the badge and uniform would look good on you." He tapped the gold badge on his chest.

"I'll leave the uniform to you and stick with flour and butter."

"Deal." He walked me out. "I'll stop by later and let you know what I learn."

I left with a new resolve to pour myself into the work. If I had learned anything these past few days it was that I may not be the richest man on paper in Ashland, but I had an abundance of wealth in the form of Helen, Juliet, and Torte.

Chapter Seventeen

The Professor shut the journal. He folded his hands to-gether, linking his fingers. "Well, there you have it, Juliet. The Pastry Case. My first solo case. Still unsolved."

"Wait, that's it?"

He unclasped his hands. "Alas, it is. I warned you that you wouldn't be satisfied with the ending."

"But I don't understand. What happened after my dad dropped out of the investigation?"

"Things returned to normal for the most part. I contin-ued questioning suspects, following up on a few anonymous tips, tracking lots of dead ends. It was frustrating, to say the very least. Your dad and I felt like we might have had a chance at catching Chuck's killer if we had had more time to work on it together, but Will made the right choice by opting out. I didn't blame him. I would have done the same thing in his position." The professor folded his hands. "I wish I could have closed the case."

"What about my dad? What about whoever was follow-ing him? The guy who left the note at Torte?"

"More of the same. Will was vigilant. He reported a few instances where he thought someone was watching the bakeshop, but when I arrived on the scene each time the guy was gone. It paralleled my frustration with the investigation. It always felt like we were inches away from solving the case."

"That was it? My mom never knew anything about my dad working with you?"

"Not to my knowledge. There was one more incident. Torte was vandalized."

"What?"

The Professor sighed. "Yes. It was about a week after Will and I decided it would be best to keep him out of the investigation. Your parents arrived at Torte to find the front windows smashed. There had been some vandalism and graffiti in town, but Will and I knew that the bakeshop had been targeted. He found a note tied to a rock that mimicked the same tone of the note on the napkin. He made sure your mom never saw it, but I sent it into the lab to have the handwriting analyzed. It came back a match."

"But you never figure out who wrote it?"

"No." He looked tired. "I made copies of the entire police report and of my notes from the Pastry Case for your dad. I think that Will kept newspaper clippings, photos from the damage to the bakeshop, and our collective case notes."

"I'll have to check the basement tonight. I remember seeing other papers, but at the time I was focused on his journal."

"If the case notes aren't there, let me know. I'd be happy to provide you with access to the old files. They're stored in archives."

"I can't believe that nothing more ever developed." It

was almost impossible to believe that any criminal could have eluded the Professor for all these years.

"Nothing." He hung his head. "This case will stay with me until my dying days. There is nothing I'd like more than to bring Chuck's killer to justice."

"What about Stewart and Shelly?" I couldn't accept that there wasn't more to the story.

"I had my suspicions about both of them, but again, nothing concrete. Certainly not enough evidence to make an arrest."

His phone dinged. "Ah, this is your mother. Duty calls."

Before he left, he reached for my hand. "I'm sorry to disappoint you and leave you wanting more. You have a taste of what it's like to walk in my shoes. There's nothing worse in this profession than an unsolved case, but I am glad to have had a chance to share these memories with you. Those were some of my best days with your father." He placed his hand on his heart. His eyes misted. "Reading his account of our first adventure has made him more alive for me too."

I fought back hot tears and a growing lump in my throat.

"There is one favor I must ask." He reached for his tweed jacket.

"Sure, anything."

"It's about your mother. I would like to tell her myself, when the time is right, but I don't want to put you in an uncomfortable position."

"It's okay. I need some time to let this sink in anyway." I cradled the journal in my hands.

He stood, kissed the top of my head, tugged on his tweed jacket, and left.

I tried to pretend like everything was normal for the rest of the afternoon, but I felt like I was walking through the motions. I checked in with the kitchen staff before they left for the day and tried to concentrate on filling out order forms for supplies. I felt like I was stuck in some sort of time warp.

"Hey, boss, we're all done upstairs." Andy tugged a gray ski hat over his amber-toned hair. "Need anything else before I hit the slopes?"

"Huh?" I looked up from the spreadsheet I'd been studying for the past half hour. It was a basic Excel document, but at the moment reading it felt like I was trying to decipher hieroglyphics.

"We're done cleaning. Sequoia locked up. I'm heading out, unless you need more help?" He posed it as a question.

"No, no. That's great. Thank you. Have fun on Mount A."

Andy stepped into the kitchen. "Boss, is everything cool? You and the Professor were talking for hours and now you kind of seem"—he paused, searching for the right word—"well, out of it."

"You're too sweet, Andy." I pushed the laptop aside. "Thanks for your concern, but I'm fine. You know what I really need?"

He perked up. "A triple-shot espresso. I can go pull shots right now."

"You have a ski bus to catch." I stretched and walked to the far wall where five cherry red aprons hung in a neat row. "And I don't need coffee. I need to bake."

"As Bethany would say, 'Bakers gotta bake.'" Andy snapped his thumb and index finger. "As long as you're cool, I'm out. The slope is open until ten o'clock. There's nothing like skiing under the lights. See you tomorrow."

I watched him take the stairs two at a time and then heard the doorbell ding as Andy opened and shut the front door. Mount Ashland ran a free daily ski bus that picked up powder-lovers at the plaza and delivered them to the lodge every hour during ski season. The shuttle made an ongoing loop up and back from the mountain, which allowed skiers of all ages to leave their cars at home and avoid long bottlenecks on the windy, narrow, mountainous road.

My statement to Andy was completely true. Maybe baking would clear my head, or at least provide a distraction from thinking about my dad. I poured myself a glass of white wine and surveyed the walk-in fridge. After considering ingredients for a minute, I landed on corned beef, red onions, potatoes, eggs, white cheddar, and fresh herbs. I would make an Irish corned beef hash for my dinner. If it turned out the way I anticipated, it could be tomorrow's breakfast special.

I started by dicing red onions. Then I added a healthy glug of olive oil to a cast-iron skillet and sautéed the onions until they were translucent. My shoulders began to relax as I peeled and diced potatoes and added them to the skillet. I finished the hash with chopped fresh herbs, salt and pepper, and a generous splash of red wine vinegar. A hash is a simple, yet hearty potato dish that can be made with practically any ingredients on hand. For tonight's dinner, I sliced strips of corned beef and cracked eggs on top. Next, I turned the heat to low and covered the hash with a lid to allow the eggs to poach.

The crisp white wine, with notes of apples and peaches, was refreshing. I returned to the inventory spreadsheet with renewed energy as the Irish hash cooked. From the columns in red, it was evident that we'd been selling more coffees with alternative milk options lately. We were running low on coconut, almond, and oat milk. I made a note to double our order. Then I reviewed the daily sales sheet. Torte had come a long way from the early days the Professor had spoken of when my parents had the one and only espresso machine in town. Our coffee sales equaled our pastry sales these days and our profit margin on espresso drinks was much higher. I was sure if my dad were here to see Torte's progress, he would be astounded to see that we literally sold hundreds of artisan coffee drinks every day.

I left the paperwork to check on my hash. When I lifted the lid, warm steam enveloped my face. It smelled divine. The eggs had poached perfectly with pale yellow yokes surrounded by lovely white circles. I removed the skillet from the heat and topped it with freshly grated Irish cheddar.

My stomach rumbled. Suddenly, I was famished. When had I eaten last? With the Professor earlier this afternoon? The day had vanished in a blur of hazy memories. I served myself a scoop of the hash and returned to my wine. The briny flavor of the corned beef and hint of vinegar married with the creamy eggs, tender potatoes, spicy onions, and touch of sharp cheddar made me groan out loud. This was definitely a keeper.

I finished two servings while going over the receipts and tomorrow's custom orders. By the time I had cleaned up my dinner dishes and filed the paperwork in the office, I felt more like myself. It was late (at least for me), and it had been an emotional day. I locked up and headed home.

Back at my house and armed with a cup of lemon zinger tea and my cozy fleece pajamas, I crawled into bed and began leafing through my dad's journal again. As the Professor suspected, he had saved dozens of newspaper articles about Chuck's death. Along with grainy photocopies of the note written on the napkin and the note he had found when Torte had been vandalized.

"STAY OUT OF IT OR TORTE WILL GET TORCHED!"

I was no handwriting expert, but the thick, heavy scroll was an unmistakable match. The lettering on the napkin had been written in all caps but otherwise the writing was very similar. As was the fact that whoever had written the notes, wrote them both in black felt-tip pen.

I reviewed the suspects. There was Chef Ronald, who had had a physical fight with Chuck the night he was murdered; Jeri, from OSF, who blamed Chuck for the fact that her job was on the line; Pat, the owner of Rumors, who had made it clear that he had no love lost for Chuck. And, last but not least Stewart and Shelly, who had poured their life savings into the Cabaret. I wondered—how many of them had stayed in town after Chuck's death?

Jeri was still in touch with the Professor, but what about the others?

A plan began to form in my mind. What if I could find them now? What if I could pick up the case now? Part of me started to stop myself from heading down that rabbit hole, but another part felt prickly with excitement. What if I could close the case for my dad? And for the Professor. What if I could bring it full circle? It would be like closing an open loop while at the same time connecting me to my father deeper than ever before *and* helping the man who had taken on his fatherly role to finally be able to close his first case.

This was the twenty-first century after all, and I had fresh eyes. What if there was something in his journal and old articles that they had missed? Or maybe not even missed but had been unable to prove at the time. The handwritten notes would be my starting point.

The Professor had mentioned that he took handwriting samples from each of the suspects. But the killer was clever. They could have easily disguised their handwriting. If I could track down each of the suspects and find a secret way to obtain current handwriting samples, the Professor could have them analyzed against the old notes.

I sat up in bed. This could work, but I needed help and I knew just the person. I reached for my phone and called Lance.

"Darling, to what do I owe the pleasure?" He answered on the first ring.

"Are you busy?" I bundled my dad's journal on the bedside table.

"Define 'busy.'" He shouted something about stage left. "We're less than two weeks away from previews and still don't have our blocking mastered."

"I won't keep you then."

"No please, I could use a reprieve." He must have covered the phone with one hand because I could barely hear him dictate orders about running the scene again. "Do tell, what's going on?"

"I need your help."

"With what? Pastry tasting? Consider it done."

"No, a murder investigation." I had no doubt that would get Lance's attention.

"Come again, darling? It sounded like you said '*murder.*'"

"I did." I gave him a very condensed overview of my day with the Professor.

When I finished, he squealed. "Juliet Montague Capshaw, you have yourself a partner in crime. Shall I raid wardrobe? How do you feel about a magnifying glass? Trench coat? Sherlock cap?"

"None of the above," I cautioned. "Lance, I want your help, but we have to be extremely subtle. The whole point is that decades have passed. None of the suspects will have any reason to believe we're looking into the case."

"Subtlety is my middle name, darling."

"Yeah right."

"Don't wrinkle that pretty brow of yours."

How did he know that I was scrunching my forehead?

"I'll meet you bright and early and we'll dive headfirst into this Pastry Case."

We hung up. I had a brief flash of regret for involving Lance. He had a tendency toward the dramatic, but he was also cunning, crafty, and well-connected. Not to mention that if I was going to open up old wounds, I wanted a steadfast friend by my side.

Chapter Eighteen

The next morning at Torte, I showed Marty and Sterling my recipe for Irish hash. Marty had a brilliant idea to finish the hash in the wood-fired oven, just long enough to infuse it with a smoky flavor. Sterling was inspired to make a traditional Irish stew for our soup of the day. St. Patrick's Day was right around the corner.

When the rest of the team arrived, we took it a step further. Bethany and Steph added dark chocolate Guinness stout cupcakes to the daily specials list, and Andy said he would experiment with an Irish cream latte and mint mocha. I hadn't anticipated that my simple hash would end up being the centerpiece for a full Irish spread, but that's typically how things evolve in the bakeshop. Everyone builds off one another. Our brainstorming and collaboration sessions were my favorite part of my morning. Rosa took on the task of decorating our front windows for the holiday. We sent her upstairs with trays of green sweets and decorations.

"Let me know when you're done," Bethany called. "I'll take a bunch of pictures for our social media." She had spread out at least a dozen cookbooks on the marble countertop. "You have to see this recipe I found," she said to me, holding a faded index card with my dad's handwriting.

"Where did you find this?" I asked as I examined the recipe for pineapple upside-down cake.

"Steph and I were going through some of your vintage cookbooks to look for other St. Patrick's Day recipes." Bethany pointed to an exposed shelf that ran the length of the far side of the kitchen. It had been positioned about a foot below the ceiling. When we remodeled the basement Mom had come up with the idea of using the high ceiling shelf to display cookbooks and some of the original items she had saved from Torte's early days, like the distressed turquoise kitchen scale that had once belonged to my great-grandmother, and the original bakeshop menu that we had framed.

"Yeah there's some funny stuff in those," Steph chimed in. Her bright purple hair, which she normally wore long, had been cut in an asymmetrical bob. The new style suited her. I liked being able to see her striking, almost violet eyes. I knew that she achieved the effect by dusting her lids with a touch of shimmery purple shadow and matching eye liner. "The eighties must have been a blast. Bethany and I want to try some of these recipes, like tiramisu and chocolate lava cakes."

Bethany flipped on her phone to show me pictures she had saved. "Steph and I are thinking we should totally do an eighties bash. You know, like, throwback to the decade of neon. I saw that they used to have dessert carts and trays at restaurants that they would bring around to each table to try and tempt you to order something sweet at the end of the meal. Do you remember that?"

I couldn't help but laugh. "I do! I had forgotten all about dessert carts. I remember going to dinner at Chateaulin, a fancy French restaurant back in the day, and they would wheel out a dessert cart draped in white linens that had gorgeous slices of New York cheesecake with fresh cherries and giant slices of four-layer carrot cake with cream-cheese frosting. You're bringing back childhood memories."

"No way," Andy said. He had come downstairs with the first sample of the special he and Sequoia planned to serve—a mint mocha with mint infused whipped cream and green sugar sprinkles. "You're barely over twenty, boss, right?"

"Something like that." I tried to wink, but ended up giving him a lopsided grin.

He passed around tasters of the sweet coffee drink. "I hope this isn't too much of a gut-bomb. You guys should come check out the display Rosa did. It's really cool. Green cupcakes, Bethany's mint chocolate chip brownies, lots of shamrocks, and even a pot of gold. We decided to go all in on the mint for this one."

I took a sip of the minty drink. It had a bright pop of flavor followed by a subtle chocolaty finish. "Oh, this is delish," I said to Andy. Shockingly it wasn't ridiculously sweet.

"Nice." Andy reached over to give Bethany a high five. "Sequoia suggested making a simple syrup with fresh mint leaves to reduce the sweetness."

"It's a winner." Marty tipped back his drink. "Can I have another?"

"Come upstairs whenever. We're working on an Irish cream next."

Marty patted his slightly plump stomach. "Then I'll save my calories for that, young laddie."

Andy returned to the espresso bar.

"What do you think, Jules?" Bethany asked. "Can you teach us how to make pineapple upside-down cake?"

It was strange that my worlds were colliding. I'd been reminiscing about desserts from my childhood with the Professor yesterday and now this morning these same recipes were laid out in front of me. I took it as a sign from the universe. "I'd love to, but I'm a novice too. I have a vague memory of my dad making the cake and I remember eating it, but I've never baked one."

"Let's do it." Bethany's enthusiasm was one of the best things about having her in the kitchen. Her energy was contagious. The three of us spent the next hour testing my dad's old recipe for pineapple upside-down cake.

We started by melting brown sugar and butter on the stove. Then we poured the melted bubbling mixture into a baking pan and arranged slices of pineapple on the bottom. The 1980s recipe called for placing maraschino cherries in the center of each pineapple slice.

"What do you think?" I asked Bethany and Steph. "Should we stick with the classic or elevate it with our Bing cherry preserves that we canned last summer?"

"Duh, classic." Stephanie gave me her signature scowl.

"Really?" I scrunched my forehead. "Bright, red, fake cherries?"

"Uh, yeah, absolutely. I'm with Steph on this. If we're going retro, we have to go retro," Bethany said.

"Okay. Okay." I held up my hands in surrender. "Maraschino cherries it is."

Stephanie used kitchen tweezers to arrange the brilliant

red cherries in the center of the pineapple slices as Bethany took a couple of photos.

Next, we mixed a simple cake batter consisting of butter, sugar, milk, eggs, baking powder, salt, and flour. The creamy batter didn't call for any extra flavoring like vanilla or almond. I knew what the answer would be, but I asked my question anyway. "Should I add a teaspoon or two of vanilla?"

"She doesn't get it, Steph," Bethany scoffed.

Stephanie rolled her eyes. "I know."

"It's in my nature. I'm a pastry chef. I'm always tweaking recipes."

Bethany tapped her short nails on the recipe. "The eighties are totally in right now, so if we're doing this we have to go with the classic."

"Deal." I handed her the bowl to spread the batter on the top of the pineapple slices.

"That's it?" Steph asked.

I picked up the recipe to make sure we had followed my dad's directions to the letter. "Yep. It's super simple. His note here says, 'Flip the cake with confidence.'" I smiled at the sentiment. "We bake it for fifty minutes and then gather up our confidence to flip it." With that I slid the cake into the oven. While it baked, we finished the morning prep and sent Marty out on our bread delivery route.

The timer dinged a little less than an hour later. Bethany and Steph dropped their piping bags and raced over to watch the unveiling. "Okay, read me the instructions again," I said, removing the golden cake from the oven. The scent of caramelized brown sugar and baked pineapple enveloped the kitchen.

"It says to immediately turn the cake out of the pan and onto a cake plate or platter," Bethany read.

Steph set a white oval cake platter on the counter nearby.

"You place the platter on top of the pan, using oven mitts. Then carefully lift up the pan but be sure to hold the platter in place."

"Got it," I replied, following her directions.

"Invert the pan with confidence," Bethany said with a wide smile.

"Here goes nothing." I flipped the platter over and tugged on the pan. It came off with ease, revealing a buttery row of pineapples dotted with maraschino cherries. Caramel brown sugar glaze dripped down the sides of the cake.

Bethany and Steph let out a collective "Oooh."

"Not bad for our first attempt." I took the pan to the sink.

"It's so pretty," Bethany gushed. "Should we serve it today or save it for ourselves?"

I washed my hands with oatmeal-and-honey soap. "This one has to be our taster. If everyone gives our retro cake a thumbs-up, then you two can make more."

Bethany cut into the rectangular cake, making sure that each piece had a perfect slice of pineapple in the center. "It's almost too cute to eat."

"Did someone say taste? Count me in," Sterling said from the stove where he was stirring a stockpot of veggies.

Steph passed around plates of the glossy upside-down cake. With just one bite I was transported back in time. The combination of buttery cake and sweet pineapple made me reach for another taste.

"This is awesome," Bethany said through a mouthful.

I took the fact that everyone else nodded and continued eating their slices as a good sign. "Alright, I'll leave you two to it. Get baking and I'll go have Rosa add this to the specials board."

I went upstairs to find Lance waiting at the front door. Seeing him awake before the sun had fully risen gave me pause. We didn't even open for another half hour.

"You're here early," I said, unlocking the door to let him in.

"As promised." He ran his long fingers across his tailored gray suit and skinny black tie. "Dressed and ready to start the day. As they say, 'The early bird catches the worm.'" His body shuddered at the thought. "Not that I have any intention of catching an actual worm. Metaphorically speaking, of course."

"Of course." I ushered him inside. "Do you want coffee?"

He gave me an exasperated sigh. "*Do* I want coffee?"

"Okay, coffee it is." I called to Andy. "Can you make two of your test Irish cream lattes for me and Lance?"

"On it!" Andy's cheeks were wind-burned, I assumed from night skiing on Mt. A.

Lance and I sat in the same booth the Professor and I had occupied yesterday. Had it really only been a day? It felt like our conversation had gone on for weeks.

"Do tell. Where do we start?" Lance strummed his fingers on the table. The early morning light pouring in through the front windows made his eyes look bluer than usual.

I lowered my voice, not that anyone was listening. My team had the morning opening routine down to a science. Rosa tended to the flowers on the dining room tables, snipping away any dead foliage and adding fresh water to the vases. Andy and Sequoia prepped their coffee station. Sequoia poured bags of whole bean coffee into our industrial grinders as Andy used a dry erase pen to mark different milk options on stainless steel frothing pitchers. Bethany lugged heavy trays of key lime tarts, pesto bacon and egg sandwiches, and dark chocolate stout cupcakes up the stairs and then begin arranging them in the glass pastry cases. "Like I said last night, we have to be extremely discreet."

"And like I said, I am the model of discretion." Lance mouthed his retort in an exaggerated whisper.

"Lance, I'm serious."

"O ye, of little faith, Juliet. You know I jest." He kissed his pinky and then held it up. "I do solemnly swear that I will be the model of discretion."

"Okay, but you have to promise not to breathe a word of this to anyone."

He crossed his heart with his index finger. "I swear upon Shakespeare's grave."

I wrinkled my brow.

"What?" Lance looked injured. "My affinity for the world's greatest playwright runs deep."

I didn't have time to argue.

"Now that we have that ugly business squared away, are you going to enlighten me on our plan of attack?"

"I was hoping *you* might have an idea." I told him about the note my dad had found on the napkin and the matching handwriting found when someone smashed Torte's windows. "It's probably a long shot, but I was thinking that if we could get handwriting samples from each of the suspects, we could compare them with the notes."

"Yes, yes. Well done. I like it." Lance waited as Andy brought us two of Irish cream lattes. "Now *this* is the way to start a morning," Lance said to Andy. "Many thanks, young man."

Andy was used to Lance's theatrics. "Let me know what you guys think. I went pretty easy with the Irish cream, but if there's not enough I can add more."

"I'm sure it's wonderful." Lance took a sip and gave me a Cheshire cat–like grin. "Subtlety is the key, after all."

The drink was masterful. Andy's expert touch shone through with a coffee-forward drink that had a rich, silky finish without being overly sweet or syrupy.

"Need anything else?" Andy asked before he left.

"The kid is skilled," Lance commented once Andy was out of earshot.

"I know. Giving him more responsibility has really helped him shine even more." I felt a surge of pride for my young coffee protégé.

"Now how to garner handwriting samples from our pool of suspects?" Lance twisted his ascot as he thought. Then he snapped. "I've got it! A survey."

"A survey?"

"Yes, of course. We've been doing so much work at the theater trying to pull in young and more diverse audiences, and what's been most successful has been the content we're producing. Not that the Bard won't always have a voice on the Elizabethan stage, but some of our most successful shows in the past few years have been contemporary and written by playwrights who traditionally weren't given a platform for their voice. We've been casting the most diverse set of actors on the West Coast and flipping gender roles." He paused. "I was just reminding the

company last night that the concept isn't entirely new—
Shakespeare was casting men as women in his day."

I folded my arms across my chest. "Yeah, because
women weren't allowed to act."

"Details, details." Lance waved his hand and winked.
"I digress. We've been toying with polling our audience and getting their input on what they'd like to see
on OSF's stages. It's perfect. Everyone on your potential
suspect list has a connection to the theater. We can approach them under the guise that we're looking for input
from influencers in the field. Everyone loves to feel like
a celebrity."

I choked on my coffee. "*Everyone* does." I gave him a
knowing look.

Lance gasped and pointed to his chest. "Moi? Never. I
simply give the people what they want."

I kicked him under the table.

He scowled. "Well, what do you say?"

"It just might work."

Lance clapped twice. "Excellent. I'll have the art department mock something up for us to look at this morning."

"Great. I'll see if I can figure out who is still in the valley. I know that Jeri is in town because I saw her talking
with the Professor yesterday. You didn't say anything to
her by chance, did you?"

"Not a word." Lance finished his coffee. "Shall we re-
convene after lunch?"

"That works for me."

"You're sure about the Sherlock caps? They could add
a certain *je ne sais quoi*." He paused for effect.

I shook my head.

"But if you were to reconsider, I'm sure I can dig something out of the props department."

"I won't reconsider."

He stood and tightened his ascot. "Your loss, darling. Ta-ta!" With that he pranced toward the door, offering Andy lavish praise for the coffee as he left.

Classic Lance. I laughed at the thought of him sneaking around the plaza in a Sherlock cap with a magnifying glass pressed to his face.

"Thanks for the coffee," I said to Andy after gathering our empty cups and taking them to the bin to be washed. "That drink was absolutely the best."

Andy's cheeks were already red from a night of skiing, but they deepened at my compliment. "Aw, shucks, boss. You're making me blush."

Sequoia arranged tasting samples on a tray at the espresso counter. Her long dreadlocks had been tied back into a loose ponytail.

"Are you giving out samples to customers this morning?" I asked.

"We decided the Irish cream is good, as long as you're cool with that?"

"Absolutely. I loved it." I picked up one of the small paper tasting cups. "What's this?"

"It's a dirty chai latte. Half masala chai and a shot of espresso with steamed milk." She waited while I tasted the drink.

"Mmm. This is delicious too." The spicy, sweet chai and strong espresso were an interesting and unexpected combination. "You guys keep outdoing yourselves."

Sequoia slowly topped off the last of the taster cups. "We like to keep it fresh, you know?"

"I do." I stopped and checked in with Rosa who was at the pastry case, ready to take the first orders of the morning. "Are we stocked up enough?"

She smiled, revealing dimples on her cheeks. "Yes. I think we are as ready as we can be." She nodded to the windows where a small line had already formed. Customers pointed at Rosa's whimsical St. Patrick's Day display.

"Shall I let them in?"

Rosa wore her dark naturally curly hair in two braids fastened with pretty aquamarine clips. She held up a finger and fixed one of the clips. Then she tightened the Torte apron around her narrow waist. "Okay. Let them eat cake."

I chuckled and went to unlock the front door. Within minutes the bakeshop was humming with happy morning energy. I touched base with the kitchen team to make sure they weren't in need of an extra pair of hands. Marty and Sterling tried to one-up each other with bad jokes as they chopped veggies for the hash special and our soup of the day.

"Why did the lazy man want to work in the bakery?" Marty asked, shielding his eyes with one hand as he diced red onions.

"Oh man, do I want to know?" Sterling added olive oil to a stockpot and tossed in chopped garlic.

"Because he wanted to loaf around." Marty's boisterous laugh reverberated through the kitchen.

"That's bad." Sterling stirred the sizzling garlic.

At the opposite end of the kitchen, Stephanie was frosting the chocolate stout cupcakes and Bethany was packaging wholesale bread orders.

"I have some ordering to do," I said to the team. "If you need me, I'll be in the office."

"Don't forget to order inventory for Sunday Supper," Sterling reminded me. "We were going to talk about a theme."

"Right. Thanks. Quick brainstorm, any ideas?"

Marty chimed in. "I make a mean soda bread. What about an Irish theme?"

"I love it. What if you make more of the stew?" I asked Sterling. "We could do a St. Patrick's Day picnic with sandwiches, potato salad, stew, an Emerald Island salad, and a hot whiskey cake."

"Kill me now." Marty pretended to stab himself with a wooden spoon.

"That's good, right?" I looked to Sterling for confirmation. Mom and I had made him our official sous chef, and I wanted to make sure that he knew he had a voice.

"It works for me, but you might get some pushback from those two." He turned his head to the decorating station where Bethany and Steph both had headphones in as they piped rainbow and shamrock shortbread cookies. "I think they have their hearts set on an eighties dinner."

"Right." I looked at a stainless steel tray waiting to go upstairs with square slices of pineapple upside-down cake.

"What if we do both," Sterling suggested.

"An Irish eighties dinner?" I wasn't sure how the two would mingle together.

"No." Sterling dabbed the corner of a plate with a paper towel. "Why not do another dinner this month? We have the space. They've been selling out, and I'd be up for working with Steph and Beth to create an eighties flash-back menu."

"That's great. Let's do it." I was thrilled to hear that Sterling wanted to take on more responsibility, and he was right. Every time we announced a Sunday Supper, tickets sold out within a few hours.

"Cool." He ladled stew into a bowl. "Can you order some parsnips and Yukon gold potatoes for the Irish supper?"

"For sure." I left to work on our inventory order in my office. While I already had my laptop at my fingertips, it wouldn't hurt to do some research into the current where-abouts of the suspects. I grabbed a notebook and jotted down a few notes as I scoured the web for any info.

Jeri was easy. She was still living in Ashland and work-ing part-time for the Camelot Theater in Talent. Shelly was currently the managing director of the Cabaret, al-though she had sold her ownership stake to a young couple from L.A., and according to what Lance had told me, was staying on for a few months to help with the transition. Stewart had retired and lived half of the year in Mexico and the other half in Ashland. I figured if Lance and I started with Shelly, she would likely know if Stewart was currently stateside. Ronald was the head chef at a hotel in Jacksonville. That left Pat. I made a call to the former home of Rumors, which was now a swanky well-reviewed restaurant, ironically named The Grapevine. The woman I spoke with on the phone told me that Pat's son had in-herited the building and was the current owner. It was a start.

I printed out a list of everyone's current or most recent address and employer. Waiting for Lance was agony. I paced between floors, probably annoying my staff by hovering. When he finally arrived a little after noon, I was bursting with anticipatory anxiety.

"Darling, take a breath." Lance pressed his index fingers and thumbs together to model a meditative pose for me.

"I know. I feel like a kid the night before my birthday or something. What if we crack the case, Lance? This might really work." I waited while he held the door open for me. A bank of gray clouds to the east threatened rain, but above us the sun was as bright as Rosa's pot of gold in the front windows.

He waved to a patron, then pulled me outside onto the sidewalk. "You are an eager beaver, aren't you? I feel like we've swapped roles."

"Sorry." I breathed in the early spring air. "Did you make the survey?"

Lance opened a leather attaché case and handed me a file folder. "Have a look."

I was impressed that the design team had been able to put together something so official in such a short amount of time. There were ten plays listed on the survey with images of each playbill and a short synopsis. Underneath the choices there was blank space with a number of leading questions about feedback, personal preferences, and if they had any objections to the proposed productions.

"I requested plenty of open space so that our unsuspecting suspects will have no choice but to fill in the blanks. A survey with simple YES or NO boxes wouldn't fulfill our purposes, now would it?"

"Good thinking."

Lance reached into his leather bag and took out a Sherlock cap. "Just in case the spirit moves you, darling." He placed the houndstooth deerstalker tweed hat on his head. It looked ridiculous with his modern, tailored sleek gray suit.

"No way." I laughed and yanked the cap off his head. "You ready?"

"Ready and willing." He tucked the file folder back into the bag. "Lead the way."

I wanted to start at The Grapevine because I'd been told that Pat's son was usually available in the early afternoon before the happy-hour crowd descended. A mix of nerves and excitement swirled in my stomach as Lance and I walked up Main Street. Were we about to close a cold case?

Chapter Nineteen

The Grapevine had gone through a major renovation since its heyday as Rumors in my dad's time. Gone was the wood paneling and red leather booths the Professor had described. Now the basement restaurant was sleek and modern with slate-tile floors, bamboo tables, and Edison-style light bulbs and succulent plants hanging from the ceiling.

"We should come here for cocktails more often," Lance said, admiring the gold-leaf wall behind the bar.

"Good luck getting a table. This place is booked months in advance during the season."

"Darling, please." Lance glared at me. "You're talking to me."

"Okay, fine, but let's stay on point." I walked up to the bar where a young guy about Andy's age wearing a white shirt with black suspenders was polishing copper Moscow mule mugs. "Hi, we're looking for the owner."

"Pat?" He asked.

"I thought Pat's son owned the restaurant now."

The bartender looked confused. "Hang on a minute." He left and returned shortly with a guy in his early forties who wore an expensive black suit jacket and slacks. He walked with the help of a matching black cane.

"I'm Pat, how can I help you?"

Lance stepped forward and introduced himself.

Pat immediately recognized Lance and invited us to sit down. The bartender brought over glasses of water. Lance launched into his fable about wanting input on next season's shows.

"I'm flattered," Pat said when Lance finished. "But I have to admit, I'm confused. You mentioned wanting feedback from members of the greater theater community, but I'm not connected to the theater."

I jumped in. "We were under the impression that The Grapevine used to be a nightclub called Rumors, is that right?"

Pat nodded.

"In doing research into the Cabaret, we learned that Rumors used to be connected to the theater and we wondered if that was still true now."

Pat looked skeptical. "Why were you researching the Cabaret? I'm not sure I'm following."

I felt splotches forming on my neck. Lance and I should have talked this through better.

Fortunately, Lance was quick-witted. "One of our artistic goals for next season, as you'll see when you look through some of the proposed shows, is to give our patrons a full-circle tour of Ashland's thriving theater scene both on and off-*Bardway*. We want to pay homage to the Cabaret's inaugural season. You'll find three selections of shows from their first year. The same is true for the surrounding area theaters—Camelot, Randal, and all the others."

Lance was so convincing that I almost believed him.

Pat relaxed. "I see. Well, I'm happy to offer suggestions as a food guy. It's too bad my dad isn't here."

"Is your dad Pat, too?"

"He was. I'm Pat Junior." He looked to his feet.

"Was?" Lance asked, his voice thick with concern.

Pat nodded. "Yeah, Dad died a long time ago."

"I'm sorry to hear that," I offered.

"It's a stressful life, the restaurant business. Especially back in the eighties. I think Dad had a steak for dinner every night at the bar. Plenty of whiskey, lots of late nights, and trying to pay the lease, mortgage on the house, salaries, and college for the three of us kids. The stress finally got to him. He had a massive heart attack three years ago. Mom has always said at least he went quick. It's pretty amazing he lived into his early eighties, actually. You can't eat like that these days." He pressed his hand on his thin stomach. Pat Jr. wasn't a large man. I would guess that Mom was taller than him. "I run up in the hills—do the Lithia Loop and Alice in Wonderland trails at least three or four days a week to stay fit. Not my dad. His idea of exercise was lifting a knife to slice into his steak."

Heart attack, I made a mental note. That likely meant that Pat Sr. hadn't been our killer's second victim, but it also meant that we had hit our first dead end. If Pat had killed Chuck, there would be no way to prove it now that he's dead.

Lance offered his condolences and went through the theater survey with Pat Jr. We were about to leave when an idea came to me.

"You wouldn't happen to have any old memorabilia

from Rumors would you? Maybe notes from your dad, photos?"

"Probably, why?"

"Since my parents started the bakeshop at about the same time, I thought it might be fun to put together a scrapbook of Ashland's renaissance."

"Let me look and see what I have in the office." Pat left us.

"Well played, darling. Ashland's renaissance."

Actually, the idea was starting to take shape in my mind. The *Daily Tidings* might be interested in doing a historical piece about Ashland in the 1980s if I could provide them with enough material. "You too," I said to Lance. "I couldn't think of anything when Pat asked why we were reaching out to him."

"You have to stay nimble on the stage."

Pat returned with an old cardboard box. "Here you go. It's everything from Rumors. Just bring it back when you're done."

We thanked him and left with the box. If nothing else, we might be able to find an old handwriting sample amongst Pat's things. It wasn't much, but it was a start.

"Now what?" Lance asked when we were outside. "Our first suspect is dead. That can't be a good omen."

"No." I shifted the box of memorabilia. "When Pat Jr. said his dad was dead, my first thought was that Chuck's killer had struck again. But when he said Pat Sr. lived into his eighties, natural causes seem more likely."

"Don't sound so glum. Chin up. There are four more suspects on our list and the day is young and so are we." Lance motioned to the Cabaret. "Next up, Shelly?"

"Sure." I followed him into the converted church

building. It was hard to imagine that the gleaming building had been run-down and abandoned. Ever since I could remember, the historic theater had been a crown jewel with its carved dark wood railings, opulent baroque chandelier, and deep red velvet curtains. Stepping inside the Cabaret always felt like stepping into a different world.

Today was no different.

The company was rehearsing onstage when Lance and I came in. A woman in her mid-thirties sat in the front row, offering input and suggestions. I assumed this must be the new owner Lance had told me about.

She turned in our direction and spotted us. "Take five," she told the actors and hurried over to greet us. "Lance, to what do we owe the pleasure?"

Lance kissed her on both cheeks. "I thought I would pop by and introduce you to Ashland's pastry muse. Amanda, meet my dear friend Juliet Capshaw."

My mouth hung open as I stared at the woman standing next to Lance. I recognized her immediately. "Amanda? Amanda Howard?"

"Yes, I mean, it's Amanda Brooks now." Her deep brown eyes lit up with delight. "Juliet Capshaw! No way! How long has it been?" Amanda leaned in and embraced me in a huge hug.

"I can't believe it's you," I said staring at my childhood friend. Amanda was the daughter of my parents' friend, Wendy. She and I had attended preschool together, but had lost touch when they moved to California when I was in third grade. "I see your mom at the bakeshop all the time, but I hadn't heard you were back in town, too."

Amanda beamed a smile. "It's been a whirlwind! The opportunity to purchase the Cabaret came kind of out of the blue and my husband, Jed, and I jumped at the chance. Of course there was no pressure from my mom." She winked. "Literally a week ago I was in L.A. packing up our condo and this week I'm getting ready to launch a show."

Lance cleared his throat. "Um, ladies, anyone care to fill yours truly in on what's happening here?"

I squeezed Amanda's hand. She hadn't aged at all. I would have recognized her doe-like brown eyes and silky straight chestnut hair anywhere. We had been like sisters when we were young. Since Wendy often lent a hand at Torte, Amanda and I had spent countless hours "helping" our moms frost cupcakes and sample tastes of buttery shortbread and banana nut muffins. We had attended dance class together and even done a handful of productions at OSF in our early years.

"Amanda and I go way back," I said to Lance. "We grew up together."

"How charming. A reunion." He placed his hand over his heart. "For the record, I approve. You two seem like you should be friends."

"Well as long as we have Lance's approval, we'll have to plan a night out and catch up."

"I would love that! Plus I'm dying to come see what you've done to the bakeshop and try your pastries. My mom has been raving about Torte."

"Yes, come by soon. We have so much to get caught up on and I'll make sure you get the star treatment." I moved the box from Pat into my other arm.

"It's uncanny that you're here," Amanda said and then looked thoughtful for a moment. "You won't believe what I found this morning."

"What's that?" I asked.

She tucked her long brown hair behind her ears. "I've been reviewing all kinds of old materials—donor receipts, actor contracts, playbills, brochures, and menus in the process of taking over and I just saw your dad's name on the original menu. I think I have some old photos from opening night, if you want to see them."

Words stuck in the back of my throat for a second.

Amanda must have picked up on my emotion. "Your dad was one of a kind. He always felt like a father to me. He was so funny and kind. Do you remember how he used to pretend to be the Swedish chef from *The Muppet Show* when he would make us pancakes for breakfast? That terrible Swedish accent. I can still hear it in my head." She was quiet for a moment. "I'll make copies of everything I can find for you."

"That would be lovely." My voice sounded shaky. I didn't want to cry.

Lance cleared his throat. "I was hoping for a minute with Shelly. Is she still hanging around?"

Amanda's face changed. She grimaced and pointed above us. "She's up in the booth." Again, she gave Lance a knowing look.

"Do you mind if we go have a word? I want to get her input on some future shows."

"No problem." Amanda forced a smile. "She's all yours. Good luck."

I didn't think she was going to say more, but as Lance and I started to move away she reached for his arm to stop him.

"Can I ask for some professional advice?" Her voice was barely audible.

"Of course." Lance leaned in.

"When we purchased the theater, part of the deal was for Shelly to stay on for six months and help get us up to speed. It sounded great at the time, but she's making me crazy. She watches over everything I do like a hawk." Amanda looked to me. "Even those old papers and photos I was telling you about. She literally stood behind my desk asking why I was bothering. She wants to shred the entire pile. I told her I wanted them for posterity. Having spent the early part of my childhood here in Ashland, I have so many memories I want to revisit. You never know when historical gems like that might be useful."

"Absolutely," Lance concurred. "Don't throw away any of it. We have extensive archives at OSF that I've tapped into on numerous occasions for donor campaigns, events, you name it."

"Right?" Amanda's face relaxed. "It's not just that. It's everything. She's micromanaging every detail from directing the cast to what we're serving for dinner. Jed and I have a different vision. We're doing away with volunteers for dinner service and hiring professional waitstaff. It's a bit of an investment, but we feel like it's going to help streamline the flow and, quite frankly, it's been a pain to get volunteers to show up. Inevitably, we're calling around like crazy for people an hour before the show to get extra help when someone bails on a volunteer shift."

The cast had begun to gather on the stage again. Amanda looked to Lance. "Jed and I were talking last night. Do we ask her to leave? I mean, be honest. You've been here. You've been helping, and you have to have seen how overbearing she is. She technically is supposed to be offering her 'input' for another six months, but I'm not sure I can handle another quarter with her on my shoulder. Right now she's up in the booth giving my lighting director her 'notes.' I don't have any notes for him. He's a pro."

Lance patted her shoulder. "Cut the cord. You don't need her. Too many directors on the stage is the same as too many cooks in the kitchen, am I right, Juliet?"

"Yeah. That sounds rough." I balanced the box in one arm. It had been a while since I'd been to the dinner theater. My eyes swept over the theater. It was much the same as the Professor's description with shiny dark wood tables in ascending rows from the stage. Small lamps with red velvet shades adorned each table, casting a romantic glow. The massive crystal chandelier that the Professor had told me about was even more impressive in person. It looked as if it belonged in Kensington Palace, not here in Ashland.

Amanda forced a smile. "I'm not excited about the thought of having that conversation with Shelly, but I appreciate your input. Thanks for letting me vent."

"Anytime." Lance kissed her on the cheek in parting. "Let's do lunch soon. Ta-ta."

I hugged Amanda tight. "I'm so excited that you're home. Seriously, please stop by Torte soon so we can catch up."

"It's a date." Amanda flashed one more smile before leaving.

We headed upstairs to the lighting booth. As Amanda had said, Shelly was reviewing pages of notes with the lighting director, who appeared to be half listening. When we interrupted, he seized the opportunity and fled. The lighting booth was a maze of buttons, wires, computer monitors, and dozens of directional lights with colored screens.

"Ah, Lance, how unusual to see you slumming here in the land of dinner theater when you're not even needed." She might have been trying to be funny, but there was a definite edge to her tone.

"Kiss, kiss." Lance blew her air kisses.

Shelly waved to the office door behind us. "Would you like to go somewhere a bit brighter?" She pushed past Lance and opened the door to the office. I was surprised by how spacious the upstairs area was with its curved windows and high ceilings.

"Do you know Juliet Capshaw?" Lance asked.

"Grab chairs from any of the desks." Shelly sat down at a desk covered with scripts, receipts, and headshots. "I don't know that we've formally been introduced, but I knew your father well and your mother and I go way back."

"I'm sure I've seen you at the bakeshop." I set the box from Pat on the floor.

"Yes, I'm sure you have." She gave me a dismissive nod. "Did you need something?" she asked Lance.

I got the impression that she and Lance weren't exactly friends.

"Indeed." Lance reached into his attaché case and launched into an over-the-top ego boost, explaining his plight to draw in younger audiences and asking for Shelly's input on potential shows.

She studied the survey as he spoke. "I see you have three of our inaugural shows."

"Exactly. We want to pay homage to the entire Rogue Valley next season."

"It's a little late for that, don't you think?" Shelly glared at him. "You've turned your nose up at the Cabaret and now that there are new young owners, you're ready to team up?"

Lance pretended to be hurt. "Turned up my nose? Dearest Shelly, how can you say such a thing when we've collaborated on so many projects?"

Was he actually upset?

Shelly pushed a stack of headshots aside. "I guess you're right. I'm frustrated. That's all. Amanda and Jed have no concept of what the Cabaret's long-standing reputation has meant to the community. Seeing them dig through photos from the early days has me feeling like I don't want to let this place go. They want to come in and modernize everything. If you could only imagine how much of myself I poured into this theater over the years."

But hadn't Amanda just said that Shelly was the one who suggested shredding the historical documents? I was confused.

"I was just reminiscing with a friend who helped get Torte off the ground about how different things were in the eighties," I said to Shelly, careful not to mention the Professor. "It sounds like every business in Ashland in those days had to scrape together loose change and put in a lot of sweat-equity hours."

"I guess. We were lucky. We had plenty of cash thanks to some high-end donors, so we were in much better shape than some of the other folks in town." She reached for a pen and began scribbling answers on Lance's fake form.

Lance stood and wandered around the office. "I understand how difficult it must be to see the theater shifting. It's the nature of the biz, things change. We can't stay stagnant. We have to evolve. We have to reflect the world around us. That's our mission as artists and global citizens."

Shelly finished the survey and handed it to me. "I'm done. I've been in this business too long. And I've definitely been in the Rogue Valley for way too long. I need a change of scenery. I'm going to follow in Stewart's footsteps and go find a sunny condo in Palm Springs."

Again, she wasn't making sense. Hadn't she just said she didn't want to let go?

Lance came back to the desk. "What is Stewart up to these days?"

She shrugged. "I can't keep track. He spends most of the year in Mexico, but last I heard he had bought a horse ranch outside of Jacksonville. I think he's renovating the property to have it ready by summer. He had some grand plan about turning it into an Airbnb for horse lovers. Don't ask me why he'd want to take on a project like that when he has a perfectly wonderful beachfront hacienda."

"I'll have to give him a call. It would be nice to get his insight too."

If Shelly was suspicious of our motives, she didn't give any indication.

"How's the transition going?" Lance asked.

I knew it was a loaded question. Shelly unleashed. It was clear that neither she nor Amanda were happy about the process. I didn't know if that had any connection with our case. The fact that Shelly wanted to destroy the old donor files, playbills, and menus raised a red flag for sure. I read her responses to Lance's survey while she lamented about Amanda and Jed's management style. I couldn't be sure until we could place the notes and the survey side by side to examine the handwriting, but at first glance Shelly's writing looked completely different from the old threatening letters. Drat.

Amanda came into the office a while later, which finally put an end to Shelly's rant. Lance and I stood to take our leave. I picked up the box from Pat.

"What's that?" Shelly asked.

"Memorabilia from Rumors. Pat Jr. shared it with me," I replied. "I'm going on an all-eighties flashback with some of this stuff."

"That's right," Amanda replied, picking up a stack of playbills on her desk. "Thanks for reminding me. I'm going to make copies of everything from the early days here the Cabaret. I'll drop it by the bakeshop later—that way I can see how Torte has changed and we can set a date for a wine night or something fun soon."

Shelly glared at us. Was she upset about Amanda sharing the Cabaret's history with me? Why? Or maybe I was reading more into it than I should. It could be that Shelly was simply upset about being pushed out of the theater she had worked so hard to build.

Lance and I left.

Two suspects in and two strikes against us. I had thought we might have been able to figure out who killed Chuck, but I was quickly realizing that there was a reason the Professor's case had gone cold.

Chapter Twenty

"Now what?" Lance sounded as disappointed as me once we were back outside.

"I don't know." I handed him the survey. "Look at the handwriting. We can compare it with the old notes later, but I don't think it's a match. Shelly's cursive scroll has all these little loops."

Lance agreed. "Yes, but don't be too discouraged. We still have three more suspects and this is only our first line of investigation. It's highly likely that the killer intentionally disguised their writing."

"Yeah but if that ends up being true for the next three people, where is that going to leave us?"

"We'll cross that bridge when we come to it. I vote that we take a side trip to Jacksonville. We can track down Chef Ronald and see about finding Stewart. I'll call my admin on the way and have him put in a call to Stewart to let him know we're coming."

"But we don't even know where his ranch is."

"I have people for that, darling." Lance rolled his eyes.

We were both pensive on the drive to Jacksonville. I watched as we passed acres and acres of organic pear orchards. Vineyards with symmetrical rows of grapes and Italian-inspired villas stretched on both sides of the horizon. The historic mining town was a short drive from Ashland. Downtown Jacksonville consisted of one main street that ran for six blocks with brick buildings on either side. It was very walkable with cute shops, restaurants, and the vintage inn in the center of town. The gold rush had created gold fever in the Rogue Valley, and Jacksonville was at the heart of it.

Lance parked on the street where the original hitching posts still lined the sidewalk. We headed for the inn, a two-story brick building with bright red awnings. The eight-room inn had graced numerous travel magazines and won awards for its amenities, including full-service breakfast, jetted tubs, and original touches like exposed brick walls.

"What's our story going to be with Ronald?" I asked, as Lance opened the door for me.

"Leave it to me."

Famous last words, I thought. We approached the reception desk. Lance played his OSF card. Instead of creating an elaborate lie, he stuck with the truth. Explaining that he was hoping to get some feedback from Ronald, due to his previous connection with the Cabaret. The receptionist would have granted us access anyway, but Lance buttered her up with free tickets.

Since the hotel restaurant was between lunch and dinner service, the receptionist showed us to a table in the dining room to wait for Ronald. The dining room was elegant, with touches of Jacksonville's history in the form of an exposed brick wall and black-and-white photos of mining and railroad crews at work in the early 1900s.

Ronald emerged from the kitchen wearing a black chef's coat and a surly scowl. I had imagined a young, edgy chef in my mind, but kept forgetting that decades had passed. Ronald looked to be in his early sixties with graying hair and fading tattoos.

"What can I do for ya?" He pulled out a chair and turned it backward.

Lance introduced himself, then me. "I believe you knew Juliet's father, back in the day. William Capshaw."

"Will, yeah, he was a good guy. I heard he had cancer. Bad luck."

I swallowed hard.

"You here about Will?" His voice was raspy with a thick rattily quality. I guessed it was from decades of smoking.

Lance took a slightly different approach with Ronald. "In a way, yes, but before we get into that, can we buy you a drink?"

"No. I've been clean for ten years. I don't touch anything other than water."

"Congratulations." Lance kicked me under the table. "We're in the process of putting together a tribute to the Cabaret. Did you hear that it's under new ownership?"

Ronald shook his head. "I haven't paid much attention since I left in the late nineties to come work here."

"Well, the new owners are a dynamic young duo and I've made it my mission to welcome them to Ashland and roll out the red carpet."

"Okay. What does this have to do with me?" He took a vape pen from his coat pocket and flipped it in his fingers.

Lance reached into his leather bag and removed a piece of paper that looked different than the survey. "We were hoping to pick your brain, as they say, and have you write down any memories of that inaugural season that come to mind. I'm having our art department create beautiful memory boards that we'll have on display at the re-opening of the Cabaret."

I had to give credit to Lance. He had obviously thought through his approach.

Ronald pushed back the sleeve of his chef's coat to reveal a watch and more tattoos. "How long is this gonna take? I've got to prep for dinner."

"No time at all. We'll walk you through our questions in a flash," Lance assured him, handing him a pen.

"I can give ya five minutes."

"That's all we need." Lance shot him a dazzling smile and proceeded to ask Ronald about his early days at the Cabaret.

"You want me to write this?" He sounded skeptical.

"Just the highlights. A sentence or two is fine."

Ronald shrugged and scribbled his first few answers on the OSF letterhead Lance had provided.

After three relatively tame questions about the menu and how service worked, Lance went in for the kill. "We've learned there was a murder opening night. Do you remember anything about that?"

"Hard to forget. Chuck Faraday. The guy was a major pain in my ass. Can't say I was upset about it. Don't think they ever said it was a murder. Where'd you hear that?" His demeanor changed. He clutched has vape pen and repeatedly tapped it on the tabletop.

Lance waved a hand in the air as if to prove that the topic was light and airy. "Oh, I don't remember, do you Juliet? It must have come up in our other interviews."

Ronald scooted his chair away from the table. "Who else have you been talking to?"

Was it my imagination or did he seem agitated? Not to mention wrong. Between what I had learned from the Professor and reading my dad's journals, it was clear that the public knew that Chuck had been intentionally killed.

"Everyone and anyone we can track down who was involved with that first season. Our goal is to flesh out the story behind the stage, if you know what I mean."

Ronald glared at him. "What does Chuck have to do with it?"

"Nothing. Or, perhaps everything. His tragic death could become paramount to how we tell the story. It's too soon to know. At this point we're gathering as much information as we can and then we'll begin to see how the narrative unfolds."

"You've got the wrong guy. Chuck and I weren't friends." The way he rhythmically tapped the vape pen against the table remained me of a drummer trying to hold the beat.

I tried a different approach. "From articles I've found about the accident it sounded like Chuck was under the influence that night. Do you know if he had a drug problem?"

Ronald stared at the vape pen. "We all did. It was the eighties. The decade of excess. Pot and coke were popular around here. Chuck was part of that scene."

"Do you think he could have been dealing? Maybe *that* got him killed."

"Chuck?" Ronald dropped the vape pen. "No. A dealer? No. That would have been way beneath him. Chuck's ego was huge. I doubt he ever paid for his drugs. He expected everyone to give him things and worship the ground he walked on because he starred in shows at the Festival and a few low-budget commercials. The guy didn't have enough work ethic to deal."

"You mentioned that you don't use anymore?"

"Nope. I gave up those days cold turkey when I got the job here. I had to turn my life around. It was a crazy scene in Ashland back then. There was a lot of drug use for sure. It was the scene. College kids, a young town, easy access, you know how it goes. Half the staff wouldn't show up for work, so I would go out onto the plaza and yell, 'Hey, who wants to work tonight?' And, then I'd hire help on the spot."

"And your relationship with Chuck was?" Lance interjected.

"Nothing. We weren't friends. I already told you that." He picked up his vape pen. "I gotta get back to the kitchen." Ronald stood and flipped the chair back to its original spot. "I wouldn't spend a lot of time on Chuck. No one liked the guy. I doubt that's the story you want to tell."

He returned to the kitchen. I reached for the paper with his notes. "Lance, look at this. Look at the handwriting."

I thrust the letterhead at Lance.

"Hmm. It's a potential match, isn't it?"

We both stared at the page. The writing was similar to what I remembered from the notes in my dad's files. I wasn't sure if it was an exact match, but it was the closest we'd come yet.

Chapter Twenty-One

Lance carefully tucked the letterhead in his bag. I glanced at the door to the kitchen. A small round window was cut out of the top of the door. Chef Ronald stood on the other side staring us down as if we were criminals about to take off with the dining room flatware. A wave of fear washed over me.

"Come on, Lance, let's go." I felt the chef's watchful eyes burning behind me as we made our exit. "He's kind of creepy," I said once we were safely outside and away from Ronald's intense stare.

"You of all people should expect no different. Aren't chefs supposed to eccentric?"

"Maybe. But did you see him staring at us from the window? I felt like he was sending us a warning—like get out of my restaurant."

Lance clapped. "Let's hope so. That could mean we freaked him out." He took his cell phone from his leather satchel, placed a call, and rattled off rapid-fire questions. "Success," he said, hanging up the phone. "My admin has tracked down Stewart's farm and arranged a meeting in an hour. Fancy a drink while we wait?"

Downtown Jacksonville truly was like stepping back in time with its weathered wood and redbrick buildings, original horse hitching posts, and keg barrel garbage cans. A green trolley rumbled down the middle of the street, taking tourists on a historic tour of the old mining town.

We crossed the street to the J-Ville Saloon and found seats at the bar. I ordered an iced tea. Lance, not surprisingly, ordered a martini. "What? Don't judge. It's nearly happy hour and my deduction powers work best with a little lubrication. Care to share a basket of tots?" Lance didn't wait for my response before ordering Cajun-style tots with spicy ranch dipping sauce.

He spread out the papers we had collected so far, comparing Chef Ronald and Shelly's handwriting. "Take a closer look, darling. How do you think this lines up with the notes you have at home?"

I examined Ronald's rough notes. The writing was angular with piercing lines that seemed to suggest a need to write fast and be done. That matched Ronald's personality. "It looks . . . exacting, don't you think?"

Lance took the paper from my hand. "Yes, as if he was slicing through the page."

"Not that we're experts or anything, but it does line up with his personality." The truth was that we had no idea how to analyze handwriting. Nor did I know where to go to ask for help with examining the writing samples.

"Speak for yourself." Lance tipped his martini ever so slightly. "I'd say we've discovered a solid lead."

Our tots arrived. I didn't think I was that hungry, but the salty potatoes with the spicy ranch hit the spot. "There was something about our conversation with Shelly that left me unsettled though. She doesn't want to relinquish control of the Cabaret."

"True, but I can't blame her. As artistic directors we set a vision and tone for the entire company. To watch someone new come in and recast that vision must sting."

"Fair enough, but there's still something about her that feels"—I searched for the right word—"I don't know. Off."

Lance made a note on the bottom of Shelly's survey. "Off."

We devoured the Cajun tots and talked through the list of suspects. Ronald fit the profile in terms of having a commanding and intimidating personality. Shelly had sounded like she still held a grudge. Pat was dead. That left Stewart and Jeri. I felt lost as we reviewed everything we knew. The Professor had been right—everyone involved in the Pastry Case had had a motive to kill Chuck.

Lance tapped his wrist as he popped the last tot into his mouth. "Our next appointment awaits."

"Are you sure you have time for this?"

"For murder, I make time." With that he tossed his jacket over his shoulder and walked out of the bar.

I had no choice but to follow after him. The drive to Stewart's horse ranch took us on winding, narrow roads outside of Jacksonville. Within minutes the historic brick buildings and wooden plank sidewalks gave way to densely treed hillsides interspersed with lush organic lavender farms. In the far distance the snowy white peak of Mount McLoughlin stood like a sturdy fortress amongst the rolling east hills. Stewart's property was only about ten minutes from town, but it felt like a world away. Llama and sheep grazed in the pasture to our left as we turned down a long dirt road leading to the house. To the right, three horses and a pony stood in a perfect line against the fence posts as if they had been sent to greet us.

"How rustic," Lance commented, steering the car into the circular paved driveway in front of the house.

The acreage surrounding Stewart's house might have been rustic, but the house was nothing of the sort. It was modern in design, with an entire wall of triangular windows and a three-tiered flat roof with outdoor decks. Potted Japanese maples and bonsai trees gave the out-of-place architecture an even more modern vibe.

"This is unexpected." Lance parked. "How would you describe this? Farm meets Frank Lloyd Wright?"

"Something like that, I guess."

Stewart appeared at the doorway. He looked younger than I expected. Not that he was young. He was in his mid-seventies, but farm life or perhaps the sunny beaches of Mexico had given him a youthful tan and trim physique. His silver hair caught the light, giving him an ethereal glow as he stepped closer to greet us.

"Lance Rousseau, to what do I owe the pleasure?" He bowed.

"Stewart. The years have been kind to you. You look fabulous." Lance's signature singsong tone came out as he clasped Stewart and kissed both his cheeks.

After their mini reunion, Lance cleared his throat. "I don't believe you know Helen Capshaw's daughter, Juliet?"

"Wonderful to make your acquaintance." Stewart gave me a kind smile. "I knew your parents well. Wonderful, wonderful people Helen and Will. We were heartbroken, absolutely devastated, when Will died."

Pursuing this case had given me new insight into how

many people had known and cared for my dad. "Thank you." I swallowed hard, trying to fight off the lump forming in my throat.

"Come in. Let's catch up." Stewart invited us inside, where the clean, futurist design continued. A twin wall of windows offered a museum-like view of the back pastures. Terrariums bursting with life soaked in the afternoon sun. Sleek furniture with pops of canary yellow, teal blue, and burnt orange had been strategically arranged to showcase the view. "Please sit." Stewart pointed to the living room.

"You have a gorgeous house," I said, taking a seat in the yellow chair with matching ottoman.

"How much land do you have?" Lance asked.

"A few acres," Stewart tried to be modest. The land surrounding the house was a few acres and the view of the back pasture stretched as far as my eye could see. He probably had hundreds of acres.

"Enough to pull you away from the tropical southern beaches?" Lance noted.

Stewart swept his hand toward the windows. He still moved like a dancer. "This is a labor of love. I've ridden my entire life, and now that I'm retired, I'm glad to be able to provide a sanctuary for horses. Not a day goes by that I don't get a call about another animal in need of rescue. I try to accommodate as many as I can."

That didn't sound like the attitude of a killer.

"The challenge is making sure I have the right team in place to care for the animals while I'm away. The bigger the project grows, though, the less I find myself wanting to fly south for the winter. Who knows, maybe I'll end up staying here full time?" He was dressed like he was ready for a yoga class in thin gray drawstring flowing silk pants and a tank top that showed off his defined muscles.

Stewart proceeded to explain the process of identifying horses in need of rescue, how he had partnered with a team of vets who rehabbed the animals, and then once they were on the mend how they could roam free on his land.

"Impressive," Lance commended Stewart for his efforts. "You are leaving quite the legacy, but it's a far cry from your theater days, isn't it?"

"In some ways, yes. I feel grateful to be in a position to do this. And, I have to say the horses kick up much less drama than the acting company."

We both laughed.

"What brings you this way?" Stewart asked, changing the subject. "Your assistant mentioned something about needing input for next year's season. I'm not sure how much help I can offer in that arena. I've been out of the game too long."

Lance proceeded to tell Stewart the same story we'd told Pat Jr. and Shelly. He listened with interest. When Lance finished, he stared at his feet. "That was a rough time. Those early days I didn't think we would make it. I didn't know how I was going to eat, let alone pay a staff of actors, crew, and kitchen staff." He looked to me. "Your parents were godsends. If it wasn't for your dad, I don't think we would have been able to open. We certainly wouldn't have been able to offer dinner service for the first few weeks. Will saved me." He caught my eye. I could see him trying to contain his emotion. "Such a shame. He was so young when he died."

I appreciated hearing his kind words about my dad, but

I didn't want to break down in front of Stewart. He was seeming less and less likely to be our suspect the longer we spoke, but nonetheless I couldn't rule out the possibility that he could have been involved.

Without prompting he brought up Chuck. "I thought the Cabaret was plagued from the start. Shelly and I wondered if the old church was cursed. We had such a struggle just to open and then Chuck Faraday was killed on opening night. It was like something out of a Greek tragedy."

"We heard something about Chuck's death," Lance said, playing dumb. "It sounded like it went unsolved and the police suspected foul play."

Stewart shook his head. "That's true. At least about it being unsolved. They never found the driver. He was killed in a hit-and-run on his way home from the theater on opening night. There were rumors that it was intentional, but I never was sure about that. Chuck was a popular actor at the time with a huge fan base. What motive would anyone have had to kill him?"

The hairs on my arms stood at attention. Now we were onto something. I knew for a fact that Stewart had a big motive for murder—money.

"He was a beloved member of the community. A rising star. Had he lived I'm sure he'd still be acting on your stages now," Stewart said to Lance.

My senses were at full attention. Stewart was making Chuck out to sound like a saint. Why? No one else we'd spoken with had anything nice to say about Chuck. Was it simply a case of glossing over the past, or was Stewart trying too hard?

Lance caught my eye. I could tell he was thinking the same thing.

"Were you and Chuck close?" he asked.

Stewart shifted in his chair and crossed his legs. "Chuck was my leading man. It was a coup to get him from the Festival. We took him on loan, so to speak. We staged the first run so that it wouldn't interfere with the opening of Shakespeare. I was distraught after his death. Replacing him wasn't easy."

I noticed that Stewart didn't actually answer Lance's question.

"Things were different in those days." He stood and picked up a water bottle to spritz his plants as he spoke. "You didn't have the level of interest from actors on a national level. We pulled a lot of our talent from the region—maybe stretching north into Portland/Seattle and south to the Bay area. Losing Chuck was a huge blow. We had given him top billing and sent out press touting his as our lead in *Dames at Sea*. We had to scramble to find a replacement. His understudy wasn't ready."

Stewart's perspective brought up an angle I hadn't yet considered—that the Cabaret didn't want to lose their star. Did that negate any potential financial motive for wanting Chuck dead? I felt more confused.

"Those were the days, weren't they?" He broke a piece off of a succulent plant. "We were in it for the show. For the production. It wasn't about making a ton of money, although that was a nice bonus. It was about the acting. The dancing. The choreography. The music." He sighed. "I used to keep a list of folks in town who I knew couldn't afford a ticket to the show and I would call them and invite them to dress rehearsals. It was my way of sharing the theater life. It was such a gift to be involved with the talent we brought in and to be able to produce new and fresh, fun family shows. Every year at Christmas I would write a traditional British Pantomime. Families came back year after year for those shows. It touched my heart."

Stewart placed his hand over his heart. "There really isn't anything like live theater. Nothing else I've done in my life compares. Nothing."

He and Lance shared a moment before Lance handed him our fake survey and got him talking more about the inaugural season. I watched his body language as Stewart reminisced and filled out the form. His hand quivered, but that could have been due to age. "I haven't thought about those days for a long time. It was a different life. A different Ashland, for sure."

He spoke as if in a trance. I could tell that he was lost in memories of the past as his eyes glossed over and his voice developed a starry quality. Stewart repeated many of the same stories I had heard from the Professor about the emerging entrepreneurial spirit of Ashland and how everyone banded together to help one another out. "Why Shelly and I thought we could buy the old pink church and turn it into a functioning theater is beyond me. I guess you can chalk it up to the naivety of youth. It was in wretched shape. Gross, dirty mattresses lined the floor. There was graffiti inside and out, water damage. Everything was pink. We had to tear out an old pink organ and completely re-work the choir loft. We thought renovations would take a year at most. They ended up taking four years and we were literally gluing tables to their bases on opening night. Can you imagine?"

Lance nodded in solidarity. "Ah, the joys of small theater. Remind me to tell you about my early stint in Wisconsin. Let's just say that it wasn't pretty."

Stewart went on to talk at length about his friendship with my dad. "Will was one of a kind." He gently massaged an aloe plant. "I had to beg and plead with him to bake for us. I would do it all over again. I still dream about his banana Bundt cakes smothered with silky caramel sauce. To this day, no dessert I've ever had compares with what Will Capshaw could bake." My mouth watered as he described the dessert my parents had created for opening night. The longer we stayed, the more I hoped that Stewart was not our killer. I couldn't let myself get swept into the past. I had to stay clearheaded if we were going to solve this case.

Chapter Twenty-Two

We left Stewart's with long hugs and a promise of cock-tails in Ashland soon. I didn't want him to be the killer, but I couldn't rule him out either.

"So about those cocktails, shall we pop into Alchemy or Pucks on the way home?" Lance asked as he started the car.

"I don't think I'm in the mood." I looked to the back seat where the box from Pat sat safely untouched. "I'm wiped out after this long day, and honestly my mind is spinning. I think I got my hopes up. I know it sounds silly, but I guess I thought maybe we might have stumbled upon a major clue today."

"There you go, sounding gloomy again. No bad atti-tudes allowed in my car, Juliet Capshaw."

"Sorry." I watched the farmland fade into forest. "It's just that I'm more confused than when we started today. I guess I had kind of hoped that this would be easy."

"If it was easy, the Professor would have closed the case years ago."

"I know. I'm not that naïve. I think it's because of my father. I feel personally responsible. Like I owe it to him to solve the mystery. The Professor too. You should have seen him, Lance. He was almost inconsolable."

"That's understandable. I'm sure that it must have been hard for him to relive the memories. But don't give up hope. We've only been at it for a day. Your dad and the Professor spent weeks—years—trying to figure out who killed Chuck. Cut yourself a little slack."

"I'll try."

We drove in silence. I appreciated Lance giving me some space to be quiet with my thoughts. He pulled in front of my house, put the car in park, and kissed my cheek. "Get your beauty sleep, Juliet. We'll tackle our last suspect tomorrow. Chin up."

I left him with a promise not to mope. Surprisingly, I didn't. After a quick bite of leftover soup and a cup of tea, I was asleep the minute my head hit the pillow. Chalk it up to emotional overload or stress, either way I slept through the night and woke the next morning feeling lighter and more determined than ever to help the Professor solve the case.

Alas, duty called. I spent the bulk of the day running up and down the stairwell between the kitchen and the dining room, restocking slices of pineapple upside-down cake, chocolate hazelnut brownies, and pistachio short-bread. Torte hummed with the sound of happy customers lingering over post-lunch lattes and blood-orange ricotta cookies.

Lance sauntered in a little after three. He wore a slate gray suit with a mint green polka-dot tie. "Are you ready for a break, darling?" He greeted me with an air kiss. "I thought about dropping by to see our"—he paused and whispered—"suspect."

The dining room was quiet. There was no need for him to whisper.

"So I took it upon myself to invite Jeri to stop by my office. Upon further consideration I decided it would be better to interrogate her on our home turf."

"Interrogate?" I chuckled.

"You know what I mean, darling." Lance tapped his watch. "She's meeting us in my office in ten minutes. No time to dally."

"Give me a second to let my staff know I'm taking off for a few." I hurried downstairs to check in with the team. Everything was running smoothly. I glanced at the box of memorabilia from Pat that I had brought with me earlier in the morning. Should I bring it? No, I could go through it later tonight when the bakeshop was empty.

I returned to find Lance pacing upstairs. "Shall we?" He offered me his arm. We walked across the street past the Merry Windsor, and up the Shakespeare stairs to the bricks on the OSF campus. "The bricks," as locals refer to the large brick courtyard border by tiered grass areas and cement retaining walls in front of the Elizabethan theater, were packed with school tour groups. It was always amusing to watch chaperones trying to herd energetic teenagers into orderly lines before the show. It seemed a lot like herding cats.

When we reached the Bowmer Theater, Lance greeted actors, company members, and patrons before continuing to his office.

Lance's office was bigger than many college students' apartments. Awards and playbills were displayed on the walls. There were stacks of manuscripts waiting on his desk. I imagined hopeful, aspiring playwrights keeping their phones glued to their bodies in hopes that Lance might call to give them the good news that their work had been selected for next year's season.

I took a seat on the plush leather couch, while he took off his jacket and loosened his tie. "Drink?" He ran his hand across the small bar next to his desk, which was stocked with expensive bottles of gin, vermouth, and whiskey along with an assortment of glasses.

"I'm fine."

Jeri arrived promptly. She beamed with delight as Lance gave the bogus story about being desperate for her insight and advice.

"I was thrilled when you called," Jeri gushed. She reminded me of an aging rocker with her go-go boots, tight black jeans, and frizzed bleached hair. "Too often it seems that the past gets overlooked. I had a storied history here in these hallowed walls and I'm happy to provide you with anything that might be helpful." She glanced around his office. "This has certainly changed since back in the day. I like what you've done. It's very homey."

Lance choked on the glass of water he had poured for himself. Jeri meant "homey" as a compliment, but the word made Lance visibly gag.

"You were involved in helping to launch the Cabaret?" I jumped in while he tried to recover.

Jeri frowned. "Not exactly. How strange to be asked about the Cabaret. I haven't thought about those days in many, many years and now within the span of a few days the topic has come up on more than one occasion. Isn't it strange how things come in cycles?"

"Was someone else asking about the Cabaret?" Lance held one pinky in the air as he sipped his water.

"Yes. I bumped into Doug yesterday and he told me that some new information regarding the death of Chuck Faraday had emerged. He asked me for a quick recap of what I remembered from that awful night."

An unsettled feeling swirled in my stomach. Was Jeri confirming my suspicions? Had new details emerged in the case, or had the Professor said that as a ploy to get her talking?

Another thought formed in my mind. What if the Professor had remembered something in retelling the story to me? I listened with interest as Jeri continued.

"Chuck was a great actor, but not a smart man. He got himself messed up in some stupid stuff. They never could prove it, but if you ask me, he got himself killed."

I couldn't believe that Jeri was being so forthcoming. Lance and I shared a look. "How so?" Lance asked, pouring a glass of water for Jeri.

"Are you two familiar with the case?"

"Not exactly," Lance lied. "We've heard a few snippets here and there, but Chuck's death was long before my time here. And Juliet was just a child then."

"Right. Of course." Jeri held the water glass that Lance had offered her. Then she set it on the coffee table. Before she continued with her story, she picked it up again, but didn't take a drink. "Chuck and I were great friends. He was a larger-than-life personality. Everyone in town had the biggest crush on him. We called him Ashland's Burt Reynolds. He could charm anyone."

The way she spoke about him with a dewy quality to her voice made me wonder if she was including herself.

"He could have made it in Hollywood. He was destined for stardom. Even though he was only with the company for a couple seasons before he died, he left his mark on the stage. After he died it was like a light had gone out in Ashland." She clutched the water glass tighter.

Jeri didn't sound like Chuck's killer, she sounded like she was speaking about a long-lost love.

"Things took a bad turn for Chuck when he got involved with the Cabaret. I warned him. I told him it was a bad idea. I thought he was going to be stretched too thin, working for both companies, but then it turned out that he was bleeding both companies dry." She went on to explain how Chuck had created a ticket scheme. Everything she told us lined up with what the Professor had shared.

"I was devastated when he was killed." She set the water glass down again. "Don't get me wrong I was upset with him for what he had done, but I didn't want him to die. He was so young. Such a waste. He was destined for more. Trust me he would have made it big in Hollywood with those eyes and that face. Such a terrible, terrible waste." She trailed off.

"You said you thought his death was intentional?" Lance asked, faking a surprised tone for her.

"Huh?" Jeri stared at the water glass. "Oh, yeah, I'm sure he was killed. It was definitely intentional. The police knew it too. They just couldn't prove it. Chuck had gotten in over his head. I believe that he regretted his decisions and was trying to make them right, but it was too little too late."

"Do you have an idea who did it?"

Jeri broke her gaze from the water and looked at me as if I had just walked into the room. "I have lots of ideas. The problem is that there were too many people who wanted him dead. Ronald, Pat, Shelly, Stewart. I could keep going. Like I said, he was in way over his head. You two might be too. You should be careful, you know. Whoever killed Chuck has gotten away with it for thirty years. If you start asking a bunch of questions, you might end up like him."

Was that a threat or was she genuinely warning us? I couldn't be sure.

We talked a little longer and then Lance went through the charade of having Jeri make notes about different potential OSF performances. He sent her on her way with complimentary tickets and a promise to meet for happy hour soon.

"Thoughts? Impressions?" Lance asked after she left.

"She doesn't sound like a killer. In fact, I got the impression she had feelings for him."

"Me too, but that warning at the end. Is she actually worried about us, or was that her subtle way of telling us to back off?" The phone on Lance's desk buzzed. He answered it. "Sadly, darling, I must cut our time together short. Duty calls. Drama on the stage. What else is new?" He pressed his hand to his forehead.

"That's okay. I need some time to process everything. And I want to go through the things Pat gave us and look over my dad's notes some more." I stood and stretched.

"Shall I come over later? I could bring a pizza?"

"No. You have previews to prepare for. I can't keep pulling you away from work."

Lance looked disappointed, but he didn't protest. "Work. It's nothing but work for me."

I knew that his work, like mine, was his life. In the best possible way.

"I should probably check in with the cast." He stood,

reaching for his jacket, and walked me to the door. "Coffee. First thing, tomorrow? You must promise to fill me in on any and every detail you might discover without me tonight."

"Promise." I blew him a kiss and returned to the bakeshop. A handful of late-afternoon coffee drinkers lingered in the dining room. Sequoia, Rosa, and Stephanie had already departed. Stephanie was taking classes at SOU and left before noon most days. Andy was cleaning up the coffee bar, and Bethany was boxing up the last few straggling pastries in the case.

"Did I miss anything?" I asked.

Bethany tucked an almond croissant into a white cardboard box and closed the lid. "Nope. Everything's been excellent. We sold like crazy. People loved the pineapple upside-down cake. I'm glad we made more today, and Steph and I think it should be on the specials board all week. You wouldn't believe how many customers said it was like biting into a slice of their childhood. This is it for the leftovers. I was planning to swing them by the shelter."

"That would be great, thanks."

"You're going to the shelter?" Andy asked. "I thought you said you might come up to the mountain and take some pics."

Bethany shrugged. "I don't know. I'm kind of tired."

I knew that Bethany had a crush on Andy, and lately she had changed tactics, appearing nonchalant and disinterested anytime she was around him. It appeared to be working.

"Come on, you have to come. It's going to be an epic night of skiing, and the lodge has a band and fun drinks.

You can take the shuttle up with me. I'll show you around."

Bethany looked at the box in her hands. "I don't know. I should drop this by the shelter."

"I can take it later," I offered. I didn't want to get in the way of Bethany's strategy with Andy, but I didn't want her to feel obligated either.

"Do you mind?"

"Not one bit. I was going to do some work downstairs and then I could use a short walk. I'll take it later."

"So you're coming, right?" Andy held up his hand for a high five.

"I guess." Bethany slapped her hand to his.

"It's going to be awesome, trust me." His brown eyes were locked on hers. I wondered if he was starting to reciprocate her feelings.

I left them to finish cleaning and went to check in on the kitchen staff. Marty and Sterling had wiped every countertop and had scrubbed each pot and pan. The space smelled like rosemary and lemon soap with a faint hint of applewood from the smoldering fire.

"Wow, this place is spotless."

Marty clapped Sterling on the back. "Thank this guy. He did most of it."

Sterling brushed off the compliment. "Nah, it was a team effort. I'm taking off, Jules. I have a class tonight."

"A class?" I was intrigued.

"Yeah, Steph signed me up for a poetry workshop at the college. We'll see how it goes. I told her I would give it a try."

"That's fantastic." I was thrilled that Sterling was pursuing writing. He had the heart of a poet. I constantly caught him sketching notes in a journal, but as of yet he hadn't been ready to share anything he had written. Good for Stephanie to encourage him to take a writing class.

Marty tossed a dish towel in the bin. "I'm taking off too. I have a hot date."

"You do?" This shocked me more than Sterling voluntarily taking a class. Marty's wife had died over a year ago and I hadn't heard him say anything about dating again.

He smirked. "Yep. With a pizza. I signed up for a pizza dinner at a new joint in Medford. Thought I would check out the competition."

They left together. I sighed with relief. Finally, I was alone and could go through the box that Pat had given me. If there was a clue about Chuck's death mixed in with the Rumors memorabilia, I intended to find it.

Chapter Twenty-Three

With everyone gone, I spread out the papers and photos from Pat Jr. and started trying to make sense of what he had given me. The ink on the carbon copies had faded with time. I had to squint to try to decipher Pat's writing. It was more masculine, like the warning note, but Pat's scroll was small with tight strokes, not large and demanding. I read through old profit-and-loss statements, early menus, the lineup of musicians (which was quite impressive), and marketing materials, like print ads that ran in the *Daily Tidings* touting well-drink specials for locals. Near the bottom of the stack I found a letter that Pat had drafted to an attorney asking for advice on how to potentially press charges against Chuck Faraday.

Interesting!

I read the correspondence between Pat and his lawyer. Pat had advocated strongly for legal action against Chuck. His lawyer had responded with empathy, understanding Pat's frustration, yet also made it clear that without a signed contract it would be nearly impossible to prove any wrongdoing.

Pat's last letter to his lawyer read: "You're telling me

I have no other recourse? I'm supposed to accept the fact that Faraday has used me and stolen thousands of dollars?"

Could Pat have become so furious about his inability to recoup lost finances from Chuck that he took matters into his own hands? But killing Chuck wouldn't have given him any money back. His only motive would have been revenge.

I made a note about Pat's attempt to sue Chuck and placed the letters to and from his attorney on the top of the pile to show Lance later. There wasn't anything else of interest. I was about to head to the shelter to drop off the box of pastries when a heavy knock sounded on the basement door.

"Jules, you still here? It's Thomas," a voice called from the other side of the door.

I was glad Thomas had identified himself. Looking into Chuck's death had me on edge. I unlocked the door to let him in. He wore his traditional blue police uniform, badge, and tennis shoes, and tonight he sported a navy blue baseball hat with ASHLAND POLICE embroidered in yellow thread.

"Hey, I spotted the basement lights on when I walked by and thought I might find you here." Thomas looked expectantly at the kitchen to see if I was baking. Disappointment flashed across his youthful face.

"Are you hungry?"

He grinned. "You know me, Jules. I can always eat. It doesn't look like you're baking though. What's with all the paperwork?"

"Come on in. I'll whip up something." I locked the door behind him.

Thomas made himself comfortable on a bar stool and

starting rifling through the papers I'd left out. "What is all this? It's ancient." He held up a flimsy sheet of yellow carbon paper.

"I got those from Pat Jr." I went to the walk-in to see what we had on hand. I decided on omelets. Simple and delicious. Omelets are such a versatile dish. They work at any meal: breakfast, lunch, or dinner. I grabbed a carton of eggs, heavy cream, fresh basil, tomatoes, a red onion, goat cheese, and salami.

"Jules, don't go to any trouble. I was stopping by to say hi." His sharp eyes immediately landed on the pile of newspaper clippings and Cabaret brochures.

"It's no trouble. Plus I could use the company right now. My head is spinning."

Thomas tapped on the stack of papers. "Let me guess. It has something to do with this."

I beat eggs and heavy cream together, adding a dash of salt and pepper. Then I poured a splash of olive oil in a cast-iron skillet and turned the gas burner to medium low. In culinary school the true test for any bourgeoning chef is their ability to make an omelet. As simple as the egg dish might sound, the omelet is viewed as the litmus test in the culinary world. Making a perfect omelet is extremely difficult and technical, requiring skill and knowledge about heat, texture, touch, time, and finish. Creating a glistening, luxurious omelet that wasn't overcooked or over-seasoned took patience and practice.

While I started our omelets, I told Thomas everything about the case. I couldn't believe how quickly details poured out of me. I barely noticed when he removed his iPad mini from his police jacket and started making notes.

"This explains why the Professor had Kerry and me pull old records."

"He did?" I diced the red onion and rolled the basil to chiffonade.

"Yeah, he had us get the records from an unsolved hit-and-run in the 1980s. I haven't had a chance to look at the file, but this can't be a coincidence."

I thought about what Jeri had said to me and Lance. Had the Professor realized something new about the case? "I feel terrible for him," I said to Thomas. "I've never seen the Professor like this, and it's my fault. I'm the one who showed him my dad's journal and brought this case back to the forefront. He said Chuck's murder will stick with him until the day he dies.

"Don't worry. I won't say anything to him, unless he brings me in on the case," Thomas reassured me. "But, Kerry and I will do our own digging." He leafed through the stack of papers from Pat. "Can I make copies of these?"

"Sure." I poured the frothy eggs into the hot pan and with a flick of my wrist coated the bottom with the mixture. "Just be sure not to bring it up around here. The Professor asked me not to say anything to Mom until he has a chance to figure out the best way to share the story with her."

"That makes sense." Thomas pointed to the salami and cheese. "Can I help with something? I feel bad, I didn't come here to mooch dinner off of you."

"I'm so glad you stopped by. I really needed to talk this through." Granted, I had already talked it through with Lance, but Thomas was a professional member of Ashland's law enforcement team. I welcomed his thoughts and perspective.

"And I'm always in need of kitchen help," I added, watching the omelet. "Go ahead and dice that salami."

He washed his hands and got to work.

"You won't believe who's back in town," I said, swirling the pan to keep the heat even. "Amanda Howard, from elementary school."

"That's a blast from the past." Thomas chopped the salami into tiny pieces. "I haven't seen her since we were in elementary school. Didn't she move away?"

"Yeah, to California." I filled him in on my conversation with her and the fact that she and her husband had bought the Cabaret.

"That's so cool. We'll have to have a mini reunion."

Another knock sounded on the basement door. No one ever used that door. It was located down around the corner from Torte's main entrance.

"That's probably Kerry," Thomas said.

"I thought you were passing by."

"I was." He scooped the chopped salami in a pile. "But she knows that I tend to follow my stomach." He went to open the door for his partner.

As expected, Detective Kerry stood at the door. "I knew it." She punched him in the arm. Her long red hair fell loose on her shoulders. She wore a pair of skinny jeans, ankle boots, and a puffy navy jacket. Kerry's style looked like she belonged in L.A. or New York, not Ashland. "He can't stay out of the kitchen, can he?"

I laughed. "It's true."

Detective Kerry and I had been slowly but surely

building rapport. I appreciated her dry sense of humor and the fact that she was usually game to tease Thomas.

"Can I interest you in an Italian omelet?" I asked.

She breathed in the scent of the freshly chopped basil. "It smells divine in here. How can I resist?"

"Excellent. I have plenty and, honestly, I'd love your input on this case that Thomas and I have been talking about." I finished the three omelets, plated them, and poured us glasses of Sterling's blood-orange lemonade.

Thomas brought Detective Kerry up to speed. "That's why Doug asked us to get the old case file?" she asked, tucking into her omelet.

"That's my guess." Thomas devoured half of his omelet in two bites.

"What do you think? Ronald's handwriting is the closest match to the notes."

"Do you have them here?" Kerry asked, her green eyes widening with interest.

I shook my head. "No, they're at my place, along with my dad's journal."

"Can we take a look?" She looked to Thomas. "It would be great if we could come up with a solid lead for Doug. No wonder he seemed so distracted. He left in a rush a while ago. He said he had to get up to the Cabaret, but didn't elaborate."

My mind went to Shelly. Could the Professor have learned something new when he pulled the old case files?

Thomas finished his omelet. "That was delish, Jules. Thank you."

"Do you want a second?" I pointed to the stove where I had left the burner on low.

"No. I can't, but Kerry's right. Can we stop by your place later and take a look at the handwriting samples you and Lance gathered against the old notes?" Thomas sighed. "I hate to say this, but that was good thinking on Lance's part."

"I wouldn't tell him that. You'll never hear the end of it."

Thomas laughed. "I have no intention of sharing that. It stays in this room. As does this case for the moment. If we can work it for the Professor and come to him with something solid, I think we will both feel great, right Kerry?"

She nodded. Their walkie-talkies crackled in unison. Thomas responded to the dispatcher while Kerry finished her omelet. "Thanks for dinner. We'll come by later tonight. Will you be home?"

"I just have to clean up and swing by the shelter. Then I'll be home all night. I want to look through my dad's notes again."

"See you then." They left with a purpose.

I did a quick kitchen cleanup, gathered the notes and handwriting samples along with the box of pastries, and left. The plaza was humming with activity. Locals and the first round of early tourists filled restaurants and wandered between shops. Shakespearean banners flapped in the slight breeze and posters advertising Irish dance celebrations and St. Patrick's Day green beer lined the information kiosk in the center of the plaza. I walked toward Lithia Park as the sinking sun cast a shadow on the Elizabethan rooftops. The sun lingered longer now. I loved spring and summer, when I could close the bakeshop and still soak in some warm evening sun. However, living in the Siskiyou Mountains meant that once the sun began its decent, it would disappear quickly.

"Juliet!" I heard someone call my name and turned to see Amanda, my old childhood friend and new owner of the Cabaret, flagging me down from the Lithia Fountains.

I waited for her.

She was breathless when she reached me. "I'm so glad I caught you. I was on my way to the bakeshop to give you these." She thrust a manila envelope at me. "I made copies of everything I could find for you. I even found some old photos of your parents from opening night that I thought you might enjoy."

"Thank you. I wasn't expecting you to make copies this fast." I took the envelope from her.

"I know, but I already had boxes of our old stuff out and I know how much some of these photos of your dad will mean to you. I figured I would do it while it was fresh in my mind. And that way I didn't have to worry about Shelly breathing down my neck. I swear if I hadn't gathered all this stuff together tonight, she would have shredded it just to spite me. She was watching my every move while I made photocopies. I'm not sure how much more I can take."

A thought flashed in my mind—what if there was something in these old donor statements, playbills, and theater programs that Shelly didn't want anyone to see?

"This is great," I said to Amanda. "I still can't believe you bought the Cabaret."

She pointed to two young girls who were running through the lush green park grass, holding bubble wands the size of their heads. Iridescent bubbles trailed behind them, floating into the fading evening light. "I know. It's surreal. In some ways I feel that was just us. Do you remember how many hours we spent at the park, searching for hidden fairy gardens and splashing in the creek?"

"Those were good times. It's funny, after having been away from Ashland for over a decade, I see it differently now. I can appreciate how lucky we were to spend our childhoods here."

"I completely agree." Amanda nodded. "It was a magical place to grow up in. We rode our bikes everywhere, to the bowling alley, the pool, for ice cream. That never happened in L.A. No joke, my neighbor once called the police because a twelve-year-old boy was walking home from school by himself and she wanted to report the parents for child abandonment. Can you imagine? We used to take quarters to the mini mart and stuff our pockets with candy and then bike to the park. I don't remember our moms even telling us when we had to be home. We would just sort of find our way back around dinnertime. Jed is astounded by how that vibe still seems to be running strong in Ashland. We see kids biking everywhere and kindergartners walking to school on their own. He's also shocked at how welcoming everyone has been. We've met more people here in a week than we did in ten years in the same condo in L.A. Am I wrong, or is Ashland still the same as the Ashland of our youth?"

"Not at all. I think you're right. If anything, I feel like it's changed for the better in that there are even more shops and restaurants now. It's become such a foodie town, but at its core it's still a small town with a lot of heart."

The girls raced past us with their bubble wands. Their moms hurried to catch up with them, shouting out reminders to stop before they got to the street. Amanda and I reminisced about sleepovers, my dad's homemade Ding Dongs, and the time her mom had taken us to see *Pippi Longstocking* at the movie theater.

"How are we in our thirties?" Amanda asked. "Doesn't it feel like we were just begging our moms to drive us to the mall in Medford so we could pierce our ears and get perms?"

"Perms." I stuck out my tongue. "Who thought *those* were a good idea? But, you're right. I wonder that all the time when my staff looks to me for answers and I realize I'm the one in charge."

She laughed and glanced at her watch. "On that note, I should go. I have another dress rehearsal to get through tonight. I'm sure Shelly will be breathing down my neck. You should have seen her when I was making copies and getting the photos of your parents together. I thought she might pop a vein or something. The woman is an utter control freak." She blew me a kiss. "Lunch or wine soon. We've only scratched the surface."

I agreed, thanked her again for the folder, and continued on to Lithia Park. In the short time we had spent catching up, the sun had fallen behind the mountains, plunging the plaza into a hazy purple light.

A strange sensation came over me as I walked to the park. It was hard to explain, but it almost felt like someone was watching me.

You're being silly, Jules, I told myself, but I stopped in front of Elevation, the outdoor store, where I used to live in the upstairs apartment and looked around me. Across the street at the Merry Windsor, a bellboy in pantaloons and tights was helping an older woman with her bags, but fortunately there was no sign of Richard Lord. Behind me on the sidewalk, a group of tourists had stopped to read the menu posted at the sushi restaurant. No one appeared to be taking any notice of me.

Jules, you're freaking out. Maybe channeling my dad was finally getting to me.

I proceeded onward, through the park, passing the duck pond and following the path that led to the creek and the children's playground. Not long from now the grassy area would be full of families picnicking and kids splashing in Ashland Creek, but this evening it was deserted.

The feeling that someone was watching me persisted as I crossed the wooden bridge and headed for the shelter. It only took a minute to drop off the box of pastries. When I returned outside, I saw someone, dressed in black from head to toe, directly across the street.

My heart thudded in my chest.

Maybe I hadn't been imagining things.

The person's face was shielded with a balaclava, leaving only their eyes exposed.

I stepped backward.

The stranger in black moved toward me with such purpose and force that I froze.

What were my options? Should I scream for help? Return to the shelter.

Think, Jules.

It was as if fear had eroded my brain synapses. I couldn't formulate a plan, and the person in black was now at the footbridge.

The box in my arms felt like dead weight.

You have to get inside.

I commanded my muscles to move, but it was as if I

were observing the scene from outside of my body. Part of me wanted to know what this person in black wanted. The other part of me was yelling at the top of my lungs to get away.

The person in black had crossed the footbridge and was directly across the street from me. Since my leaden feet didn't want to move, I was about to let out a scream for help, but at that moment a pair of runners with headlamps and reflective shirts raced past.

They must have spooked whoever was stalking me because the stranger in black made a break for it, sprinting across the footbridge and out of sight.

I let out a long sigh of relief, but knew that it was only temporary. The late-evening purple light had shifted to blackness. Aside from a few glowing golden streetlamps, the park was plunged in darkness. I had to get out of here.

Unfortunately I was too encumbered with the box of paperwork from Pat, our fake OSF surveys, and the new folder from Amanda to run, so I hugged the edge of the sidewalk in order to stay as visible as possible under the streetlights. I kept glancing behind me as I power walked to the plaza. There was no sign of the person in black, but the fact that someone had been watching me could only mean one thing—I was close. Really close.

Chapter Twenty-Four

My nerves were scattered on the drive home. I made a quick call to Thomas to let him know that someone had been watching me at Lithia Park. He told me to hang tight, that he and Kerry would be by soon. Then, I commandeered the dining room table and spread out every piece of information I had connected to Chuck Faraday's death. The photocopies that Amanda had made included relics from the Cabaret's opening. A wave of tears flooded as I looked at photos of my parents and the Professor smiling on opening night. They had their arms wrapped around one another and reminded me of the three musketeers. If my dad hadn't died, what would things be like now? Would the Professor still be alone? Would he have ever found love?

I felt torn. As much as I longed for my dad, I was glad that Mom and the Professor had each other.

Focus, Jules. I forced myself back into the moment, combing through receipts and playbills from the Cabaret. What could be in there that Shelly didn't want me or Amanda to see?

Could Shelly have been the one following me? That

person was wearing a baseball hat, but the build was about right.

I found her handwriting sample. It looked nothing like the notes my dad had received. But did that mean she was a dead end? It was possible that she had disguised her writing or had someone else write the note.

Someone else.

Why hadn't I thought of that sooner? Could two of the suspects have been working together?

I reviewed my list. First there was Jeri. She had admitted that her job was in jeopardy due to Chuck's scheme. Yet, when Lance and I had talked to her, I had gotten the distinct impression that she had held a torch for Chuck. Unless they'd had some kind of lover's quarrel that she hadn't told us about, my instincts told me that she wasn't a killer.

Pat Sr. was a possibility. He had sought legal advice. If he had been unhappy that there was no course of action against Chuck, could he have exacted his own revenge? But, again, why? It wouldn't have served a purpose. He wouldn't have been financially compensated with Chuck dead. If he had hoped to get any of his money back, then having Chuck alive would have been paramount. Not to mention that Pat was dead. If he was the killer, then justice would never be served.

I moved on to Stewart. He too had financial motive. Why would a prominent theater owner kill his rising star? It didn't make sense. And my impression of Stewart had been grandfatherly. He had sounded sad about the circumstances surrounding Chuck's death, not like he was harboring an old grudge.

My two top suspects were Shelly and Chef Ronald. Could they have been working together?

Ronald's handwriting was the best match. As if to prove my thought process, I held it up next to the notes. It needed proper analyzing, but with my untrained eye I could see similarities in the style and force.

What I couldn't figure out was Ronald's motive. Why kill Chuck?

They had fought, but it seemed like a huge risk for Ronald to take the drastic step of murder. Unless he was lying. Maybe he and Chuck had been dealing at Rumors. He had admitted to having a drug problem and sobering up. Chuck had plenty of other schemes, what if dealing drugs was one of them? If he and Ronald had had a falling out over profits, that could be a motive for murder.

Last was Shelly. Something about her felt off to me. Why didn't she want Amanda to pass on the archive materials from the Cabaret? Plus her reaction to my comment about my parents having to scrape money together was odd. She had said the Cabaret had plenty of cash. How could that be? And was that why the Professor had raced over there?

I went through everything Amanda had copied again. This time, I studied every picture in detail. The very last photo made my skin tingle. It was a photo of the cast on opening night. Everyone was gathered onstage, hamming it up for the camera. Except for Chuck. He and Shelly stood off to the left of the stage.

I looked closer. Chuck was handing her something. A large envelope.

With what?

Money?

Were she and Chuck working together?

My mind worked overtime trying to connect the dots. Is that how Shelly had been able to buy the theater? Was she in on Chuck's schemes? Or could she have been behind it? I frantically flipped through the donor statements that Amanda had copied for me. What if Shelly had been running the scam? Maybe Chuck was her pawn.

Could I have had it wrong all along? We had assumed that Chuck was pulling the strings of his scamming operations, but what if he had been the puppet?

I scoured every donor receipt. Names and dollar amounts had been written out by hand in a spiral notebook. I ran to the kitchen to find a calculator and began to tally up the amounts. It didn't take a math whiz to quickly realize that something was very off. Large sums of money had come in for the Cabaret's opening under the initials C. F.

As in Chuck Faraday?

The doorbell rang, giving me a start.

That must be Thomas and Detective Kerry.

I went to answer it, and immediately regretted my decision.

Shelly stood on my front porch, dressed in black from head to toe, and holding a gun. "Hello, Juliet."

Stay calm, Jules. Stay calm.

I pressed my thumb and index fingers together as hard as I could, and willed myself to take a long, slow breath.

"Aren't you going to invite me in?" She lifted the gun, so it was level with my heart.

"Do I have another choice?" I moved to allow her entry.

"No. You had to snoop around. Like your father. Why couldn't you leave things alone?"

I was wondering the same thing.

She pushed me toward the kitchen. "Let's go. Get inside."

I tried to think of a way to signal Thomas, but nothing came to mind. Instead I left the front door unlocked and walked to the kitchen.

"I don't understand, Shelly."

"Right. I'm sure you don't. You were born into an easy life. You've never known hard work and having to fight for every dime."

What was she talking about? It was hardly as if my parents had been well-off. Far from it, but I let her talk.

"Your dad was so smug about the bakery and how wonderfully things were going. Well good for him, but he should have tried running a theater. Do you know how much money we were bleeding out? We were gushing blood. Gushing."

I wasn't sure I appreciated her metaphor, especially since she kept the gun pointed at my chest.

"There was no way we would have made it without my intervention. Stew was so stupid and naïve. He thought we were actually going to make enough to stay afloat with ticket sales. Idiot. I knew from the first dry run that we were going to have to find other revenue streams, and fast. We wouldn't have even opened if it weren't for me."

As she spoke, I reviewed my options. Shelly was older than me by a couple decades, and smaller. I could probably take her. The only issue was the gun. What if she shot before I could take her down?

Thomas and Detective Kerry had said they would come by. When? They could be on their way now, or it could be another hour before they arrived. I didn't have that much time. I was going to have to find a way to keep her talking until I could come up with a plan.

"Did you and Chuck work together?"

"Chuck was an actor," she scoffed. "He did as he was directed. I was his director and I gave him specific directions about how and when he was going to get us the cash. It was easy. Like taking candy from a baby. People are so gullible. It helped that Chuck was devastatingly handsome. All he had to do was flash his pearly whites and the little old ladies would be running for their checkbooks."

"I don't understand. What exactly was your strategy?"

"Keep up." She sounded disgusted. "It was as easy as pie, as your dad would have said. I came up with the targets, Chuck sweet-talked them, took their hard-earned cash, and we split the profits fifty-fifty. That is, until he decided to go and get morals."

"You mean he wanted out?"

"He wanted out, but that was not going to happen. We were in it together and I wasn't about to let him ruin everything I had built. He threatened to go to the police. He was going to confess. I told him that he would do jail time too, but he said he didn't care. That the pressure was getting to him. He only cared for himself. I knew the truth. He was going to throw me under the bus and keep the cash. I couldn't let that happen, and then in a stroke of the most wonderful luck, he was drunk as a skunk, dancing around the middle of the street when I was on my way home. I seized the opportunity. No one ever suspected me, except for you and your father." She narrowed her eyes and gave me a stare that sent fear running down my spine.

"I warned your father—twice. If he hadn't stopped meddling, I wasn't about to give him a third chance. Now you have to get involved and ruin everything. Too bad daddy isn't here to save you."

"Shelly, I don't know what you're talking about."

"Don't play dumb with me. I've been in the theater far too long. I know a con when I see a con. You know exactly what you're up to. I didn't buy that ruse for a minute today. And then I watched Amanda put together a nice little packet of 'memories' for you. Yeah right. You and Lance are trying to find Chuck's killer. Success, honey. You found her, but I bet you didn't think through what you were going to do next, now did you?"

Her syrupy voice sent another chill through my body.

"You didn't really think that I would let my dirty little secret come out after all these years, did you? Oh no, no, no, no. That's not the way this works. You should have stuck with the baking."

"Shelly, you don't want to do this. If you kill me, the police will know. I've already shared everything with two Ashland detectives."

"Shared what?" She glanced around the kitchen. "Where is it?"

"Where's what?"

She stepped closer and pressed the gun to my skin. "The file that Amanda gave you. I was watching. I followed her to plaza and saw her give it to you. Where is it?"

"It's in the dining room."

"Excellent. Let's go grab it."

"Even if you take whatever evidence you think is there, the police are still going to figure it out, Shelly. I told them my suspicions." That was half true. Where was Thomas? Please come soon.

"Pick it all up." She motioned for me to gather the papers and photos laid out on the table.

I followed her directions. Once I had everything stacked, she pointed to the chair. "Take a seat."

"You're going to shoot me in my own house?" If I could figure out what Shelly's intention was, maybe I could find a way out.

She looked at her watch. "No, no. I'm not shooting you. My dear friend will be taking on that responsibility. Sadly, then he'll be so remorseful that he'll kill himself. A double homicide. Such a shame in charming little Ashland, Oregon."

The gun stayed focused on me.

"Who? Ronald?" I asked.

"You figured that out too. My you are a smart one, aren't you?"

"Did he write the notes and leave them at the bakeshop for my dad?"

"He did. He owed me a favor—or a dozen favors. That's the nice thing about addicts. They are always so helpful when they need their next hit, so I took him up on his services. He had no idea why of course. And if he did, he never said a word because he knows better than to mess with me."

The longer she kept talking the better chances were that Detective Kerry and Thomas would arrive. I just hoped that they would get here before Ronald.

Chapter Twenty-Five

"Let's go," Shelly commanded. "Get those papers—all of them. I think it's chilly in here. Time for a fire, don't you think?"

I shuddered, but followed her directions.

"Move, move." She used the gun to force me toward the fireplace.

She was going to burn the evidence.

I heard the front door open. I wasn't sure if Shelly heard it too, she was still consumed with rage over my dad and his "meddling." Was it Thomas? Why wasn't he calling for me?

"Your father was such a do-gooder. He should have minded his own business. A young wife and daughter. What was he doing running around town trying to play detective?"

"He was asked to help by Doug—the Professor."

"Doug. What a joke. What did *he* know? He was as green as they come. I had a good laugh watching him make a mess of the case. He had no chance of figuring it out. I'm surprised he kept his job."

Shelly's cockiness surprised me. I would have thought

that having the case resurface would make her nervous, not boastful.

She kept talking with the gun lasered at me. My senses were on high alert. I heard soft footsteps in the hallway and then the kitchen. Was it Chef Ronald, coming to be of service again, or was it Thomas and Kerry?

My heart thudded in my chest.

Keep her distracted, Jules.

Maybe Ronald would refuse to help her this time. If he really didn't know that she had killed Chuck, maybe he would come to my rescue. He had turned his life around. He wouldn't want to risk his career and everything he had worked for in the last ten years for Shelly, would he?

"William and Helen Capshaw, Ashland's love birds. Weren't they the cutest? That's what everyone said. They used to complain about their expenses. I would have liked to have had a small bakery to run."

The footsteps were close now. Right behind me.

I didn't dare turn around.

Shelly glanced at her watch again. "Where is he?"

"He's not coming," a familiar voice boomed.

I turned to see the Professor standing in the dining room doorway with his gun pointed at Shelly. She didn't flinch. She kept her gun on me.

"What are you doing here?"

"I'm here to arrest you for the murder of Chuck Faraday and the attempted murder of Juliet Capshaw." The Professor's tone was calm and even.

I felt neither of those emotions.

Shelly wasn't budging. She kept the gun pointed directly

at my chest. Her eyes weren't crazed. They were unnervingly focused. "Go ahead. Try. I'll shoot her."

I didn't doubt that she would. I clutched the papers so tightly my fingers had turned white.

The Professor gave me a reassuring nod. "You won't shoot. This ends tonight. It should have ended long, long ago."

Shelly cocked the gun.

I tried to swallow, but my tongue felt like it had swollen to twice its size.

"No. You'll put the gun down and come with me, Shelly. It's over. We have you surrounded."

"What?" She turned just as Thomas and Detective Kerry appeared on the opposite side of the dining room.

For the first time since Shelly had shown up on my doorstep, I took a real breath.

Everything happened in a blur. Detective Kerry had the gun out of Shelly's hands and her wrists in handcuffs in one deft motion. The Professor read Shelly her rights, and Thomas came to check on me.

"How you doing, Jules? You look a little pale."

"I'm okay." I scrunched my head. "The Professor. How?" I couldn't form complete sentences.

"Kerry and I met up with him back at the station after we took care of a traveler panhandling by the theater. We were going to try to keep quiet about the case, but he was reviewing the old file when we got there." He guided me to a chair to sit down.

"I'm so glad. She was going to kill me. She said that Ronald was on his way, and she intended to have it look like a murder/suicide."

Thomas patted my knee. "It's cool. You just take it easy for a few. I'm going to get you a glass of water, and then I'm sure the Professor is going to want to take a statement while everything is fresh."

"Okay."

He went to get me water while Kerry and the Professor took Shelly out to their waiting squad car.

"Here you go." Thomas handed me the water. "Drink slow."

"I'm fine," I insisted.

Thomas frowned. "You've just had a gun pointed at you and your life threatened. If you're fine, Juliet, then you're not human."

The glass shook as I tried to bring it to my lips. "Okay, maybe I'm a little shaken."

"Yeah." Thomas sat next to me.

The Professor returned. "You and Detective Kerry can process Shelly. I'll be along shortly."

Thomas gave him a half salute. "On it." Then he pressed his hand on my shoulder. "Good work tonight."

"Mind if I take a seat?" The Professor nodded at the empty chair next to me.

"Please."

"I'm sorry to have put you through that, Juliet."

"It's my fault." I told him about Lance and our excursions. "I know we shouldn't have gotten involved. I guess after you told me the whole story about my dad, I sort of felt responsible. Like if I could solve the case, it would connect us somehow. And, to be honest, I wanted to solve it for you. You've done so much for me. You've been like a second father."

His voice became husky. "Juliet, let me assure you that

you never need do anything to be more connected to your father. He is you. Every time I look at you, I see Will's laughing eyes and his giant, open heart. He lives on in you, and nothing—absolutely nothing—gives me more pride then being able to fill his shoes in any small way, shape, or form."

Emotion overcame me. I broke down.

The Professor sat in silence, holding me tight. His arms wrapped me in comfort. When I regained control of my tears, he encouraged me to drink more water. "I do believe this is my fault. I shouldn't have burdened you with the case. It's been weighing on me for so long, that I feel I unfairly put you in the middle. Will you please accept my apology?"

"Of course. I'm not upset. Hearing about my dad and Torte's early days has given me a new perspective and understanding."

He nodded, but I wasn't sure he agreed with me. "I must beg you to walk me through what you recall."

I relayed everything that had happened, including each of the suspects that Lance and I had visited and Shelly's confession. "There's no sign of Ronald though?"

The Professor made a final note in his Moleskine notebook. "He's already been taken into custody for questioning."

"Do you think he was in on it?"

"Off the record, I would say that he must have suspected something. Why else would Shelly have asked him to write threatening notes? If he was involved, that will make him an accessory to murder. And withholding critical information pertaining to the case will also land him some jail time."

"I can't believe that it was Shelly."

"It is a puzzle, but it makes sense when I think back. She was so driven those days. Too driven, obviously. I have you to thank, actually. When I pulled the old case files, I realized that there were a number of financial records missing. I'm sure you're familiar with the old adage 'Follow the money'?"

I nodded.

"I should have done a better job at doing just that. Reading Will's journals brought it to top of mind. I had forgotten how piecemealed the Cabaret's financial records had been. At the time, I chalked it up to their newness and lack of funding, but with fresh eyes, I realized that was exactly what she wanted me to think. Donor receipts were scribbled on notepaper, intentionally hard to read. What a grave mistake I made by overlooking that. I assumed, like everything else in Ashland in those days, that it was a lack of time and organizational skill, but now I see we were wrong."

"I was just looking over the same thing, and there was a lot of money exchanged." I explained how Amanda had made copies for me. "Now I know why Shelly was so desperate to get her hands on the old paperwork. I wonder why she kept it. Why wouldn't she have shredded it years ago?"

The Professor shrugged. "Overconfidence perhaps? Time? I would guess that it was our renewed interest in the case that triggered her panic."

"She showed up before I had time to look everything over. What exactly were she and Chuck involved in?"

"From what I've gathered, she repeated the same scheme again and again. Promising high-end donors special access, special recognition, private early screenings of plays, and much, much more—none of which ever came to fruition. Chuck was her front man. He sold them in and Shelly took their money. My aha moment came when I reopened the case file and saw the bank statements we pulled back in 1988 for the Cabaret. I should have picked up on this at the time, but Shelly was the sole signer on the account. She had complete access over every single cent coming in and out of the theater."

"And, when Chuck wanted out, she killed him," I added.

The Professor sighed. "Such a shame."

"Now what? What about Mom?"

He frowned. "I think the time is long overdue to explain this to your mother. I feel better knowing that we have a suspect in custody, but I'm not looking forward to coming clean myself. I hope she'll be able to forgive me."

"She loves you." I reached for his hand. "Do you want my dad's journal and everything we've found? That might help."

"I would love for you to share that with her once I've had a chance to speak with her."

"Deal."

He stood. "I must get to the station . . . and then I have a date with your mother."

"Good luck."

I locked the door after he left and went to bed with my dad's journal. I had planned on reading it again, but fell asleep with it resting on my chest.

Chapter Twenty-Six

The next morning, I woke feeling refreshed and ready to meet the day. I knew what my first order of business had to be—a conversation with Mom. When I arrived at Torte, she was already in the kitchen. The Professor must have confessed everything last night.

Classical music played overhead. The smell of baking bread and coffee flooded the kitchen. Mom pressed buttery tart crust into tins. Her cheeks were dusted with flour and bright with color.

"Mom, you're here." I walked to greet her with a hug and ended up bawling in her arms.

"I know, honey. Doug told me everything last night," she whispered in my ear, as she brushed a tear from my cheek.

"It's weird, I've never felt this close to Dad."

She kissed my head. "Haven't I always told you that you are your father's daughter?"

"Yeah, but I guess I never knew how much until now." I showed her his journal. Tears poured from her eyes as we looked through his notes.

"You know what comes through the most?" she asked, when we finished.

"What?"

"The fact that he loved us more than anything."

We leaned into each other.

"Torte sounded amazing back then."

She wiped her eyes with the edge of her apron. "It was. It really was, but it still is, and I know if your dad were here, he would be so proud of what you've built and how you've grown it."

"Stop, Mom, you're going to make me cry again."

She brushed her hands together. "We can't have that. There's bread to be made. We'll get a head start before Marty gets here."

We got to work baking. "How did your conversation last night go? Doug was so worried about telling you."

She rolled her eyes. "As if I didn't know."

"Mom!"

"Juliet, what? Give your poor mother a little credit." She used the weight of her arms to press the tart crust into a line of fluted tins.

"I can't believe you knew." I measured milk and butter for my cinnamon-roll dough.

"Of course I knew. William was like a little kid. He was so excited to be working side by side with Doug. Ashland is a small town now, but back then it was even smaller. I would've had to have been hiding under a rock not to know. I also knew the reason he didn't tell me was because he thought I would worry. He was wrong about that. I wouldn't have worried. I knew he was with Doug, and Doug was already the best detective we'd ever had."

"You knew!" I repeated.

"I can have my secrets too. Sometimes a touch of mystery is good for a relationship. I didn't know about the threatening notes, or the fact that Torte was broken into by Shelly—or maybe Ronald—and not kids. I'm grateful that your father gave up the case then, because I wouldn't have wanted to see anything happen to you or for Torte to have sustained more damage." She took the first batch of tart crusts to the oven to blind bake.

"Poor Doug. He was so worried."

"To tell you the truth, I had forgotten all about the case. It never crossed my mind when we got married. I never felt like Doug was hiding a secret. You have to remember this happened almost thirty years ago."

"Right."

She returned to the next batch of tart crusts "I never told your father this, but I was pleased that he was working the case with Doug. He was so consumed with Torte at the time. Don't get me wrong. It was good. We needed his energy and commitment to making the bakeshop a success, but he was obsessed. He didn't sleep well at night those days because he was so worried about money and whether or not we were going to succeed. Helping Doug with the case was a break from all of that. I guess that's probably one of the reasons I never let on that I knew."

Her explanation made sense. And, yet again, it made me understand my own compulsions. I guess if nothing else, now I knew that I came by them naturally.

We went through the routine of proofing yeast for bread dough and mixing vats of cake batter. I couldn't believe how much things at Torte had changed while at the same time how much they had stayed the same.

Bethany was one of the first staff members to arrive,

breaking our morning of reminiscing. Her cheeks were flushed with color and she had a bit of spring to her step.

"How was the mountain?" I asked.

"Great. So great. Andy is hilarious. He's a really good skier too. I had no idea." Her skin blotched as she spoke. "I mean, I got a ton of fun outdoor shots that we can use on social."

"Of course. That's great."

Her cheeks turned a deep shade of maroon, so I changed the subject. "Did Sterling talk to you and Steph about an eighties dinner?"

She clapped. "Yes! Yes, and we love it. We have so many ideas. The three of us were brainstorming yesterday afternoon. I know we're doing the Irish feast this week, which is actually good because it gives us more time to plan and get the word out." Her words ran together as she spoke. "Let me run upstairs and bring down some of the ideas we mapped out."

When she was out of earshot, Mom winked. "Young love."

I smiled and returned to baking. By a little after six, the kitchen was buzzing with activity and energy. Things were back to normal, and I'd never felt more grateful.

"Hey, Sterling," I called. "I brought something for you."

He tied an apron around his waist and walked over to me. "What's that?"

"Some gems of inspiration for the Sunday Supper." I showed him some of the old photos I'd found of Torte along with the copies Amanda had given me.

"Check out the mustache on the Professor," Andy joked.

"I keep telling him he should bring the stash back," Mom bantered.

"Maybe he will for our flashback dinner." I slid a tray of cookies into the oven. "It can be a party to celebrate our roots."

"These are so great," Sterling said, gathering the photos and newspaper clippings. "This might be our most popular Sunday Supper yet."

"Totally," Andy agreed. "I'll come up with some, like, totally gnarly eighties drinks to serve."

"And we'll have to put together an eighties playlist," I suggested. "Wham!, Madonna, you know, the classics."

"Don't forget about the desserts," Bethany chimed in. "Steph and I have a list of desserts from the 1980s, but what else was popular back then, Mrs. Capshaw?"

Mom shared some of her favorite retro recipes with the team. Everyone was excited about the event and eager to lend their input. The Professor had been right. I was my father's daughter, but I was my mother's daughter too. Torte was my legacy. They had created the bakeshop as a place of comfort, where delicious food was served with love. It was my job to carry on that tradition, and I was ready for the task.

Chapter Twenty-Seven

For the next few weeks, I savored the pages of my father's
journal every night before bed. He had puzzled over
Chuck's killer. I could tell that it had been hard for him
to let it go. Each passage in the weathered journal solidi-
fied how much he had cared for Mom and me. We were
his priority. I wondered if he might have continued helping Doug with the Pastry Case if it wasn't for us. There
were more entries after where the Professor and I left
off. The paragraphs slowly changed from his obsessions
with the hit-and-run to more news and musings about
Torte and me.

Juliet landed the part today. Helen and I are
bursting with pride. I hope it's not too much pres-
sure for my little sweet pea. She has her first fitting
tomorrow, and Janet called to let us know that A
Rose by Any Other Name is going to be designing
a true flower crown for the show. I can't wait to
see Juliet's face when she learns that she's going to
be a real princess. I'm excited because we'll get a
season pass to the Festival. Prices are steep these

*days. Eighteen dollars for good seats. Juliet will
also receive a stipend, which Helen and I agreed
will go directly into her college fund.*

*Our espressos are starting to gain traction.
Today, we actually had a line of customers waiting
for lattes and cappuccinos. Helen told me I needed
to be patient and give it some time. The other exciting news in the bakeshop is that we've been invited
to cater the Feast of Will. The renaissance feast in
Lithia Park is one of my favorite traditions of the
year. I never imagined that we would have the honor
of baking for the feast. I'm scouring Elizabethan
recipes for inspiration.*

Reading small snippets of my parents' life brought me
more closure. On the night before our 1980s flashback
Sunday Supper, I turned the yellowed pages in the journal
to realize that there were only three pages left. I didn't
want this journey to end. And, yet, I knew that it had to.
My time with Dad's journal had made him whole again.
Examining my past had given me new insight into my
future. It was soon going to be time to move on. To close
the leather-bound journal, return it to a secure shelf in the
basement, and carry my dad's memories with me in my
heart.

Read on, Jules, I told myself.

All capital letters on the next page caught my eye.

BREAKING NEWS IN THE PASTRY CASE!

*Doug and I are still at a loss as to who ran
Chuck down, but I believe that I have solved one
piece of the puzzle. I bumped into Richard Lord
this afternoon. It was a classic Richard interaction.*

He puffed out his chest like a peacock and started spouting off about his record-breaking numbers with his dance parties. I half listened. I was in a hurry to go meet Helen and Juliet at the Black Swan for her first costume fitting. Not to mention that everything Richard says must be taken with a grain of salt. Or maybe a full shaker of salt.

Why he needs to try and impress me is a mystery.

Here's the interesting part. The man is paranoid. Completely paranoid. I realized that he's the guy who's been following me around at night. He had to be the one who followed me up to my van on my way home from the Mark Antony and who was behind me on the plaza. That's why he was sweating profusely at the dance party. He hadn't been dancing. He'd been stalking me.

His whole story about me and Doug playing detective had no merit. He's been convinced that I'm trying to steal his business plan. Yeah right!

I can't wait to tell Helen about our conversation today. She'll get a good laugh out of the idea that we would ever try to intentionally copy anything that Richard Lord is doing at the Merry Windsor.

He actually accused me of spying on him and trying to pilfer his business ideas!

Of course! I flipped the journal shut. I could picture Richard sneaking around the plaza in the dark trying to figure out what my dad was up to. Classic. I placed the journal on my nightstand and clicked off the light. Tomorrow was our 1980s party. It felt like things had come full circle. Throwing a flashback feast was fitting, just the sendoff I needed to put the past behind me. There was one

last page for me to read in the journal, and I would save it
for tomorrow night.

The next morning, I woke up with renewed energy. I
tugged on a pair of jeans, a Torte T-shirt, and my tennis
shoes. Then I packed a bag with my costume for the party.
The mood at the bakeshop was alive and frenetic. Everyone had a long list of tasks to complete before we opened
the doors to our dinner guests at six.

Bethany and Steph were in charge of our dessert course.
They whipped marshmallow cream filling for our Ding
Dongs and baked extra pans of pineapple upside-down
cake. Sterling and Marty had prepared a menu straight out
of the 1980s. We would be greeting guests with sparkling
wine coolers and platters of jalapeño poppers, jelly-glazed
meatballs, and spinach dip. The main course would consist
of a Caesar salad, baked potatoes with all the fixings, and
blackened chicken and salmon. Our pièce de résistance for
the evening was the retro dessert cart, for which Bethany
had repurposed an old delivery cart. We would drape it
with white tablecloths and wheel it through the dining
room with our beautifully plated desserts.

Andy blasted Debbie Gibson after we closed the bakeshop for the day. Rosa and I pushed tables together and
covered them with black butcher paper. Andy and Sequoia
hung posters of 1980s rock stars on the walls and fes-
tooned the bakeshop with fluorescent glow-stick bou-
quets. I had ordered an assortment of retro candy—like
giant jawbreakers—that we scattered on the long tables.
Sterling helped me rig a black light and disco ball from
the ceiling. Rosa taped the front windows with more of the
black butcher paper in order to block any light from coming in.

"This is awesome, Jules." Sterling flicked off the lights and turned on the disco ball.

The bakeshop was transformed into a scene straight out of the 1980s. Rosa's white T-shirt glowed under the black light, and the colorful neon glow sticks lit up the room.

"It's pretty cool," I agreed. Then I called everyone upstairs. "Great work today, team. Guests will be arriving in thirty minutes, so go change. Tease up your hair and pull on your legwarmers."

When it was my turn in the bathroom, I left my jeans on, but swapped my tennis shoes for a pair of rainbow Chuck Taylors that I had scored in the vintage store along with the scoop-neck pink T-shirt that draped over my left shoulder. I pulled my hair into a side ponytail and applied a generous amount of bright blue eye shadow. I stood back and appraised myself in the mirror.

Not bad.

My already blue eyes looked almost fake beneath the layers of eye shadow. The side ponytail showed off my jawline. I felt like a teenager as I joined my team in the dining room.

From Bethany's neon green legwarmers to Andy's red tracksuit, everyone had outdone themselves. We danced to the beat of the Beastie Boys under the flashing disco lights.

Lance was the first guest to arrive. He was dressed like Don Johnson from *Miami Vice* in a baby blue suit with a tight white T-shirt and pair of black sunglasses. "This is, like, totally rad, darling." He tipped his wine cooler to me in a toast.

The Professor and Mom even got in the spirit. He arrived sporting a fake mustache and a Hawaiian shirt. Mom opted for an ode to Joan Collins with her yellow jacket and its massive shoulder pads and form-fitting white miniskirt.

"Oh, honey, this is hilarious." She squeezed the Professor's hand. "It takes us back, doesn't it, Doug?"

He pressed the fake Tom Selleck mustache to his upper lip. "So much so that I'm considering bringing the stash back. What do you say, Juliet?"

I winced. "I think that trend died a while ago."

"Thank you." Mom leaned in to kiss my cheek.

"Oh dear lady, wait. I thought you *wanted* me to bring the stash back." The Professor pretended to be injured. He stabbed himself in the chest with his fist. "Say it isn't so."

Mom wrinkled her brow and bit her bottom lip. "Let's just say that I may have been teasing."

She got whisked away by Wendy and Janet. The Professor watched her bop to the music with her friends.

"Any update on Shelly?" I offered him a wine cooler. "Have you been able to determine whether she was working with Chuck or masterminded the entire plan herself?"

He took one of the chilled fluted glasses. "At this point, it's unclear. Her story continues to change. My guess is that she had some involvement in Chuck's schemes, but that's for the DA to determine. The good news is that we have a solid case now. Her attempt to take your life as well as threatening police officers will ensure that she will serve time."

"That's good." I reached for a Ring Pop on the table and placed it on an index finger.

"And, my dear, given all that has transpired, how are things with you?" His kind eyes were full of concern.

"I'm doing well. Really well. It's been hard to drag up

painful memories of loss, but honestly, I think I needed this time in my dad's head more than I could have ever known."

He folded his hands together and closed his eyes for one brief minute. "Yes, I understand."

Lance swept over to us. "Darling, fabulous party." He bit into a jalapeño popper. "Everyone is absolutely raving about the eighties theme. You've outdone yourself."

The Professor excused himself.

"Thanks," I said to Lance. "Credit my staff. It was their idea."

"Well color me impressed. They are brilliant." He lowered his voice. "Do tell though, what are we going to do now that we've cracked another case?"

"What do you mean?"

"I mean it's another win for Rousseau and Capshaw. What's next? You know me, I yearn for adventure."

"Right, but don't you have a new season at OSF and your work at the Cabaret to concentrate on?"

Marty circulated with a tray of jelly-glazed meatballs on tiny toothpicks. Lance helped himself to two. "Pshaw, that's work. I mean adventure. I feel something new brimming. Don't you feel it too?"

"No." If anything I felt more grounded to Ashland than ever.

Lance wasn't having it. "Mark my words, Juliet, there's a difference in the air. I do believe that surprises are in store. Keep your chin up and your eyes on alert."

"Okay." I agreed mainly to get him to stop and because I spotted Amanda and her husband at the front door. Amanda wore her hair in two ponytails and was dressed like Punky Brewster. Jed had gone with more of a Beastie

Boys approach with parachute pants, a backward baseball cap, and three silver chains around his neck.

"Thanks so much for inviting us," Amanda said when I greeted them. "This is amazing. I feel like I've stepped back into our childhood."

"Let's just say that my staff got very into the theme."

"I don't think you two have officially met, but I've been talking about you nonstop to Jed, so I'm pretty sure he feels like he already knows you, right, hon?" She looked up at Jed, who was taller than her by at least six inches.

He shook my hand. "All I've heard about since you two bumped into each other is Juliet Capshaw. I'm so happy to finally get to meet you and that you and Amanda have rekindled your friendship. It's even more validation for our move. Not that we needed any. Ashland has rolled out the welcome mat for us."

"Except for Shelly." Amanda shuddered. "I can't believe she was arrested. To think that we were convinced she was controlling and didn't want to hand over the reins for the Cabaret when in reality she had been trying to cover up an old murder. It gives me the creeps every time I think about it." She shivered again. Jed reached out his arm to console her.

"According to what the police told us, she's behind bars now and we have nothing to worry about." He took a neon green cocktail from a tray that Rosa was passing around the dining room. "The police mentioned that you were involved in her arrest. I hope it wasn't too stressful."

"No," I lied, taking a cocktail from Rosa. "It wasn't too bad." I didn't want to ruin the retro vibe of the evening with the memory of Shelly pointing a gun at my chest. We chatted for a few minutes more about their plans for the

Cabaret and made a date to meet at Uva for a more leisurely catch-up over a bottle of wine.

Mom waved from the opposite side of the room, giving me the cue that dinner was ready. I showed Amanda and Jed to their seats, then I clinked my fork to an empty glass. "Thanks so much for joining us for this throwback bash. We're excited to transport you and your taste buds to the 1980s, so please take your seats."

Everyone applauded as Marty, Rosa, Andy, Sequoia, and Sterling arrived in unison with trays of Caesar salads, baked potatoes, and blacked chicken and salmon. Dinner was a lively affair with plenty of music, eighties trivia, and flowing bottles of wine.

When it was time for the dessert course, our guests whooped and hollered with delight at the sight of the dessert cart and the delectable assortment of retro sweets. There wasn't a crumb or morsel left at the end of the evening, which I took as a favorable sign. Everyone lingered late into the night. We pushed aside the tables and cranked the music louder. Watching friends, family, and my staff move to the pulse of the music made me grin. I disagreed with Lance. I didn't need new adventures. I had them right in front of me.

Epilogue

Later, once we had run the dishwasher and taken down the eighties décor, I tucked into my bed with a mug of hot tea. The last page of my father's journal awaited. Before I read it, I took a deep breath and sent out gratitude for the gift of his words. His death had changed me. I had spent years living in the wake of grief, wishing that he were alive for so many milestones and average rainy Tuesday afternoons alike. I had held tight to regret, to craving his presence, his calming voice, his comforting arms. I had lived under the shadow of loss.

In the pages of his faded journal, I had realized something monumental. Something that I knew would alter me for the better. And that was that he had been with me this entire time.

Armed with this new understanding, I opened the journal.

To my loves,
According to my bank account I'm far from a rich man, but one look of love from Helen's eyes and the sight of Juliet's wide smile tells me that I'm

*the wealthiest man alive. I might not be able to
give you diamonds or pearls. I might not be able to
show you the world, but I can give you this.*

> A work in progress for Helen and Juliet:
> I dreamed of distant lands last night,
> Of stars, of moons, of skies, and seas,
> I dreamed of places never traveled
> Of shores left unexplored,
> I steered my vessel toward adventure
> Seeking danger, a rambling stranger,
> It turned,
> and led me straight to home,
> I found you waiting,
> A sturdy stance, a welcoming glance,
> A knowing smile, a sweet caress,
> For you, my loves, know me best,
> My heart is full,
> With dreams of you,
> I need not venture far from here,
> Because with you I'm whole, my dears.

These were my father's last words, at least in the form
of his journal. No sentiment could be more fitting. The fact
that his poem reflected his thoughts on the sea resonated
deeply with me. I had fulfilled his need for wanderlust and
found my way home.

I didn't shed a single tear as I closed the journal. Instead, I drifted off to sleep with dreams of Ashland, of
my life here on solid ground, and of the many adventures
that awaited me.

Recipes

Ding Dong Cake

Ingredients:

For the cake:
½ cup butter, softened
1 ½ cups sugar
1 tsp vanilla
2 eggs
1 ½ cups flour
½ cup cocoa powder
1 tsp salt
1 baking powder
1 cup milk

For the filling:
12-15 large marshmallows
½ cup butter
1¾ cup powdered sugar
1 tsp vanilla

For the ganache:
1 12 oz. bag semi-sweet chocolate chips
2 tbsp butter

Directions:
Preheat oven to 350 degrees. Combine butter and sugar in an electric mixer and mix on low until creamy. Add vanilla and eggs. Sift flour, cocoa powder, salt, and baking powder together in a separate bowl. Slowly alternate adding flour mixture and milk. Do not over mix. Coat two eight-inch round pans with baking spray and evenly spread batter into pans. Bake at 350 degrees for 20 minutes. Allow to cool.

While cakes are cooling, make the filling. Melt marshmallows. As soon as the marshmallows have melted refrigerate. Whip butter, powdered sugar, and vanilla in a mixer until light and fluffy. Add cooled marshmallows and whip until the filling is smooth and creamy.

Spread filling in between the cakes, reserving a small portion for the design on the top of the cake. Melt semi-sweet chocolate chips and butter on medium-low heat. Once a silky ganache has formed, pour over cake. Allow the ganache to set. Pipe a squiggly line of the filling on the top of the Ding Dong cake.

Corned Beef Hash

Ingredients:
2 tbsp olive oil
1 red onion, chopped

2 cloves garlic, chopped
1 bag frozen diced potatoes
2 tbsp Worcestershire sauce
1 tsp white pepper
1 tsp salt
1 tbsp fresh parsley, chopped
8 slices of corned beef (sliced thin for sandwiches)
   diced into small 1 inch strips
8 eggs
1 cup shredded Irish cheddar cheese

Directions:
Heat olive oil in a large frying pan and add the chopped onions and garlic. Cook until soft and translucent. Add frozen potatoes and cook for 5 minutes, stirring occasionally. Add Worcestershire sauce, pepper, salt, and fresh parsley. Mix in corned beef. Crack eggs over the top, cover with lid, and turn heat to low. Cook until eggs are poached (10-12 minutes). Serve hot with fresh grated Irish cheddar.

Pineapple Upside Down Cake

Ingredients:
   ¼ cup butter
   ⅔ cup brown sugar
   6 slices pineapple in juice (drained)
   6 maraschino cherries (no stems)
   ¼ cup butter
   1 cup sugar
   1 egg

1 tsp vanilla
1 ¼ cups flour
1 baking powder
1 tsp salt
¾ cup buttermilk

Directions:

Preheat oven to 350 degrees. Once oven has come to temp, place ¼ cup of butter in a square glass pan and bake for 3 to 5 minutes, or until butter is completely melted. Remove from oven and immediately sprinkle the brown sugar onto the butter. Carefully place pineapple slices on the butter and brown sugar, setting a cherry into the center of each slice.

Add butter and sugar in an electric mixer, cream together. Add egg, vanilla, flour, baking powder, salt, and buttermilk and mix until a batter forms. Pour the batter over the pineapple slices. Bake 45 to 50 minutes or until the cake is golden brown. Once the cake has been removed from the oven, place a serving plate upside down and turn the pan over. Let the brown sugar mixture drizzle over the cake for a minute, then remove pan and serve warm.

Deep Dish BBQ Chicken Pizza

Ingredients:

For the crust:
1 package quick rise yeast
½ tsp sugar

1 cup warm water
3–3 ½ cups flour

For the topping:
1 jar BBQ sauce
2 chicken breasts (cooked and shredded)
1 red onion (chopped)
1 large bunch cilantro (chopped)
2 cups pizza blend cheese (mozzarella and cheddar)

Directions:
Preheat oven to 425 degrees. Add yeast, sugar, and warm water in a mixing bowl. Stir, and allow to rise for 5 to 10 minutes or until yeast begins to bubble. Using a dough hook, slowly combine flour (1 cup at a time) and yeast in an electric mixer and combine until a ball begins to form. Once dough is fully formed, cover with a towel and set aside for 1 hour. Dough should double in size. Divide into two equal parts and press into cast iron skillets. Top with BBQ sauce, shredded chicken, chopped red onions, cilantro, and cheese. Bake at 425 degrees for 12 to 15 minutes.

Banana Bundt Cake

Ingredients:
½ cup butter
1 ½ cups sugar
2 eggs
1 tsp lemon juice
1 tsp vanilla

   3 ripe bananas
   ½ tsp baking soda
   ½ tsp salt
   ½ cup milk
   2 cups flour

Directions:
Preheat oven to 350 degrees. Combine butter and sugar in an electric mixer, beat on medium speed until fluffy. Add eggs, lemon juice, vanilla, and bananas. Mix well, then add dry ingredients. Coat a Bundt pan with baking spray, making sure to fill in every crack and crevasse. Pour batter into Bundt pan and bake at 350 degrees for 45 to 50 minutes or until the cake is golden and a toothpick comes out clean. Remove from the oven. Allow to cool for 5 minutes. Then place a plate on top of the Bundt pan and flip the pan over. Dust with powdered sugar or serve with a scoop of vanilla bean ice cream.

Pistachio Rose Latte

Andy and Sequoia teamed up for this decadent latte with lovely floral notes and a nutty finish. It's like a taste of blooming spring roses in coffee form.

Ingredients:
   2 shots of good quality espresso
   1 cup milk
   2 tsp pistachio syrup
   1 tsp rose syrup
   Pistachio shavings

Directions:
Prepare espresso and steam milk. Mix pistachio and rose extracts in the bottom of your favorite coffee mug. Add steamed milk and stir. Pour over espresso. Top with pistachio shavings.

Read on for an excerpt from

CHILLED
TO THE CONE

— the next Bakeshop Mystery from Ellie
Alexander, available soon from St. Martin's
Paperbacks!

They say that every new beginning starts with a single step. As of late, it felt like my steps were taking me in opposing directions. Fortunately, our little corner of Southern Oregon wasn't too large. Ashland is nestled in the Siskiyou Mountains just north of California giving us long, glorious stretches of sun, stunning vistas, and an abundance of fresh pine-scented air. Not only are we tucked between deciduous forests and gently rolling golden hills, but we are also home to the world-renowned Oregon Shakespeare Festival. Throughout the year tourists came from near and far to take in a production of *The Tempest* in the Elizabethan, beneath a ceiling of stars, or experience an intimate performance of new works by innovative playwrights in one of the many theaters on the OSF campus.

When I had returned to my childhood home a while ago I hadn't been sure what to expect. I had thought my stop might be temporary, but Ashland captured me under her spell. I knew now that this was where I was meant to be. It was an exciting time to have a renewed appreciation for the place I had grown up. Maybe that was the gift of leaving. Distance and time away from my beloved hometown had made me want to embrace and experience all that the the Rogue Valley had to offer. Thus far, I had barely scratched the surface. Ashland is known as the spot where the palms meet the pines. Leafy palms give rise to a conifer canopy of Ponderosa pines, cedars, and white firs. Our temperate climate and fertile, organic valleys are ideal for growing pears, fruits, herbs, and grapes. Vineyards dot the hillsides throughout the region along with alpine lakes, pristine rivers, and hiking trails so remote that you can disappear into the forest and meander for hours without seeing another soul, except for the occasional black bear that might amble past.

From the healing Lithia waters to the wild deer that nibbled on lush green lawns to the constant bustle of activity on the plaza and the bevy of friends and family who had welcomed me in, I could finally declare with confidence that nothing could ever make me want to leave again.

That was especially true with Torte's latest endeavor. Our family bakeshop had been expanding. It happened organically. First, we learned that the basement space beneath the cozy bakeshop my parents opened thirty years ago had become available. Mom and I couldn't pass up the opportunity so we secured some grant money and city loans to break through the floor and build our dream kitchen, complete with a wood-burning pizza oven, state of the art kitchen, and cozy seating area in the basement. The renovations meant that we had been able to expand our offerings with a kitchen twice the size as well as additional seating in the basement and a new and improved coffee bar and pastry counter upstairs.

My next venture had been a total surprise. My estranged husband, Carlos, at the urging of my best friend, Lance, had made us partners in Uva, a boutique winery just outside of town. I left Carlos on the ship where we had both worked, after I learned that he had a son, Ramiro he had never told me about. In hindsight, it might have been a rash decision, but leaving Carlos meant that I had returned home to Ashland, a decision I didn't regret.

The bakeshop and winery should have been enough. I had plenty on my plate with managing Torte, growing our staff, and trying to figure out what to do with Uva. However, the universe had other plans for me. Sterling, my young sous chef, had been experimenting with a line of concretes—rich, custard-like ice creams with decadent and unique flavor combinations like lemon rosemary, dark chocolate toffee, pear and blue cheese, and strawberry balsamic with toasted pecans. We had added a small cold case during the remodel to house our daily concrete offerings. They had become so popular that on busy days we sold out by early afternoon no matter the season.

In a twist of fate, my friend Laney Lee had called to inform me that a seasonal space in Ashland's up-and-coming Railroad District was available for lease. Laney owned a Hawaiian street food cart, Nana's. We had become fast friends after I had tried her passion fruit lemonade one hot afternoon last summer. She had been keeping her eye on the outdoor space adjacent to where she parked her cart on summer days. The lot in question was attached to a ground floor yoga studio with an apartment above. It had been used as a walk-up coffee kiosk, but the owner of the coffee shop had jumped ship and moved to Paris, leaving the space unexpectedly vacant. Laney had initially hoped that the garden with its sweet outdoor counter and small covered area with a fridge, cooler, and sink might serve as a permanent location for her food cart. Alas, it wasn't meant to be. The city wouldn't approve any upgrades for the site. Laney needed a stove and oven to make her delicious fusion Kaluha pork tacos and sweet and sugary Malasadas.

She had called me a few days ago with the news that the seasonal space was about to go on the market. "Jules, you have to come take a look at this place. It's perfect for Torte Two."

"Torte Two?"

"Yeah, think about it. It's a perfect opportunity to expand. You could do walk-up coffee, even bring pastries over from the bakeshop. This area gets great summer traffic. With exorbitant rent prices on the plaza I think we're going to see a lot more action here in the Railroad District."

"That's so nice of you to think of us, Laney," I had said. "But we just finished a major expansion. I'm not sure a second location is in the cards right now."

"Come take a look at the space," Laney had pleaded. "I've had my truck here for ten years and I want to be neighbors with something complimentary like Torte— you would draw customers into the area with your name recognition alone. That would be great for you and for all of us trying to build a new shopping destination. I don't want to see a big investor or corporate coffee take over. There are rumors swirling that a huge national chain is considering doing a build out. They want to tear down the garden and turn the lot into a mega industrial coffee shop. We can't let that happen. If you are even a little interested, I can put you in touch with Addie. She owns the property and I know she'd give you a deal. Plus, the space is only open from May until September. It would be a great way for Torte to hit a new market and it's really low risk."

I had hesitated on the call. "I don't know, Laney. We're already short staffed. I'm not sure we can take on another project, even if it is seasonal."

"Opportunities like this don't pop up often in Ashland, Jules." Laney was nothing if not persistent. "You know that. Come by later this week. I'll show you around and introduce you to Addie. She's young and ambitious. Her yoga classes have attracted a lot of new faces to the Railroad District. She likes the idea of keeping the space a walk-up restaurant. No pressure, I promise."

Laney had been convincing. I agreed to stop by and take a look—more than anything to get off the phone, which is how I found myself making the short half mile walk from Torte to the intersection of A St. and Fourth Street on a spring afternoon.

Downtown Ashland was extremely walkable with relatively flat streets and sidewalks. I crossed Main Street, with Andy and Sterling in tow, and passed the blue awnings of the police station. To call it a station was an exaggeration. It was a contact point in the plaza, staffed by three officers and Ashland's park cadets who patrolled downtown and the surrounding parks on foot and by bike, handing out minor citations and alerting the police of any dangerous situations or criminal activity. The station looked more like a welcome center with its dish of water for dogs, stacks of maps, and window boxes with cheery geraniums. We continued along Water Avenue, paralleling Ashland Creek that flowed heavy with snow melt.

Andy was my resident barista who had recently opted to drop out of college in order to broaden his coffee knowledge. I wasn't thrilled with his decision to leave school, but if I had learned anything in my thirty plus years it was that we all have to follow our own path. Andy's ultimate dream was to open his own coffeeshop. Mom and I had assured him that we would support him in any way we could from sending him to regional barista competitions and trainings to giving him a larger role in our vendor partnerships and more management responsibilities.

Sterling was in a similar position. Since he'd landed in Ashland, he had become an integral part of our team. His natural talent and willingness to learn made him a leader in the kitchen. Most days he planned our lunch menus. Customers raved about his speciality soups, charred flatbreads, and herb-infused salads and pastas.

I felt so grateful to have both of them on my team. However, I probably should have thought through bringing them to meet Laney. They both buzzed with eager excitement as we made our way past the lumber yard that smelled of pine and cedar shavings and the hardware store with its friendly staff who were always ready to direct customers to the light bulb aisle or consult on paint colors. Next we passed Ashland Grange, a long tan ware-house with a green metal roof that sold everything from horse feed to festive terra cotta pots.

"Boss, this could be so cool. I mean ice cream is hot right now. Ha ha, pun totally intended," Andy said, step-ping to the side to allow a guy wheeling a cart of cans to recycle at the Co-Op across the street. "Me and Sterling have a ton of ideas for you."

"Don't get too excited," I cautioned, removing a pair of sunglasses from my purse. A drizzly morning had given way to a brilliant late afternoon sun. "This is simply a tour. I'm not making any promises."

Andy's freckles looked more pronounced when he grinned at Sterling. "Told you she would say that."

Sterling unzipped his dark gray hoodie and tied it around his waist. "Don't worry. She'll cave once she real-izes how great this could be."

"Hey, I'm still here, guys." I pretended to be insulted. In reality, I enjoyed the easy banter and rapport I had with my staff.

Laney's pink food truck, Nana's, was painted with yel-low and white flowers. It stood out like a bright spot in the otherwise semi-industrial area as we approached the gated garden and vacant coffee stand. What once must have been an inviting and charming garden reminded me of something out of Grimms' fairy tales. Wooden trel-lises sagged under gnarly twisted vines of ancient ivy. We entered through a weathered gate and were greeted with an assortment of rusting bistro tables and chairs and faded and broken sun umbrellas that were scattered throughout the overgrown garden. Cracked pots that may have once housed fragrant strawberries and potted herbs now sprouted weeds. No wonder a corporate coffee chain was interested in bulldozing the space. It was definitely in need of some TLC.

Laney sat at a rusty table with a young woman who looked vaguely familiar.

"Jules, so glad you made it." Laney stood to hug me. She was closer to Mom's age with long dark hair, deep-set eyes, and a friendly smile. I recognized her hibiscus flower apron. It was the same design that was painted on the side of Nana's truck. "This is Addie who owns the building," she said as a way of introduction. "Have you two met?"

Addie stood to greet me. She was significantly younger than both of us. I wasn't always the best judge of age, but she couldn't be much older than Andy.

"I don't think so," I said extending my hand.

Addie moved with the grace of a dancer. "Nice to meet you. I'm pretty new to town. I moved here from SoCal last year." She wore a pair of sleek aqua blue yoga pants, a plush cashmere wrap, and Uggs.

"How are you liking the Rogue Valley?" I asked, after introducing Sterling and Andy.

"Great. It's such an awesome community. Everyone's been really open and welcoming and my yoga studio is thriving." She pointed behind us to the two story building. A sign reading "NAMASTE YOGA" hung on the covered porch that led to the lower level. Tibetan prayer flags flapped in the slight breeze. "My parents helped me invest in the building. They were pretty concerned about competition because everyone in Ashland is into yoga, as you know, but my classes are packed. I've had to hire three instructors to keep up with the demand."

It was a bit of an exaggeration to claim that *everyone* in Ashland practiced yoga. I did agree that as a whole Ashland's free-thinking population was focused on health and wellness. Yoga, Pilates, meditation, Qi Gong, and Tai Chi classes were plentiful in our little artists' mecca. I enjoyed being part of a community that prided itself on health and well-being. Perhaps it was embedded in our DNA. The Lithia Waters that flowed through the plaza had long been revered for their healing properties. Ashland offered abundant opportunities to unplug. I had come to realize that was because we were a part of nature, literally surrounded and embraced by mountains in every direction. It was common to spot black bears lumbering through the vast network of trails above Lithia Park or to see flocks of wild turkeys strutting around a neighbor's front yard.

Addie stretched her limber arms. "Want to check out the kitchen?"

"Sure." We followed her to the back of the garden.

As Laney had mentioned on the phone the prep kitchen wasn't more than about ten feet long. It was covered by an overhang that, like the entrance, was wrapped in even more decades old ivy. A walk-up coffee counter and a large chalkboard menu served as barrier from the small outdoor kitchen with a row of cabinets, a prep space, fridge, and sink. The wooden counter was rotting with large splinters that could prove dangerous. The fridge had been tagged with purple graffiti and two of the cabinet doors were missing hinges.

How long had the place been empty?

"It's not much, but it also won't take a lot to make it prettier," Addie said, reaching into the waistband on her yoga pants and removing a single key. She proceeded to unlock a door next to the sink. "This is a storage closet for supplies. You and your staff will also have access to the bathrooms inside the yoga studio. I know it's not a full commercial kitchen, but it's perfect for coffee. Electric, water, and wifi are all included in the lease. The train is a nuisance, but you'll get used to it. It only passes through twice a day and it's short cargo cars. I learned not to schedule yoga at noon because when it passes behind us it lets out a shrill whistle and shakes the building. No big deal—I pushed back our start time to 12:15. It shouldn't be a problem for you, other than hearing the noon and five whistle."

She was talking as if the space was already ours.

"Basically, it's move-in ready now." She glanced up at the ivy ensconced pergola that looked like it might collapse on our heads at any minute. "That should give you plenty of time to put your own spin on the space for a late spring or early summer opening." Her attention veered as a man wearing a long purple cape pedaled past us on a rusty bike.

I recognized him immediately. He was affectionately known around town as "The Wizard" due to the cape, his wiry silver hair, and the trail of gold and green metallic streamers that flapped from his bike. As far as I knew, he was homeless by choice. He tended to travel in a radius throughout the Railroad District. I often spotted him in Railroad Park making figure eights on the paved bike path or holding court on his favorite bench, orating to no one in particular. The Wizard was famous for his elaborate balloon art. He delighted kids in the park with balloons shaped like monkeys and mermaids. Once he'd recreated the Elizabethan theater, our version of the Globe, out of balloons. It was so impressive that one of the local art galleries had put it on display for a month.

Addie muttered something under her breath that sounded like, "Stay away, crazy."

Laney waved to him. "Stop by the truck later okay? I have a bento box saved for you."

The Wizard gave her a slight nod of acknowledgement and steered his bike toward the path that led to Railroad Park.

I wasn't surprised that Laney helped feed the Wizard. That was on par with the rest of the community. At Torte, we delivered day old pastry and breads to the shelter and had an unspoken policy to cover the cost of a hot coffee or warm bowl of soup for anyone who might need it, especially during the cold winter months.

Addie didn't appear to share the same sentiment. "That guy creeps me out." She kept her eyes narrowed on him until he was out of sight.

"The Wizard?" Laney wrinkled her brow. Her golden-flecked eyes were filled with confusion. "He's harmless."

"Hardly," Addie scoffed. "You should try being here after my late night hot yoga class. He's always hanging around on the railroad tracks, just staring me down." She licked her thumb and tried to rub graffiti from the fridge. "I'm sure he's responsible for this damage and I never walk to my car alone now."

I caught Laney's eye. She shrugged in confusion.

Addie pointed to the roofline of Namaste. "I've installed surveillance cameras in the front of the building and up there. I'm going to catch him in the act, one of these days. Trust me, you're going to want to keep an eye out for him. I make one of my students come with me because I'm waiting for him to attack."

"Attack?" Laney laughed, making her long braids shake. She wore her dark hair in braids tied with small pink hibiscus flowers. "I've known the Wizard for years. He's a gentle, tender soul. If anything he's a bit of a free spirit, but dangerous—never."

Sterling who had been quiet thus far backed her up. "Yeah. I've run into him a few times and he seems like he's kind of in his own world, dancing to his own beat as they say, but I've never gotten a dangerous aura from him."

"That's because he's harmless," Laney insisted. She untied her raspberry sherbet colored apron and folded it neatly.

"I totally disagree. He's weird." Addie scowled and rubbed the spray paint on the fridge harder. It was futile. Removing the graffiti was going to take more than scrubbing. An industrial cleaner was in order. "Anyway, what do you think of the space? Should we get an agreement put together?"

"Well, I don't know." I floundered. "I would have to discuss things with my mom, as she's a partner in the business, and run some numbers on the viability of opening a second coffee spot so close to the bakeshop."

"This isn't that close, boss," Andy chimed in. He had

flipped his faded red baseball hat backwards. Strands of his auburn hair escaped from beneath the cap. "And it would be an awesome space for a summer ice cream shop. Am I right, Sterling?"

"For sure." Sterling's piercing blue eyes studied the space. I had a feeling he was making calculations in his head. "That back wall could be transformed into a larger menu. We could hang a Torte banner there." He pointed above us. "It definitely needs a deep cleaning and gutting, but there's potential here for sure."

"Yeah, and imagine if we string twinkle lights from the front gate to the awning," Andy added. "Boss, you've got to give this some real thought. This could be really cool. We could serve our signature concretes, ice cream sandwiches, and a very small line of coffees so that we're not competing with ourselves. I'm thinking cold brew, affagatos, and blended coffee milkshakes." His face lit up as he spoke, making his freckles more pronounced.

"It's a good idea," Sterling said, using his hands to measure the counter space. "We could easily fit a cold case here. And, if you wanted to go crazy and offer cold sandwiches or pasta salads for summer picnic lunches we could probably swap out this half fridge with a tall narrow one."

Laney smoothed out a crease in her folded apron that she had set on the dilapidated coffee counter. "Smart staff you have here, Jules. They're right. You can create an entirely new Torte experience. And coffee and ice cream would go beautifully with my teriyaki pork and fried jasmine coconut rice. Like I said on the phone it would be great for business. Bringing the Torte brand to the Railroad District would give us real cachet."

"So, should we go put paperwork together?" Addie brushed her hands on her yoga pants.

"Not yet. Let me talk this through with Mom and the rest of our team."

Addie blew out a long breath, as if she was trying to center herself. "I guess, but don't take too long. There are a lot of other interested parties, but because of my yoga vibe, I'd like to keep the garden pretty chill. Laney highly recommends you, so if you want it, we can make it happen. But if you don't, I'm putting it on the market on Monday."

"Deal. I'll let you know one way or the other before Monday." I shook her hand.

We parted ways. Laney left me with a hug and a promise to stop by Torte and help brainstorm if we wanted any other input. Sterling and Andy chatted about concrete flavors and potential shop names all the way back to Torte. I did appreciate their enthusiasm and I could definitely see the potential, but I had to be realistic, too. Was I ready for another new venture? Things at Torte had finally started to feel settled. We had an easy routine and a highly capable staff. Did it make sense to disturb that balance?

And, there was one more major issue that I hadn't voiced—Carlos. My husband had opted to take an extended leave from his work as head chef on the Amour of the Seas. He had been in Ashland for the past three weeks to give things a go. This was our last chance to try to figure out what we both needed from our relationship, or whether it was time to say goodbye for good. If I took on yet another project, would I be intentionally sabotaging any hope for a future with him?